His Just Desserts

HIS JUST DESSERTS

John Raymond Williams

His Just Desserts

iUniverse books may be ordered through booksellers or by contacting:

iUniverse
1663 Liberty Drive
Bloomington, IN 47403
www.iuniverse.com
1-800-Authors (1-800-288-4677)

Because of the dynamic nature of the Internet, any web addresses or links contained in this book may have changed since publication and may no longer be valid. The views expressed in this work are solely those of the author and do not necessarily reflect the views of the publisher, and the publisher hereby disclaims any responsibility for them.

Any people depicted in stock imagery provided by Thinkstock are models, and such images are being used for illustrative purposes only. Certain stock imagery © Thinkstock.

ISBN: 978-1-4917-4908-1 (sc)
ISBN: 978-1-4917-4909-8 (e)

Library of Congress Control Number: 2014918735

Printed in the United States of America.

iUniverse rev. date: 11/10/2014

CHAPTER 1

Money. Can any of us really get enough? The popular thought has always been that it was love that made the world go round. If you live in a dream world, then that may be true. However, in the real world, it is money that has a stranglehold on what people do. Those of us who some think have too much very rarely get to keep a good portion of it. This was what Burt Donaldson had to deal with for a long time.

For years, he has had a running battle with the Internal Revenue Service. As a result, he was one of the most highly taxed persons in the United States. To be fair, Burt has to bear some responsibility for his tax woes himself because of his stubbornness.

His main aim now was to find a way to keep most of the money he made. The question was, could he do it legitimately and just how far would he be willing to go?

Burt was a self-made millionaire—no heir of a huge fortune like some others. He started with ten dollars his father gave to him just before he died. It was a lot of money to a little kid of seven. From an early age, Burt learned the power of investing wisely. He used to invest all of his pocket money in oranges he bought from a fruit stall at a

Boston market. He'd then sell them for more than double the price he'd paid. The more oranges he sold, the more he could buy and resell. As business increased, Burt hired others to do some selling for him. He would pay them a set wage for each orange sold and pocket the rest. This setup netted him a nice profit, and as he grew into a teenager, he developed an acute business sense.

Burt was quite young when he discovered that eating was more important than anything else. Since this was the case for him, he figured it would be the same for everyone else. As a result of this logic, Burt put most of his money into foodstuffs.

In the early seventies, when Burt was just twenty-four years old, he noticed that most families had more than one car. Burt saw the importance of oil and wisely developed partnerships with others. He then made inroads into the oil industry.

Burt's business sense told him not to rely on just one type of investment but to diversify.

He decided to stick with the oil investments for the present, and he bought out his partners and some of his competition at a fraction of the real cost. As he grew into a stealthy young business executive, Burt became greedy.

He bought old houses, had them torn down, and built apartment buildings in their places. He used cheap labor and inferior materials. On two occasions, he went before the housing commission. This was after two apartment dwellers died when a small section of one of Burt's buildings collapsed. Burt escaped any charges, mainly because he had some friends on the housing committee. This experience scared him to such an extent that he got out of the housing business.

By his late forties, Burt had his own finance company, a chain of travel agencies, and a major food company. His pride and joy, though, was one of the largest casinos in Las Vegas. He had unwisely unloaded the oil companies a few years earlier. Others considered Burt a very wealthy man. The tax collectors liked him a lot, but the feeling was far from mutual. In fact, he had a growing hatred of the IRS. He frequently fought with them over what he described as stealing from those who were willing to work to give to those who were not.

"If people don't want to make anything of themselves, why should I support the bastards?" he often shouted.

Now in his early sixties, Burt added to his empire with various other enterprises too numerous to go into detail. All were perfectly legal, of course. Burt always tried to keep on the right side of the law, although he wasn't averse to bending it a little. As long as he could justify it to himself, then it was okay.

Burt resisted all attempts from organized crime to be infiltrated and ran a very honest casino. Burt had moved to Las Vegas in 1998, mostly to control his main asset but also to take advantage of the warmer weather. The Las Vegas police had never had reason to visit Burt's casino in an official capacity. He ran a very tight ship.

The sun was rather warm as it shone through the open window of Burt's office. Being on the twenty-second floor of the Starlight Hotel, he could get a good view of the city. He sat there in his swivel chair, turning to catch the sun that was beating in through the window. He turned his chair slowly so the sun would caress as much of him as it could. He was a big man, just over six foot with shoulders to match. There was no potbelly, as customarily found in men of his age and considerably younger. He was extremely fit for his sixty-three years. He jogged two miles twice a week and took great care of his body. He would walk as often as he could and was adept at tennis. He had given up squash a few years earlier.

His blue eyes sparkled as the sun's rays struck them. His hair, dark brown with many gray streaks, was thinning, but he would die with most of it.

As he sat there staring out of the window, he played with his pencil as some men do when they're thinking. The constant tapping of the pencil was just enough to break the deafening silence in the office.

The lone picture on the office wall was a painting of a World War II Spitfire fighter plane. The heavy, wooden dark-brown desk was strewn with contracts for signature. The other furniture consisted of a black leather couch and two black leather chairs. The only article of interest in the office was a little figure that sat on Burt's desk. It depicted a man on his knees praying with the caption. "Oh God, the IRS has taken everything I have to give. Please don't let them take my soul." Nora, Burt's second wife, had bought it for him to inject some humor into the office. Burt's first wife had died in childbirth more than thirty-five years ago. The baby died at the same time. To date, Burt remained childless, and it didn't look as though he would father any offspring, unless some miracle happened.

With his assets bringing in more than $10 million in income each year, his annual tax debt was more than $4 million, which left only a paltry $6 million in take-home pay. That may not sound bad to the average person, but to give nearly 40 percent of your income to the government didn't seem fair, according to Burt Donaldson's philosophy.

An interruption by his secretary broke the silence, as she asked if he would like a cup of coffee. Burt had been miles away in his thoughts, and it took two requests before he even knew that she was there.

"Pearl," he said, "do you have very many money problems?"

This question surprised the secretary, and she fumbled for an answer before blurting out. "Do I!" She continued with a two-minute oratory on her money woes.

Burt wished he had not even asked her by the time she had finished.

"How do you save on your taxes, though?" he asked.

"I claim everything allowable and some that aren't."

"You don't mean that you, of all people, would ever cheat the government, do you?"

"It's not cheating," she replied with downcast eyes. "It's an American tradition—or better still, it's part of our heritage."

"How the hell do you come up with an answer like that?" Burt said.

"I take it you mean the tradition part."

Burt nodded.

"Well, sir, this country was really founded when it broke away from the British. The beginning of that breakaway started at the famous Boston Tea Party. This was where our forefathers thought they were overtaxed and refused to pay the tax on tea."

"I know the story," said Burt, wondering where this was going to end.

"If trying to get out of paying unfair taxes was good enough for our ancestors, then it is good enough for me," Pearl concluded. She felt good that she had said that. She left the office forgetting the real reason she went in there in the first place.

Burt began to think about her words. To some degree, he could see it was traditional to get away with paying as little tax as one could. Although it wasn't a foreign country that was receiving the tax, it made a big difference to Burt. He was a true patriot, having fought in Korea. He was a supporter of the Vietnam War, or Conflict, if that's what they officially called it now.

The afternoon paper arrived, and Pearl brought it in promptly for her employer to read. Normally, Burt would look at the financial pages first, but today he happened to glance at the front page. A little editorial caught his eye. The title read: "Where Our Tax Dollars Go." Burt sat back in his chair and began to read the editorial. It was but forty lines long with a mere twelve words to the line. However, it packed a punch that sent strong emotions hurtling through Burt's body. His pencil snapped in his fingers as he reread the passage. The message the writer was trying to get across came through loud and clear to Burt.

The main gist of the editorial stated that most of our tax money was being used to support the welfare budget. It went on to say that in future years, the percentage of the taxes going to add to welfare payments would increase. This made Burt furious. He could see those people who snubbed their noses at him for making so much money. They were now being supported by the very money they ridiculed.

What an absurd situation, he thought to himself. *No, not absurd; it's downright criminal.*

He reread the passage again to make sure he was understanding it correctly. Burt believed that if the government would just stop paying welfare, those who were capable of working would seek employment. The money the government would save could then create jobs these welfare recipients could apply for.

With the thought of his hard-earned money being used for these purposes, Burt started to think about what Pearl had said. Burt's frustration with his tax situation caused him to quickly draft a memo to his executives to come up with some ideas on how he could save on his taxes. They had three weeks to come up with some good ideas.

To Burt, those three weeks seemed like an eternity. He tried to guess what their ideas would be. The executives were all very individual, though, so Burt expected a good cross section of ideas. *Some will be quickly discarded, of course, but a few will probably be accepted*, he thought. They were all very professional people, and he knew they would take to this task with enthusiasm.

Burt set the date of the meeting for a Sunday. The weather on that particular day was warm with just a slight wind, but conditions were still quite comfortable. The three senior executives and three other executives assembled at Burt's country mansion, each with his or her own view of solving Burt's problem, even if it was just a little.

The mansion was home to Burt; it was as much a part of him as his first company. It was situated about an hour's drive from Las Vegas. The grounds were very spacious and had a good-quality dark-green lawn. The groundskeeper did an exceptional job, making sure the grass was cut to the perfect length and devoid of weeds. There were several statues on the property, which were obviously Nora's doing. They were hidden among the bushes where one would come upon them by accident. It was as if Nora knew she should have them to show a touch of class without flaunting it.

The pool was basic, rectangular, and large. The water was very clear and reflected the pale-blue color of the bottom and sides of the pool. The rest of the estate consisted of a neat row of hedges. They surrounded a well-manicured garden of colored flowers of all descriptions. A big white brick wall, more than nine feet high, surrounded the grounds. The other security feature on the estate was a very modern surveillance system with direct access to the local police. Big wealth attracts big criminals. The house itself consisted of six large bedrooms with six bathrooms. The kitchen contained a kitchen island, and the living room was very spacious. There was also a divided dining room. When opened up fully, the dining room could seat up to forty people.

On the business side of the house was a large meeting room and a den. The den contained a pool table, which looked as though it had never been used.

The decor of the home was rather drab. Nora had little taste when it came to decorating. Her major talents came to the forefront when she was on her back. There was precious little color in the decorating, mainly browns and grays with just the greenery of some plants to inject a semblance of color.

Burt was not one to lay on a huge spread of beluga caviar and imported fine wines to his own employees. They were stuck with barbecued hamburgers and roast beef. Nora liked to entertain but rarely got the chance unless it was a business meeting like this one.

Nora married Burt when he was already in a successful position with his own company. She did some investigating to see what his future prospects were like. The reports she received back were convincing enough for her to accept his marriage proposal. That had been fourteen years earlier. Nora's past was a little on the shady side. She got out of the call-girl racket before she had met Burt. He knew nothing about her past and didn't want to know too much.

There was a difference of twenty years in their ages. The years Nora had spent on her back did not increase her looks in the present. She stood five feet six inches tall and still had a shapely figure. Unfortunately, her best attributes had begun to sag quite a lot. Nora had long black hair. Whenever a gray hair appeared, she would immediately have her hair dyed again. She was very fearful of growing old and was grateful that she had latched on to Burt, so she could spend the rest of her future in comfort.

She was not unattractive and always tried her best to look presentable, but she knew that no matter how good she looked, it was now wasted on Burt. It was only when they had company or went out that she did much about her looks.

In the past few years, Burt had been unfaithful on a couple of occasions that she knew about. As long as he was discreet about it, she turned a blind eye to these little indiscretions. They hadn't made real love in quite some time, so she wasn't missing anything. Burt always bought her a little gift when he knew he'd done something wrong.

Each of the executives arrived by themselves within thirty minutes of each other.

There were two women at the little gathering besides Nora: Jane Coe, assistant lawyer, and Paula Pratt, assistant accountant. The others in attendance were Jack Smedhurst, chief accountant, and the three senior vice presidents. The vice presidents were the men Burt relied upon the most.

They were Bill Smythe, the company lawyer; Peter Rush, vice president of marketing; and John Fix, vice president of administration.

All the staff knew each other, and there was a friendly ambience over the gathering. Tables were set up on an outdoor entertaining area. Because this was a business meeting, there were no spouses invited. The general conversations evaded the issue, and no one spoke directly of the preassigned task.

Nora moved around the group chatting to each guest in turn, trying not to give any one person more time than another. This was very difficult, because she found it much easier entertaining the men than the two women. It wasn't that they were catty or anything, but Nora just felt a little uncomfortable around women who were attractive. It probably stemmed from her early years on the street and the competitiveness she had to endure.

There was no alcohol served because Burt wanted them all to be in complete control of all their faculties. The strongest drink available was Coke.

Burt brought the festivities to a halt, as it was time for the business side of the day to begin.

A typical meeting with Burt followed a set pattern. Everyone would get a turn to speak, and when all had finished, Burt would call for questions. He would not ask or answer any himself. He would insist that everyone speak. There were to be no exceptions. He felt that anyone who was invited had to be able to contribute something, even if it was shot down in flames by the others or himself.

Once all had their say, Burt would get up out of his big chair and turn his back on the group. He would pretend to ponder what was said for about thirty seconds. Then he would whirl around and deliver his interpretation. This, of course, made most of the participants sweat like hell.

However, this was not just a meeting but more like the planning of the Normandy invasion. The estate guests were a little more uneasy than they would normally have been. Burt conducted his meetings in the general meeting room, a rather large but cozy room able to seat twenty-five people comfortably. There was no assigned seating, but the three senior executives always managed to get the seats nearest to Burt's big chair.

There was an electronic whiteboard behind and to the right of Burt's chair. Most whiteboards are okay to work with, but the electronic ones are far more complicated. They have the advantage of containing five screens to use. They also have the ability to print any of the screens at the press of a button. This just added to the tension everyone would be under.

All knew the topic. They'd had three weeks to have their ideas prepared. The only stipulation Burt had was that their ideas could not involve any fake sons, daughters, or other nonexistent kin.

Over the past years, Burt's financial advisors had pleaded with him to set up dummy corporations in the names of his relatives.

He was loath to do this for two reasons. It would weaken his total control, and he didn't feel that he could trust any of his relatives.

As everyone took their seats and nestled back with their own ideas neatly in hand, Burt officially welcomed them to the meeting. He opened the proceedings by saying that he felt sure there would be some great ideas presented today.

He then told the men to take their jackets off to be more comfortable, as this was going to be a relaxed session.

He always enjoyed picking who was to speak. There was none of that going-around-the-table nonsense. He found a distinct pleasure in seeing people squirm and sweat. He felt that they were all overpaid for what they did. They deserved to suffer some of the stress that comes with the high-priced territory.

The first person called upon was Jack Smedhurst. Jack was a short, chubby man and looked like a used car salesman. Jack stood up. He was always a nervous man. Badgered at home by his oh-so-righteous and domineering wife, he tended to sweat a lot when he was under stress. This meeting was a bona fide stressful situation, the kind that would call for about a gallon of sweat at least. He began to shuffle his notes to give the impression that he had something concrete to add to this exercise. As he did so, he mumbled some barely audible explanations of what he had figured out with the help of his staff. Once the paper-shuffling routine was complete, Jack began to talk.

Burt interrupted him by saying, "No, not there. Come up in front of everyone and use the board if it will help." He then motioned Jack toward the whiteboard.

Jack took a deep swallow and nervously stepped up to the whiteboard but had no intention of using it. He had never used the electronic board before and didn't want to start at this particular meeting. He was not very good at standing up in front of a group of people to speak. Doing it at the front of the room made him dread it all the more. He was very proficient on a one-on-one basis. However, to get to the position he now occupied in business as chief accountant, he had done very little public speaking.

Jack used a lot of facts and figures in his presentation. It dealt mainly with buying a large yacht, outfitting it like a home, and spending a minimum of two weeks on the yacht each year. Burt could then class the yacht as a second home for tax purposes. There would be a savings of about a quarter of a million dollars in the first three years.

After Jack had finished, he returned to his seat to prepare for the onslaught of questions from his peers. However, before anyone could raise questions, Burt rose from his chair and strolled up to the whiteboard. He wrote Jack's name with a single word next to it: "yacht."

Burt returned to his seat and called upon Peter Rush to give his plan. Peter was one of those people who always appeared to be "with it" according to the language of our time. He could always be counted upon to do his share and would have his work completed on time. He was a very logical person and always tried to figure things out rather than just accept what was presented to him. A bachelor for all of his thirty-four years, Peter was never romantically linked with anyone of note. He gave the impression that his work was everything to him. Because of his boyish good looks, quite a few people at the office thought he may swing with a different crowd. However, there was nothing definite to this, just hearsay. Peter stood just over six feet two inches tall and used every inch to gain a psychological advantage over his opponents.

Peter, with the confidence of a 200-to-1 shot at Aqueduct Racetrack, strode to the front and got straight into his spiel. Forty-five minutes passed before he stopped talking and sat down. The main point Peter was making was to diversify into various other endeavors. The examples he gave were the oil industry, which Burt had already been associated with, or the lucrative but speculative film industry. The reasons for this tactic was that the tax allowances for those types of companies were almost totally written off. Of course, Burt would have to sell some of his successful companies to try to effect this plan. The return would be a $2 million savings over the next two years.

Burt wrote Peter's name on the board with the word "diversify."

Burt slowly looked around the room, trying to pick who the next victim was to be. He had a sadistic streak and tried to find the most frightened of his staff. He seemed to feel that it kept them on their toes.

"Bill, how about you?" asked Burt.

Bill Smythe, who detested being called Bill Smith, put forth a tame presentation. It included the purchase of nontaxable stocks and bonds. Bill was a straight-laced sort of guy. The oldest of the vice presidents at sixty-two, Bill had lost almost all of his hair. He had a faithful wife who lived for him and their two children. If it was possible to have 0.6 of a child, Bill and his wife would have achieved it just so they could epitomize the typical American family of having 2.6 children.

Bill was always a little afraid of his position with the company. He knew the best years were well behind him. He had probably just a slim chance of making it to the mandatory retirement age of sixty-five. The main part of Bill's plan was for Burt to put part of his payday in a deferred-compensation plan instead of taking it all at once. This allowed earnings to grow tax-deferred up to ten years. The savings in the first five years could be around $2 million. Alongside Bill's name, Burt wrote "deferred-compensation."

The two women must have known that it was about time for one of them to give a presentation. It was Paula who got the nod first. Paula was a little on the chubby side and wore her black hair in a bun. She wore contact lenses but was not very comfortable with them. To flash a smile was not a daily occurrence for Paula. Her attention to detail and her enthusiasm allowed her to move up the corporate ladder at the early age of thirty. She wasn't bad looking and had a certain beauty about her that some people could see but others couldn't. She'd been married once but divorced after a year. Some say that her marriage suffered due to her drive to push her career.

She prepared for this meeting by studying tax-savings plans at the library. She had her sights set on Jack's job and wanted desperately to make a good impression in front of Burt. She had stayed up late every night for the past three weeks letting her social life be nonexistent. All eyes were upon her as she strode to the front.

It was the first time for her to talk in front of such a select gathering. She was more than a little nervous. Her presentation, she felt, was very professional and thorough. It would save Burt about a quarter of a million dollars a year in taxes. The main thing she had to say was to invest in options rather than stocks. Most options are only taxed when they are exercised. Although they could be of little risk, the return on the dollar would not be exceedingly high.

Burt again moved to the whiteboard and wrote the name Paula and "options."

John Fix, who, along with Peter, was the most level headed of the group, was the next one to give his presentation. It was a concise but descriptive speech. It centered upon moving investments offshore. Overseas tax havens have always been a big favorite for rock stars. John quoted the Cayman Islands as a possible source. Such a course of action would net a savings of $2 million in the first year. This would be followed by a half a million dollars in savings for the next four years. Burt showed no emotion as John continued his presentation to its end. Burt wrote "offshore" next to John's name.

The only person left to make an appearance at the front was Jane Coe. Undoubtedly one of the most beautiful women working for Burt, Jane was all business today, dressed very smartly in a pink velour suit and a white blouse with pin tucks. Jane had medium-blonde hair, a fantastic figure, and stood five feet seven inches tall. She had an innocent beauty and was a fitness fanatic. She looked far younger than her thirty-two years. Often pursued, though unsuccessfully, by all the men, she was considered very beautiful. Burt had taken a liking to her and had taken her to dinner on several occasions, purely for business reasons, of course.

She walked to the front of the room and gave Burt a little smile, which he eagerly returned. All the men watched Jane move to the front, and most of them fantasized about what her clothes hid. There were rumors about Jane, but none of them had been proven. They'd probably started by men who had tried to date her but were unsuccessful. They made up stories to try to hide their disappointment. Jane was a professional in every sense of the word. She gave her all to her job and was quite capable of giving presentations. Jane stated that incorporating was the way to go and backed up her argument with facts and figures. Next to John's idea, hers would save Burt the most money.

As all eyes followed Jane back to her seat, and Burt

moved to the whiteboard again. "Incorporate" was written next to Jane's name.

It was close to six o'clock, and without any further discussion, Burt decided to break for dinner. He asked that his guests not mention the contents of the meeting at the dinner table. They would return to the meeting room at seven thirty when discussions would then take place.

Burt had a modest dinner laid out. It consisted of a buffet of chicken, boiled potatoes, carrots, and green salad. For dessert, there were cold apple tarts.

Conversation around the dinner table consisted of mainly small talk and a smidgen of flirting between Peter and Paula. Peter often flirted with the girls at the office. He thought he was a lot more attractive to the opposite sex than he really was. He had also made a play for Jane Coe, but she spurned any interest.

She was one of those women who people often thought to be stuck up at first. However, after speaking to her for a little while, they changed their minds very quickly. She was astoundingly beautiful, a former model who at the first hint of anything like "special favors" quit that business immediately. She had never married and had only a couple of romantic affairs. Maybe she wanted to give her all to her work, because she wasn't giving it to anyone else.

Nora always struck up conversations with the participants at these affairs. She knew what they had been going through for the past five hours. It was as if she were trying to put them at ease to make up for the pressure her husband must have put them under. For some reason, the conversations Nora did have with her guests seemed to put them at ease quite a lot. It was just her smile or her soft-spoken voice. One of her favorites who she liked to chat to was John Fix. He was a very likeable sort of person. An ex-jock, he had been captain of his school football team and an outstanding track-and-field athlete who almost made the Olympic team. Married at twenty-three and divorced at twenty-eight, he still retained his good looks. He kept in shape by playing tennis as much as he could.

It was hard for the participants to relax at these affairs, especially when Burt took careful note of what everyone did or said. It was as if they all had to be on their best behavior always.

At 7:25, Burt began to make his way toward the meeting room, and the others started to follow suit. At exactly 7:30, everyone took a seat.

Without saying a word, Burt walked over to the whiteboard and stared at the six suggestions. He pondered for a while with his back to the group. He stepped back a few feet, still looking at the board, and then turned to face his audience. He sadistically looked at Jack Smedhurst who turned on the sweat glands to full. He knew his suggestion was going to be the first ridiculed. Burt said nothing, turned back to the board again, fully knowing they were all going through their own personal hell. They all waited for their suggestions to be torn to shreds. Some of them knew they could have done better. If they could get another chance, they would have come up with a more realistic solution. As he made his way back to his chair, Burt instructed them all to study the board very closely. They were to write down the one idea they thought was the best. Everyone looked at each other in bewilderment but quickly complied with the edict. Jack seemed almost disappointed that he'd done all that sweating for nothing.

Burt instructed John to collect all the votes and give

them to him for tallying. Burt quickly ascertained that only three of the suggestions were popular. Burt announced the three suggestions very slowly, giving the participants time to digest each. He surveyed the quorum with a rather deadpan look.

"So these are the best solutions the top people in the company can come with," said Burt quietly. And then he exploded. "Is this *all* you bunch of so-called highly intelligent university grads can come up with?" shouted Burt. He placed a high emphasis on the word *all*. There was a short silence and much seat squirming before Bill Smythe got up the courage to affect some sort of defense.

"Well, sir," he said, "maybe if you offered a reward."

"A reward," said Burt.

"A reward of, say, ten thousand dollars. Then we could come up with something better," said Bill.

John hoped Bill was not talking for the whole group. He felt that for them to do their job, a money incentive was a mistake. He also knew that such an unprofessional statement made by Bill would just make Burt even madder than he already was.

At this point, all restraint in Burt's voice had ceased. He yelled, "None of these suggestions are acceptable—not one. They are all *totally un*acceptable."

"An incentive, Bill?" Burt continued "Why not make it a hundred thousand or even a million dollars. Where would it stop? Not one of these suggestions could achieve what I wanted. I'm not wanting to save a few thousand dollars. I want to cut my taxes in half. None of these so-called great suggestions of yours will allow me to do that."

He stopped talking for a moment to let what he had said sink into their minds. He looked around the room to try to make them all feel ashamed before continuing. "No, I am very disappointed and see no point in discussing the matter anymore."

With that, he declared the meeting closed and left the room.

The executives just sat there in stunned silence for a few minutes. Burt achieved what he wanted. The group left the room in total quiet, and each made their separate ways to their cars. The only talking was between the three chief executives.

Bill called Peter and John over to his car. He said, "You know, I think the old man has really flipped out on this."

"He is just under a tremendous strain," said Peter. "He is trying to save money on his taxes like the rest of us. The only difference is his are about one hundred times more than ours."

"Well, I know one thing," said John. "He is going to be a real bear for the next few days. I would advise that we all try to keep as far away from him as possible."

Burt decided to spend some time at home. He felt this would have a twofold effect. The first would be to put a lot of pressure on his executives by forcing them to dig deep. This would make them come up with some better solutions. The second reason was to give himself some time also to possibly come up with some solutions. If those were the best solutions they could come up with, then he felt sure that he could do no worse himself. Yes, that's what he would do.

I'll show them, Burt thought to himself, cursing the incompetents. *They are not the only ones who can think.*

Burt was a man who had accepted the twentieth-century philosophy of visualization put forth by some sectors of the community. In sports, they had used this process for a number of years. The acceptance of it in the business world was not widespread. It only existed in pockets of successful businesses. He had trained himself to visualize a whole plot in his mind, while he was at rest, just before going to sleep. He would give his mind a problem and then sleep on it, and the answer would come to him in the next few days. In this case, the answer came very quickly. So quickly, in fact, that Burt didn't even recognize it as an answer. It wasn't until the end of the three days that the realization dawned upon him.

It was almost like a fantasy. Excitement began to well up inside of him. He called to Nora and told her he was going into the den for a few hours. Nora knew she would not see him for the rest of the day once he entered the domain of the den.

Burt started by writing down a few notes. He would look at them, add to them, and discard the ones he didn't like. This process went on for hours. Nora interrupted him on a couple of occasions to bring him some coffee. He thanked her and then called her back on the last occasion and asked her to sit on his lap.

This is a rather odd request, thought Nora. She hadn't sat on her husband's lap since, well, she couldn't remember the last time. It must have been a long time ago. As she sat perched on his lap, Burt gave her a little kiss on the side of the neck. This was another thing that he hadn't done spontaneously for quite a long time. Obviously, Burt was in a good mood.

"And what do I owe this to?" she inquired.

"Oh, just for being you," Burt replied.

Burt sometimes had these little three-minute trips of

euphoria. The unfortunate part was that they only lasted about three minutes at the maximum. Even he didn't know what brought them on, but he really enjoyed those three minutes. However, when it was over, it was over. Much to the disappointment of Nora, who was just beginning to enjoy this attention.

"Now I must get back to work," he said, ushering Nora off his lap.

Burt gathered his thoughts again, trying to remember exactly where he had left off. As his plan started to take a positive turn, excitement began to come over Burt. He could now see that it was possible to save a lot of money on his taxes. In fact, he envisaged the saving of a lot more money than even he thought possible. He excitedly began to go deeper into this mysterious plan, trying his hardest to find any flaws with it.

It's going to take quite a bit of research, he thought to himself. *I hope it will all be worth it in the end.* As the thoughts literally flowed out of him and onto his notepad his excitement grew stronger and stronger.

He called his secretary and gave her a list of things he wanted her to find out for him. A few more phone calls, and his plan began to take shape.

It was another two days later when Burt felt he was ready with his plan. He called his three chief executives to come to a special meeting, again at the estate. Burt sent a limousine to pick up all three at the office.

CHAPTER 2

As Burt waited for his three visitors, Bill, Peter, and John, he continually went over his plan in his mind. He was also trying to anticipate the many questions and concerns they would have. He began pacing back and forth. Nora hadn't seen him like this for such a long time. He was like a little boy waiting for a present to be delivered.

Nora didn't meddle in her husband's business and only knew what he decided to tell her. Just before Burt would fall asleep, he would tell her some of the doings of the day. When she had asked what had taken up all his time in the den, he replied that he was working on a tax-saving idea. He then explained that it was going to be a very complicated procedure. He also mentioned that he had invited his three senior men to come over to go over his new plan in private.

He continually peered out the window, waiting for the limousine to appear in the drive. This was totally out of character for Burt, but the excitement he felt about this plan was overwhelming.

He hadn't had to use his brain like this for a long time and felt young again. He had been a little in the doldrums as far as his personal aspirations had been of late. He felt if he could pull this off, it would give him a new lease on life.

It was about ten minutes after Burt had begun his window peering that the limousine finally arrived.

Burt was all smiles as he welcomed the three men and ushered them into the meeting room. He wanted to get the meeting started as soon as possible. They would be served coffee in about half an hour. He told them to relax and explained that it was to be an informal meeting. In fact, it was to be one of those meetings that never took place.

The three guests, already bewildered by Burt being in such a good mood, could not believe their ears when confronted by these later facts.

Excitement raged through Burt as he prepared to divulge the contents of what he considered the best tax-saving idea of them all. Burt took an unaccustomed seat on the corner of his desk. That way, the three would have to look up to him. It was purely a psychological edge for Burt and was interpreted by the guests as a signal that this conversation was going to be very heavy, with Burt in control.

Burt started by saying, "What I am about to say to you must not be divulged outside of this room. I have had to resort to coming up with a tax-saving plan of my own, seeing that no one else could come up with a satisfactory one."

This last remark was meant as a dig at the three listeners. Burt continued. "You may feel that it is an off-the-wall idea. I have had all the facts checked out and am convinced that it will work. I would prefer it if you would hold all your questions until I have finished with this presentation."

With that, Burt began. "Let's say we have a hypothetical situation." A wry smile came across his face. "A person who owns a casino that always generates a large winning percentage comes up against a man with an infallible system at roulette."

"There is no such thing as an infallible system," said Peter.

"There is if you know what numbers will be coming up," replied Burt.

"That's not a real system; it's like cheating," argued Peter.

"Of course it's bloody well cheating. That's what this is all about. I want to cheat the government and get back what is rightfully mine. After all, everyone cheats the government. It's an American tradition," Burt snapped back, a little disgruntled at being interrupted. He again asked that all questions be held until he had finished.

"The main ingredient in this idea is a man," he continued. "A man who has a great memory. He must be married, honest, and an immigrant from one of just a handful of countries. He must also have kept his original citizenship. Now, before you barrage me with questions, let me continue. He will be given a set of prearranged numbers to play at one of my roulette tables. This will enable him to win a huge amount of money in one night. He must also have signed a contract. In this contract, he agrees to return to his own country and give me back 90 percent of the money he won. The other good thing about this is that I can also write off the whole loss as a tax deduction. Well, that's the plan in a nutshell. I welcome your comments."

The three men sat there stunned for a while, not really believing what they had just heard.

Bill was the first to talk. "I have been making a few mental notes, and my first impression is that it would depend on too many uncontrollable factors to succeed. Firstly, who can you find that you can trust to do this? Secondly, speaking as a lawyer, it leaves room for embezzlement charges."

"The first objection I will deal with later, but as to embezzlement, no way," Burt quickly replied. "I have checked into this already. Provided we can cover all the bases, only the people in this room will have full knowledge of what is going on. Besides, how can you embezzle your own money? Since I am the sole owner of the casino, the only one who would be losing the money would be me."

"That's not strictly correct," argued Bill. "For starters, the ones who would lose the money would be the government."

"Granted," said Burt, "but if I closed the casino down and made no money this year, would that be cheating the government?"

"No, of course not, but that's completely different," Bill countered.

"Look," said Burt, trying to make his point clear, "as long as I don't make the money, I should not have to pay tax on it."

"I know what you are trying to say, sir," said Bill, "but you are splitting hairs here because you are making the money."

"Ah, that's where you are wrong. I am not making the money. It will be a gift from the mystery gambler to me and outside of the United States, so there would not be any taxes to pay by me. Listen, I have tentatively had this point checked out by a tax expert. He says that although it really skirts the law, it is a unique situation. It would have to be proven conclusively there was wrongdoing. Believe me, I have given this a great deal of thought.

"As long as the people concerned follow their predefined roles, then everything will pan out correctly. Trust me on this. Now what I want to know is, can you see anything that would prevent this from working that I may have missed?"

"And what about the mystery gambler?" asked Bill.

"He will only know what he has to know," answered Burt.

The next question was one that they were all thinking, but it was John who first asked.

"How much money are we talking about here?"

This was the question that Burt knew would be asked, and before answering, he watched all their faces with an intense expression.

"You all know I make more than $10 million a year, but my take-home pay is barely $6 million. Now, by my method, I could earn the same in a few months that it would normally take me two years to earn."

"Ten million dollars," all three exclaimed almost in unison.

"Now why would anyone in their right mind hand over $10 million just like that?" said Bill.

"Like I said," returned Burt, "we will have this signed agreement, and the person chosen would have to be of the best possible character. Also, he will be getting over $1 million to keep for himself."

John, who had been unusually quiet, asked the next question. "Just how thoroughly have you gone into researching all this?"

"Just the surface," came the reply. "I do know that the person we need must come from either Australia, Belgium, New Zealand, or Switzerland. The reason these countries have been chosen is that they all have the following characteristics: they have a relatively low rate of tax, including gift tax, thus making the venture more appealing to the gambler. Their governments are very stable, and the long arm of the IRS cannot reach them. There may be other countries that fall into the same category, but these readily came to mind."

"Too simple. It is too bloody simple. There must be a flaw in it somewhere," said John.

"Well, if you can come up with one, come up with it now. I want to get right on with this because there is a lot of preparation and planning to do in a very short time."

"Do you have anyone in mind to be the gambler?" said Bill.

"No, I haven't the faintest idea. That's where you all come in. I want one of you or all of you to find him. No one outside of this room must know anything about it, and I do mean no one. So I don't want any of you telling your friends, girlfriends, or wives. And, John, I don't want Jane to know either." As he ushered the last phrase, Burt was looking straight at John.

When John's eyes met Burt's, it was like the glare of a new bull moose waiting to displace the old chief.

"How you find him is your business, but you may have to do a lot of the leg work yourselves, unless you can come up with some excuse as to why you are looking for such a person," said Burt. "Of course, there will be a large bonus for the one who finally tracks down the perfect candidate for the job. Provided he accepts the task."

"Where do we start?" said Bill. "Do we just go up to a complete stranger and ask if he would like to make a million dollars?"

"I know you are just joking, Bill," said Burt. "The first thing we have to do is to check the personnel files of all the companies under my umbrella. This will be to come up with a short list of persons with the qualifications that I have outlined before and that I will repeat. Number one, he must be from one of those four countries. Number two, he must be married. This will give credence that it was an innocent win and not a fraud. The wife, of course, will not know anything about the plan."

"I don't understand that point," questioned Bill. "What does having a wife got to do with not being fraudulent?"

"It is a known fact that the majority of gambling frauds are done by gamblers who are alone. Admittedly, some of them have been married, but the wife was very rarely with her husband when the fraud took place. I admit that I don't know the logic for this. It is just a fact," replied Burt.

"So the wife must accompany the gambler in this plan of yours?" asked Bill.

"Of course," replied Burt in a manner that indicated he felt the question was unnecessary.

"Now, if I may continue," said Burt rather sarcastically. "Number three: he must have a good memory. Before you all jump on me to ask why this is important, let me say that I will explain later. Probably the best way to determine this would be to give all those on the short list a little test. Finally, he must not have a criminal record of any kind or even associate with any shady characters. He must be so far above reproach that we must leave no stone unturned to try to find anything bad about him. We can't afford even the slightest hint of any wrongdoing in his past. This must be the most perfectly conceived operation ever. We cannot afford any slipups. The risk is very great, but the rewards are far greater."

"It seems like there is one other thing we must consider also," said Peter. "That's the croupier who I imagine will make sure that the prearranged set of numbers does come up at the proper time."

"Quite correct," said Burt. "I'm glad someone is finally on the ball here. I purposely didn't mention the croupier, because he will have to come from the pool of employees already working here. However, you can leave that selection to me. Now, is there anything else you can see that would prevent this from working?"

They all stared at Burt with the look of desperation on their faces.

Bill was again the first to speak. "Maybe if we could have a little time to think about this. You must remember that this is the first we have heard of the scheme, sir. For some of us, if not all of us, it may take a little time to digest it all."

"Fair enough," Burt agreed. "I will take an early extended lunch. There will be sandwiches sent in for you, and the three of you can discuss it. Then, in exactly four hours, I will return. If there are no serious objections, we will go ahead with the plan. I feel sure that any objections or concerns you do come up with can be explained away."

With that, Burt left the room.

The three men all looked at each other with disbelief written on their faces.

"I've never heard of anything as stupid as this," said Bill, rather astonished.

Peter also aired his displeasure at the scheme. He was more resigned to begin finding fault with it rather than criticize haphazardly.

"We should try to come up with some good reasons why the plan won't work," Peter said. "I know whatever reasons we come up with for it to fail, Burt will ignore one way or another because this is his project. I would even say it is his pet project, and nothing we could come up with will sway his decision. We have to come up with some objections to justify his faith in us as the senior members of his company."

John was about to comment when the door opened, and one of the servants came in with a trolley of assorted sandwiches. Pots of tea and coffee were also on the trolley. They each helped themselves to the goodies and relaxed for a while.

"Bill," said John, "from a lawyer's point of view, could this really be construed as embezzlement?"

"I would have to say yes," replied Bill. "The fact that Burt will get the money back from overseas should not make any difference in my book. However, embezzlement laws differ from country to country and from state to state. Even if it did fall within the law, it is an awfully risky venture. Before answering completely, I would have to check into the various laws very thoroughly."

Peter interjected. "Look, we may as well forget about that tactic, as Burt will argue all day on whether it's embezzlement. We should concentrate our attention more on the workability of the plan."

With that, the men began to picture the plan in action. Peter quickly began to write some notes when he could see some blatant concerns. He shared them with the others, who both agreed with him that they had at least come up with something to discuss. They had resolved themselves that no matter what objections they had about the plan, it would make no difference. Burt had already made up his mind. They did discuss the merits of the plan and if the right person, could be found then maybe, just maybe, the plan could succeed. The chances of that happening would be extremely slim.

They each tried to come up with some feasible reasons why Burt's plan would not succeed. Peter volunteered to take notes on the proceedings. The three managed to surprise themselves with the number of real objections they were able to come up with. However, in the end, they knew it would be a waste of time. Once Burt has made his mind up, it would take a lot to shift him.

"If Burt was not so excited about this plan, then maybe we could persuade him against it," said Bill.

"Well, we'll do our best," said Peter. "If he is dead set on it and he can satisfy us that it is not just a pipe dream, then we should get behind him."

"So you agree with his harebrained idea then?" asked Bill, taking the negative point of view, as usual.

"No. I didn't say I agree with him," answered Peter. "I just think we should give his plan a fair go rather than attacking it without any foundation."

Burt returned at exactly four o'clock. He sat back in his chair and waited for the questions.

Because Peter had done the note writing, he was the first to speak. "We have collectively come up with the following objections. To begin with, there are some concerns about the person to be selected as the gambler. How can we be sure he won't tell anybody about it?"

"We can't be 100 percent sure," said Burt, "but it would be in his own best interest to keep it to himself. This is why the selection of him is so very important. When I interview him, I will have some idea of his true character. If I have any doubts, then he will not be selected, and I will move onto the next candidate. What's next?"

"Still with the gambler: what happens if he makes a mistake and bets the wrong number?"

"This will depend on a number of things. If it is just one bet that goes astray early in the game, then there will be a contingency plan to cover it. However, if the bet is late in the game when the money has mounted up, then the croupier will abort the game that night. They would regroup a couple of nights later. Next," said Burt.

"Our final concern with the gambler is that we assume he will be given instructions to bet a certain amount each time. This will be measured to give the required amount at the end."

"That's right," said Burt.

"Well, what if he thinks to himself that because he can't lose, he should bet more to make a little extra on the side?"

"That's a good point. Into the calculations, there will be built an over and under figure. If the gambler exceeds the over figure or for some reason undercuts the under figure, the game will be aborted for him by the croupier."

"What if the croupier and the gambler get together and double the bets?" asked John.

"They will not have met until the first dry run and cannot be seen together at all," said Burt.

"Well, that takes care of the gambler," said Peter. "The next set of questions is about the croupier."

"If I may interject here a minute," said Burt. "All your questions about the gambler were valid, and that is why his selection will be a long, drawn-out process. The interviews with him will take days, and if I have the slightest doubt about him, he will not be selected. You may continue, Peter."

"Our concerns about the croupier are not as extensive

as those of the gambler but need some clarification. What happens if the croupier makes a mistake?"

"As with the gambler, if the mistake is early in the game, the game will continue. If it is past the point of no return, so to speak, the game will be aborted by the gambler. After a day's delay, they will begin again. These rules will be given to both parties, and they will have plenty of time to absorb them," answered Burt.

Peter continued to look at his notes. "What if someone just happens to notice that the croupier is cheating?"

"What do you mean someone?"

"Someone who is a member of the casino staff, such as one of the undercover security staff who frequently wanders around to try to uncover cheats."

"The staff are normally looking for the gamblers who are cheating, not the croupiers. Although they do, on occasion, check on the croupiers, it is normally only if they have reason to. Croupiers who cheat normally do it with small bets so they will have a better chance of going unnoticed. However, your point is well taken. When someone is winning big, both the gambler and the croupier do come under close scrutiny. We cannot interfere with the running of the casino, as this would be too much of a coincidence when the big win is announced."

"What about the surveillance cameras?" asked Peter.

"As you all know, at one point, the surveillance cameras will zoom onto the gambler's table," replied Burt. "The resulting tape will be reviewed by security and later by myself. As there will be no sleight of hand, there is nothing the cameras will be able to pick up. However, the head of security is very stubborn and will not let go easily. The execution of this scheme must be perfect. Not that this is any of your worry, apart from the selection of the gambler. This is why the croupier picked will have to be one of the best out there—so he can avoid all the checks thrown at him. You don't have to concern yourselves about the selection of the croupier; you can leave that part to me."

"The next question has to do with the document that the gambler is to sign," said Peter. "Although this person will be of the utmost character, there really is nothing to prevent him from keeping all the money himself. This document would have to be very powerful to entice the gambler to do exactly as you ask."

Burt had not anticipated this question at this stage and fumbled with an answer.

"You are quite right, Peter. This is the biggest part of the gamble—this time, by me. The document will just be an ordinary agreement type, one quite enforceable by law. It will be worded in such a way that it won't state where the money will be coming from, just the amount that will be owed to me. That way, if the gambler does abscond with the money, we would just have to track him down and get law enforcement in his own country to force him to live up to the agreement. Also, there will be something I will say to him that will entice him to give back the money. You need not concern yourselves with any of that. Again, I reiterate that the selection of the gambler is the most vital part of this plan."

"We have one technical question, sir," said Peter. "That is, how can the roulette wheel be rigged effectively?"

"I'm glad you asked that. It is actually quite a simple thing to rig a wheel when you know how. The important thing is that these wheels will be rigged very professionally. The croupier who I have in mind for the job could do it in the dark with his eyes closed. There will be three tables used, two for trial runs and the third for the big win. Each of the tables will be rigged so when a certain number comes up, the rigging system will be activated."

"What if this rigging of the table is discovered by the security staff?" said John.

"That's the beauty of this system. It is virtually undetectable," said Burt. "I say virtually, because there is a way to detect it. It is a costly system that I have been approached about before and turned down as being too expensive. There is nothing that could be detected by the equipment we have now."

"To that end, sir," said John, "you have mentioned that you already have a croupier in mind."

"That's right."

"Will he be willing to go along with the rigging of the tables?"

"Now that's a question I will have to put to him very delicately. I don't want to expose the nature of the plan, just in case he doesn't want to go along with it," said Burt.

"However, knowing his financial situation at present, I feel he would jump at the chance. If he doesn't, I do have some others who could also do the job."

"That's another thing," said John. "What happens if you can't find a croupier who will do this?"

"Then the plan will not go through. However, I doubt that anyone, especially the person I have in mind, will pass up a huge amount of money for a few hours of work."

"Our final question," said Peter. "To accumulate the kind of money you had mentioned, it would mean some very large bets. What if the casino manager blocks the bet as being too large?"

"I will advise the casino manager to allow no-limit bets for a month once we know when the big night will be," said Burt.

Bill, who always liked to have the last question, chimed in with some questions about the legalities of such an action. Burt dismissed them by saying that no one would be able to tie them to anything illegal. As was stated before, they would not be really doing anything wrong. All knew that it was useless to try to argue this point with Burt, so they accepted his answer.

Since there were no further questions, Burt moved onto the next step.

"For the selection of the gambler, I want you to split up all the companies I own between the three of you. You will then obtain the personnel files of all the employees. It will be necessary to go through these files and extract any of the candidates you think would meet the stated criteria. I have cleared it with all personnel departments in question to allow you access to their records."

As there were no more questions, Burt adjourned the meeting. They were to meet again in exactly three weeks. He also reiterated that no one else was to know about the plan. Once again, he stared straight at John.

"Oh, by the way," Burt added. "When we meet again, I feel sure we will each have a good number of names. Also, I had forgotten to mention that whoever comes up with the name of the person who is selected will get a bonus of one hundred thousand dollars."

The mention of such a large bonus made the executives more interested.

"Oh, and another thing, only one of the four of us will get the bonus."

"The four of us?" exclaimed Bill. "You mean that you are included too? I don't think that is fair."

Burt just smiled and said, "Don't worry, Bill. We will all select who the lucky guy is to be, not just me. So you will still all have a chance at the bonus."

With that, the three vice presidents left.

CHAPTER 3

After the three men had left the estate and were on their way back home in Burt's limousine, they had a chance to express their true thoughts.

Bill started the conversation, as he invariably did, with the negative side. "Well, as for myself, I don't like going along with the old man's harebrained scheme. After all, it is his money he is trying to save, not ours. The only reason I would go along with it is to keep my job."

"Of course, you wouldn't be interested in the bonus as well," said Peter.

"That's probably why any one of us will be doing it," said John. "What do you really think of the idea, Pete?" he asked, knowing that he'd get an honest answer from Peter.

"There are a lot of ifs about it, but it may work. I think it all hedges on who we come up with as the gambler. This is the most risky part, because whoever this guy is, there really is no hold on him to give back the money. I know Burt has said the guy will have to sign an agreement, but how valid is that? If he returned to his own country, it could take Burt years to find him, if he ever found him at all."

"I have a feeling there is something more to this agreement than we are being told," said John.

"What makes you think that?" said Bill.

"Oh, I don't know. It's just a hunch," John replied. "It's not like Burt to leave something this important or expensive to the good nature of someone he will have just met, no matter how thoroughly he will be investigated."

The rest of the conversations consisted of small talk dealing with the current topic.

"Mark my words: this is not going to be as simple as Burt thinks it will be," said Bill.

John was the first one to be let off at his townhouse. After alighting from the limousine, John leaned on the rolled down window and said to the other two, "Well, I know what I am going to do—come up with a few names to bring this stupid thing to an end. You know I can't stand the way the old man is suspicious of me even talking to Jane. You'd think I was making it with her or something."

"Are you?" interjected Peter with a hint of knowing yet not really knowing.

"No, of course not," blurted out John. "Not that I wouldn't mind, but I hear she already has a steady boyfriend. It's just that Burt sometimes rubs me the wrong way when he talks about Jane like that. Besides, he has a nice wife. Why should he go chasing after some gorgeous young woman who feels she owes him something for trusting in her? She probably thinks she could further her career by going out with him or something like that. I imagine that is what the attraction is. Christ, how the hell should I know?"

While John was staging this tirade of the evils of Burt and the innocence of Jane, Peter and Bill eyed each other. They began to wonder if there had been anything going on under the sheets at either John's townhouse or Jane's apartment. They both had the presence of mind to keep their suspicions to themselves for the moment.

As the three men parted, they all had one common goal—to find some guy, any guy, who would fit the task and to do it with the least amount of running around.

Peter saw it as a chore, another in the long line of chores he had to do for Burt. He decided to use his many contacts to obtain key personnel files. He set about it the next day.

John had other things on his mind at the moment. He lay on his bed thinking of Burt going over to see Jane. It was not just any Jane, but his Jane—the Jane who on many nights cuddled up beside him just where he lay now. He never could understand the relationship she had with Burt. She had sworn it was purely a platonic one, but for some reason, John could not bring himself to believe that. On the other hand, he had no proof of the opposite either. These thoughts had often tortured him in this way.

Jane was the first person whom he really did love, and he was inwardly jealous of the hold Burt had over her. They often quarreled about it, and John had come very close to accusing her of having an affair with Burt. Even as he lay on his bed, he still wasn't sure. It wouldn't be that she had slept with someone, just that it was Burt, if indeed it was anyone at all. What he was really mad about was the way Burt made sensual comments about Jane—nothing heavy, of course, just little niggling things that probably only John noticed. He felt that Burt did it on purpose to get under his skin.

He wasn't sure how much Jane had told Burt about him, but the chances were that she had told him enough to make him jealous.

Christ, why should that old bastard be jealous? It's me that should be jealous, thought John.

The more he thought about the situation, the madder he got. He felt that he could never really trust Jane. There was nothing concrete; it was just the way she would keep away from him when Burt was around, and that really bugged him. Was she just trying to further her career, or was there something else? John often had this conversation with himself after he had seen Burt and heard him make some dig about Jane. John decided to call Jane. Her line was busy.

Who the hell is she talking to? he wondered.

Burt was the first person he thought of, so he immediately called Burt's private number. It too was busy.

The bitch, was the first reaction he had.

He tried Jane's number every five minutes, and it was a good forty minutes before he got through to her. When Jane picked up the phone, it was barely thirty seconds since she had hung up from talking to Burt. She made the mistake of thinking that it was Burt calling back to tell her something that he had forgotten.

She answered the phone with, "What is it now, Burt?"

When John heard that, he didn't really pick up on it at first and took a few seconds to respond. "It's not Burt."

Jane was taken aback and fumbled with her words. The only thing she could say was, "Oh, it's you, John."

"Yes, it's me. Were you expecting somebody else?"

Jane had to think very quickly again, because she knew that John was deadly jealous of her relationship with Burt, not that he needed to be. She quickly surmised that it would be more prudent to tell the truth than to lie.

"I had just been talking to Burt for a few minutes, and I thought it was him calling back," she explained.

At this point, it suddenly became clear to John that

maybe Burt was telling Jane about his plan. This made him angrier, because Burt had specifically asked him not to mention it to Jane.

"Why was he calling you this late at night?"

"He's not going to be in the office tomorrow, so he wanted me to check out a few things for him."

"Like what?" John questioned.

"You know that I can't tell you anything that Burt has told me in confidence."

John hated it when she used this excuse, because he had no way of attacking it. He decided to drop the inquisition to stay in Jane's good books. He decided to tease her with some tidbits of his own.

"I am not supposed to tell you this, but I have some very interesting information. I would rather not say it over the phone, so I was wondering if it would be okay if I came over tonight."

Since it was after ten o'clock, he was probably pushing his luck a bit. He thought that Jane would use some excuse about the lateness of the hour. She did, but John started to turn on the charm. This was something he could do very well, and they both knew that Jane would put up a fight for a while. However, they also knew that she would give in eventually, just to stop John's whining.

"Oh, all right," she said, "but no staying the night."

John agreed and quickly packed one of his suits and the other necessities required for an overnight stay. Jane's apartment was only a ten-minute drive from John's townhouse.

On the way over, John wondered how much he should say to Jane about the plan. After all, he was only guessing that Burt had already told her. Maybe he hadn't. If Burt had told her, then it would be all right for John to mention it also. On the other hand, if Jane had no knowledge of the plan and John told her in the strictest confidence, then Jane would feel that she could really trust him.

Decisions, decisions, what should I do? he wondered. *I'll play it by ear.*

John prudently left his overnight bag and suit bag in his car. When Jane opened the door, he got the distinct feeling that he should just say what he had to say to her and then leave. Jane was dressed in blue track pants and a white T-shirt—not something that would illicit a seduction, although Jane would look good in anything she wore. At first, Jane was a little cold toward him, as she was peeved that he was checking up on her conversations with Burt. John realized that she was not happy with him and knew why. He sat down on one of the two couches in Jane's living room.

"Coffee?" asked Jane.

"Yes, please."

One of the things that Jane admired about John was his impeccable manners. After she served the coffee, Jane curled up on the other couch.

"Okay," she said. "What is it that is so important that you had to see me tonight?"

"Well, you must promise me that none of this, and I mean none of it, will be repeated to anybody."

"Do you want me to swear on the Bible?" replied Jane jokingly.

"Seriously," said John. "This is that important."

Jane could tell that he was indeed serious and began to pay more attention.

"Did you know that Burt had called a meeting earlier

today with Bill, Peter, and myself?" asked John. "I must have complete honesty here, Jane."

"I didn't know until Burt called tonight," said Jane.

"Without betraying Burt's confidence in you, do you mind if I ask if he said what was revealed at the meeting?"

"No, he just said that you guys had a top-level meeting that, by its nature, he couldn't divulge."

"How long did you talk tonight?" asked John, getting into the personal area now.

"You know Burt; he tends to rave on about nothing. The main gist of what he wanted to tell me was that he needed some special lists."

"What sort of lists?"

"Darling, you know I can't tell you," she said, repeating herself.

"Okay, but if I tell you what the lists were, you would just have to agree or disagree. Now that wouldn't be betraying Burt's confidence, would it?"

"I suppose that would be okay," she agreed.

"They were personnel files from some of his companies."

"You guessed it," said Jane, showing a little more interest.

"Did he say why he needed these lists?"

"No, he said that it was just something that he needed in a hurry."

"He said nothing else then?"

"No, the other stuff we talked about was just everyday lawyer stuff he wanted me to do while he was away."

"Nothing out of the ordinary then?" said John.

"No," replied Jane. "Look, John, what is this all about? What the hell is going on? You are not leaving until you tell me," she said in a voice with a lot more interest.

"I don't know if I can tell you too much about it," said John.

This just made Jane all the more intrigued, and she insisted that he tell her what he had promised. Now John was in a quandary and knew he had to tell her something.

"Okay, darling, I am going to tell you. However, you have to promise me that you will never tell anybody what I am going to say to you."

"For the umpteenth time, I promise. Now get on with it," she said.

"Oh, I almost forgot," said John with an inquisitive look on his face. "After Burt told us not to tell anyone what was divulged at the meeting, he looked straight at me and said, 'Including Jane.' How much does he know about us?"

"Well, he knows that we have dated a couple of times, but I haven't told him too much of our relationship. You're probably reading more into what he says than he actually means," Jane replied.

"I will tell you the main thing, but I won't go into details. I don't want you to get into trouble by accidentally saying something to Burt that would let him know you knew. I hope that came out right."

"Oh for Christ's sake, John, will you get on with it?" yelled Jane impatiently. She was now bursting to find out what had gone on at the meeting.

"Okay, okay, don't get your tits in a tangle. Come over closer so I don't have to shout."

Jane eagerly leapt onto his couch.

"Because he didn't like anything that we had come up with the other day, the three of us were called to the estate this morning. We had listen to a tax-saving plan that Burt devised all by himself."

"Boy, he was a real bastard that day, wasn't he?" interrupted Jane.

John continued. "Now, you are not going to believe this, but the essence of the plan is that we have to find some guy who will win $10 million at the casino. He will then leave the country, and Burt will go to see him and receive back $9 million. Burt could also claim the loss as a tax deduction. There. I've said too much already."

Jane sat facing him with eyes wide and her mouth gaping. She was too stunned to talk.

"Well, what do you think of the idea?" he asked.

"Wait a minute. Will you run that by me again? A little slower this time. I need to get a grasp of what is really going on."

John repeated the story.

"I can't believe it," said Jane. "No wonder he asked me all those questions the other day."

"What questions?" asked John.

"Just some questions about certain laws in other states and overseas. I didn't think much of it at the time, but now I can piece together why he wanted those questions answered."

"We all thought the idea was quite off the wall," said John. "He wants Bill, Pete, and me to find the person to play the gambler. We all think it's a waste of time, but it's a job. Now, I know that you've probably got a million questions to ask. I'm sure they're the same questions we all asked, so I shouldn't really answer them."

"Can I ask just one question?" she pleaded.

"Okay, but just one."

"How could Burt be sure this gambler, whoever he may be, will win $10 million and also give back the money?"

"That's two questions," said John, "but I will answer both of them anyway. The amount will be won with prearranged numbers."

"That's cheating," she said.

"Of course it's cheating. Now I will continue with the second answer. This person who will be selected as the gambler will sign a document to give the money back."

As Jane listened to this, she couldn't believe that Burt would be quite that dumb. "That sounds a bit suspect," she said.

"Look, darling, you know that, I know that, and both Bill and Pete know it too, but as long as Burt thinks that it will work, the plan will continue. Now no more questions about this stupid plan, Jane; I've already told you more than I intended. I've also broken a promise I made to Burt that I wouldn't tell you. Well, it wasn't exactly a promise; I just agreed that I wouldn't tell you. Now I want you to forget everything I told you tonight, darling. I only told you because of our relationship. Whatever you do, don't ever let Burt know that you know anything about it. If he does say something to you, just pretend you know nothing at all about it."

"I've got the picture," said Jane, rolling her eyes. "Do you think he will get away with it?" she added as one final stab at a question.

"I don't think it will ever get off the ground. Oh, I'm sure a lot of time will be spent looking for the right candidate to play this phantom gambler, but I doubt if it will actually be achieved. Look, let's leave this subject for now."

Jane asked John if he wanted another coffee and also offered him some cake she had bought earlier. She was a lot more relaxed now, and John fancied his chances of getting an invitation to stay the night.

The cake was a chocolate cake with unsweetened icing. Jane didn't like to eat too much sugar so she could keep her figure in good shape.

As they both sat on the couch drinking coffee and nibbling at the cake, Jane said, "Why did you give me the third degree earlier about Burt calling me?"

John had to think quickly and didn't want to blow any chance of an overnight stay by admitting jealousy.

"Well, to tell you the truth, I had called you earlier and your phone was busy. So when you thought I was Burt, I knew you'd been speaking to him. Since it was just after our meeting, I thought he may have mentioned his plan to you. Now, normally that wouldn't have made me react the way I did, but it was after he had specifically asked me not to mention it to you."

Jane seemed to think his answer was a logical answer. John finished his coffee and got to his feet. Jane also got up and put her arms around his neck. She gave him a kiss. Not a good-night kiss but a real kiss.

"I suppose you're going now," she inquired with a sarcastic look on her face.

"I suppose so," said John with a little pout that he had perfected and used to his advantage in all his relationships.

"Knowing you, you've probably got your overnight things in the car," said Jane with a smile.

"Does that mean I can stay?" John asked with a bigger pout and a hangdog look with pleading eyes.

Jane could never resist that look.

"Well," she said in a drawn-out response, "seeing that it is quite late, you may as well go down and get your things."

John didn't need to be told twice as he cheerily obeyed. They had done this on many occasions, but because it was not a regular event, that made it all the more exciting.

Jane was just coming out of the bathroom when John came back upstairs.

She was dressed in a sheer black negligee. She slowly walked over to John, put her arms around his neck, and pulled him close against her. "I really love you so much," she said.

"And I love you too," John replied. John took her by the hand and led her into the bedroom. He began his seduction by slowly undressing Jane and kissing every part of her body from where he took her clothes. This titillation began to excite Jane, and she eagerly started to undress him. They had made love on many occasions, but it was different every time.

Once they were both down to just their underwear, John unhooked Jane's bra. As it dropped to the floor, he kissed her breast very gently, making sure not to touch her nipple. His searching tongue went around the nipple of her left breast and then the right one. As this was going on, Jane closed her eyes; she was in ecstasy. John now concentrated on the nipple itself as his lips ever so gently imprisoned the right nipple. His tongue helped as the nipple by now stood erect, ready to burst.

Jane was, to say the least, very excited by this stage. She was oblivious as John laid her gently on the bed. He took off her panties in almost the same motion while continuing his attack on her nipples. Jane was powerless to resist even if she wanted to, and she didn't want to.

John's hands now concentrated between Jane's legs,

and her passionate moans were his reward as the foreplay reached its apex.

"Put him in," Jane moaned.

"Not yet," said John as he continued the caress.

"Do it now," she pleaded. "I can't wait any longer."

John had held back as long as he possibly could and then made love to her. It wasn't very long before they were both fulfilled.

Just before she went to sleep, Jane said, "Do you think he will go through with it?"

"Who?" came the reply.

"Burt, of course. Do you think he will go through with this plan of his?" Jane said.

"Oh we're back to that again," said John. "I am sure he will."

Jane then moved closer and gave him a nice long good-night kiss and snuggled into his side. When they slept together, John would often turn on his side facing away from her with his knees tucked up. Jane would snuggle up to him in a tuck position. This brought them very close; they had a beautiful relationship in bed, even when they were both asleep.

I wish she hadn't brought that plan up again. Now I will be thinking of the damn thing all night, John thought to himself as he lay there with his eyes wide open.

When John awoke the next morning, Jane had already showered and was putting on the finishing touches of her makeup. She always rose early, because she claimed she needed her relaxation time. It only took John thirty minutes to shower, shave, and get dressed. Over breakfast, John again reminded her about keeping quiet about Burt's plan.

They drove to work in separate cars so as not to fuel any rumors.

When he came into the office, John saw Bill and Peter, and the three of them disappeared into Bill's office.

"I hear Burt isn't going to be in today, so I thought we could mull over the events of yesterday," said Bill.

"Like what?" said Peter in a rather perplexed manner.

"Well, now that we have all had a chance to sleep on the idea, are we going to go along with it?" asked Bill.

"I don't know about you two, but Burt has given us a job to do. No matter how we personally feel, I think we should do our best and come up with the necessary names," said John.

"Boy, you have sure changed your mind in a hurry," said Bill.

"I agree with him," interjected Peter. "No matter what we say, it isn't going to alter the fact that Burt wants this particular job done, so we may as well do it. We don't have to like it or even put much effort into it, as long as it gets done."

Bill, not wanting to be alone, quickly came around to their way of thinking. "Well, I suppose you're right. It won't do us any harm to carry out our assignments," he said. "After all, there is a large bonus in it for one of us."

"There's one thing we should do," said Peter, "and that is to make sure we don't overlap each other by looking at the same lists."

They decided to draw straws, as that seemed to be the fairest way to go about things. They divided the companies into three groups, and because the number of Burt's companies was not divisible by three, whoever drew the long straw would get the extra company.

The drawing of the straws was like waiting for the start of the one-hundred-meter sprint at the Olympics. No one wanted to go first, and it was John who eventually volunteered. He drew the small straw. Peter was the lucky one with the long straw. Next was the task of selecting which companies they would each take. This process took a while, because a lot of thought went into each individual's choice.

After they had all been accounted for, amid some groaning from Bill when he realized he had made a bad choice, John and Peter went to their own offices. They then set about making phone calls to the companies they had chosen.

As Burt stated at the meeting, he had already sent a special memo to all his companies. This allowed the release of the personnel files to any one of the three executives.

Chapter 4

The job of going over the personnel files trying to select some likely candidates was, to say the least, a tedious task. Peter and John took to theirs with enthusiasm, but Bill seemed to think it was a complete waste of time—valuable time that he could not afford.

The three-week deadline came upon them very quickly.

Peter had gone over a list of thirty prospects but had eliminated ten of them, thinking that twenty was a good, round number Burt would be pleased with.

John had not gone over to Jane's apartment at all during this three-week period, although they kept in touch by phone and saw each other as business associates at the office. John kept the subject of the plan out of their conversations, and if Jane asked about how it was going, he would give her a very vague answer until she realized he definitely didn't want to talk about it.

As John painstakingly went through the personnel files, he came across a name that was very familiar to him. A smile came to his face as he sat there looking at the name and thought back to a time a few years ago, when he had a whirlwind romance with this Australian girl. This was one name that he would definitely include as a possible candidate. John ended up with eighteen names he considered worthy and thought he had a good chance of winning the bonus.

On the day of the meeting, Bill, John, and Peter all climbed into Burt's limousine. It was a quiet ride to the mansion, because they had all agreed beforehand that they would not divulge how many candidates they each had.

They were ushered into the meeting room for the customary waiting for the chief. Burt walked in with a big smile on his face and a bunch of papers in a manila envelope.

He opened his comments with, "I'm sure that since we have so many people to choose from, we have come up with some quality candidates."

Burt strolled over to the whiteboard and put their names up. All four names were written down.

"The only advantage I will have," said Burt, "is in the final interview, but by then, we will all have a pretty good idea of who the candidate is going to be. Firstly, how many candidates do you all have?" He looked straight at Bill as he spoke.

Bill took this as a cue to answer first. "I've got five quality ones," he said.

Burt put the number five next to Bill's name. The other two men gave their numbers to Burt, and he wrote them on the board. When Bill saw that the other two had a lot more candidates than him, he started to feel insecure. When Burt wrote the number five next to his own name, Bill felt a little relieved.

"Now, before we start, do any of your candidates not have all the requirements, and I mean *all* the requirements, that I had determined?" said Burt.

"I don't think any of us can tell from a personnel file

if a person has a great memory," commented John in a somewhat sarcastic tone.

"Okay, apart from the memory, do all the candidates meet the other requirements?" snapped back Burt.

They all agreed.

"And I assume you have all brought the files of each of your candidates," said Burt.

Again, the three answered in the affirmative.

"May I ask a question before we get started?" said Peter.

"Go ahead," said Burt.

"Since the three of us had decided it would be better not to overlap each other, we divided all your companies between us so we each got a similar portion. Since we covered all of your companies, it would stand to reason that the names you have, we would have also."

"If that is the case, then whoever had the name amongst the three of you would get the bonus. However, I'm sure there are many names you have chosen to ignore for various reasons that would fill the bill, and I may have some of them. So let's see who we all come up with," said Burt.

"Peter," he continued, "you have the most names, so you can go first. I think I will admit one thing before you start. I have the personal dossiers of everyone on my payroll who meets most of the requirements. I will refer to that to weed out those not suitable. Okay, Peter, who is your first candidate?"

Peter stood up and shuffled through his orderly file. "Roger Beatty," he said.

Burt asked him to stop while he checked through his own files. "No good," said Burt. "Although he is married, he and his wife separated recently."

"How did you find that out?" asked Peter.

"I have my sources," came the reply.

Peter appeared a little miffed at the way Burt dismissed his first candidate so quickly. It seemed that each name Peter mentioned, Burt had some problem with. All but two of Peter's names were rejected. On the board under the heading of Peter's name, Burt wrote the two acceptable names. Peter sat down feeling very vulnerable.

John was next. He did a little better with three names. All of Bill's names were rejected. Finally, it was Burt's turn. The first name Burt mentioned was one Peter had originally included but rejected when he was preparing his list. Apparently, this person had a bad reputation of mistrust, but nothing was down on his file about it. Peter had questioned his supervisor, and this information was confidentially given to him. When Peter relayed this to the group, Burt was pleased someone was actually taking this seriously in addition to himself.

The next name Burt mentioned was okay, and so was the third, but the following two were questioned by John, who also had them on his original list before rejecting them. The first one was from New Zealand but had gone to live in South Africa and actually took out South African citizenship, so he was an automatic disqualification. Burt's final candidate was married but also had a mistress. John had really done his homework on this one by speaking to the mistress by phone after a fellow staff member had casually mentioned it to the candidate's supervisor.

The first run of candidates was two each for Peter and Burt, three for John, and for Bill, well, Bill was just along for the ride.

"So now we have the numbers from forty-eight down to seven," said Burt. "Of those seven, we need to check to see if there is anything else we have not discovered that would exclude any one of them."

"I suppose we could call each of their supervisors to find out what each is really like, because some things just do not show up on personnel files," suggested Peter.

Burt agreed and gave Bill the files of his two candidates for calling. He instructed Peter to give the files of his two candidates to John and for John to give his to Peter. That way, no one would be calling their own candidates, and Burt knew that they would actually try a little harder to get information. This would rule out more of the candidates, so their questions would take on a more probing and personal tact.

With that, Burt told them he would be back in three hours, as he was going into town for a luncheon. A light buffet was also provided for the vice presidents.

During the lunch break, the three discussed the morning's proceedings.

"You know that Burt will be pushing for one of his candidates to be the one selected," said Peter. "You better make sure you get all the dirt from those supervisors," he added, looking at Bill.

"Provided that there is any dirt to get," answered Bill.

The conversation switched to generalities when the buffet came in. Burt had outdone himself this time. There was an assortment of salads and a selection of three hot dishes of chicken, veal, and fish. Vegetables were not forgotten either. There was a wide selection of scalloped potatoes, green beans, baby carrots, and squash. When the three saw the feast that was to be theirs, they stood opened mouthed in disbelief.

"Boy, is this actually for us?" said Bill.

While the other two stood and just looked at the food for a second, Bill was all ready to eat with a plate in his hand.

"You know he is just trying to bribe us to make sure we do a good job in finding the right person," said John. "And I expect it will probably do just that."

"Who cares," stated Bill. "We don't get a good feed at Burt's expense very often. I intend to eat and drink as much as I can hold in the next couple of hours and then do my best to come up with enough negative reasons why Burt's candidates will not be chosen."

After lunch, there was almost an hour and ten minutes left for them to do their telephone tasks. There were several phones available, and it didn't take long for the respective supervisors to get on the job. Since they were all senior vice presidents, they would have no trouble eliciting the necessary information.

As the three waited patiently for their callbacks, they drank the endless supply of coffee that was on hand.

"The two supervisors of Burt's guys were very happy to get any info on them for me," said Bill with a sense of pride in his voice.

"We just have to hope they have some bad habits, at least enough to exclude them from being selected," said Peter. "I don't mind John winning if it can't be me, and I'm sure he feels the same, as long as it's not Burt."

John agreed.

The first phone to ring was for Bill, and he patiently wrote down quite a lot of detail. The other two phones began ringing almost simultaneously, and soon they were all busy gathering details. With just ten minutes to go before Burt was due back, there was only one name that had not been reported on. It was one of John's picks. Just as Peter started to say, "I hope he calls back before Burt arrives," the phone rang. When all the details had been gathered, the only one to talk was Bill, who appeared pleased, as if there was no doubt in his mind that Burt's candidates were not going to be chosen.

Like clockwork, Burt arrived back just at the three-hour mark. "Well, have you all received your information?" asked Burt.

They all replied affirmatively.

At that moment, it dawned on John that Burt had probably had lunch with Jane, and his jealousy started to well up inside of him. That was put aside, however, when Burt asked Peter how John's candidates stacked up.

"Two sound like very good candidates," said Peter, "but the third apparently has a bit of a drinking problem. It's not enough of a problem to appear on a personnel file but enough to put him in the doubtful category, especially under the pressure that this task will create."

"And you got this information from the guy's supervisor?" asked Burt.

"Yes," said Peter.

"Extraordinary," said Burt. "What exactly did the supervisor say?"

"Well, he was a little reluctant to talk about it. I could sense there was something amiss, so I put some pressure on him. He eventually filled me in on all the details about the candidate after I assured him it was strictly off the record and as long as he no longer has the problem, it would not go against him."

"And what are these details?" asked Burt.

"Apparently, almost every night this man was seen at

his local watering hole till the early hours of the evening. Up until now, it hadn't affected his work, but his supervisor thought it was going to be just a matter of time."

"Well, that's good enough for me," said Burt. "If we are all in agreement, I will strike his name from the list."

They all agreed, including John.

Burt continued. "There was nothing the supervisors could give you on the other two that may exclude them also?"

"Nothing," came the reply.

Burt then asked John for his assessment on Peter's selections. John replied that both of the candidates seemed to check out okay according to the supervisors.

"Good," said Burt.

"How about mine?" Burt asked Bill.

"Well, sir, the first one is okay, but as for the second, I'm afraid he will have to be taken off the list," said Bill with a little nervousness in his voice.

"Oh?" said Burt with one eyebrow raised.

Bill continued. "According to his supervisor, your candidate has been having an affair with a girl at the office, although he is married."

"Well, we can't have anything like that," said Burt. He then voluntarily took the name off the board. "So now from a top roll call of forty-eight, we are down to just five. This seems like a perfect number for interviewing."

"What about the memory part?" Peter reminded Burt.

"That will be the first part of the interview," came the reply. "I have devised a little scheme that will test them as to their memory for figures. The next step will be to interview all five men. If they fail the memory test, they will not continue to the actual interview. Of course, none of them will know what this is all about. They will be told they have been selected as the five finalists in a company-wide lottery for a top prize of one hundred thousand dollars. The four runners-up, so to speak, will get a prize of five thousand dollars each." Burt felt that giving away twenty thousand dollars was a small price to pay to get the right man for the job.

"The interviews will be in two stages at least and will take place at our San Francisco office," said Burt. "Hopefully, we will have more than one candidate going through to the second interview. Now, are there any questions?"

Peter was the first to react. "Who will be at the interviews?"

"Everyone here will be at the first one. Any other questions?"

When no one else had anything to say, Burt continued. "Now I would like this done as quickly as possible. I will arrange to get the five candidates here by Thursday, three days from now at, say, ten o'clock in the morning."

Burt asked whether there were any additional questions, and when no one spoke, he told the three men that a car would pick them up from the office at eight thirty on Thursday and bring them back to the house. He also stressed the importance of keeping their meetings confidential. Again, he glanced fixedly at John. John just stared back as if he didn't know the stare was directed at him. Burt also stressed that the next phase was probably one of the most crucial and delicate ones they would face. He asked the men to come up with a list of possible questions, no matter how personal they were, as long as it would give them a better understanding of the personality of the people being interviewed. The questions needed to be submitted to Burt by ten o'clock Wednesday morning.

"Would it be better if the three of us got together and pooled our questions? That way, we might come up with some better ideas," said Bill.

"As you wish," replied Burt, "just as long as I receive them before ten on Wednesday morning."

With those words, the meeting was adjourned. The three were taken back to their homes by the same limousine that had brought them to Burt's house. The drive home was again relatively quiet. They arranged to have a meeting in Bill's office around ten o'clock the following morning to come up with questions for the candidates. The others knew why Bill suggested that they all get together to make up the questions, but they kept quiet about it. John and Peter realized that they would be the ones supplying all the questions, and Bill would just agree. Oh, he would suggest some of the questions, but they would probably be the ones to be rejected. Since he was the most senior and the oldest, out of respect, John and Peter said nothing.

Bill broke the silence again with the negative attitude that the scheme would not work. Peter, who was getting a little sick and tired of these negative comments from Bill, suggested that he had been of the same opinion, but after listening to the latest events, he had changed his mind. John took up the challenge also and agreed that he had been of a negative opinion before, but seeing how far they had all progressed, he could see that maybe the plan would work. However, they realized that it was going to be mainly up to them to make sure that the right person was selected. This seemed to appease Bill, and he retracted a little from his previous statement, admitting that maybe it could work. He agreed that it was, in fact, really up to them to make sure the plan succeeded by picking the right man for the job.

Bill had a new burst of enthusiasm and couldn't wait for the meeting the following day. He stated that he was going to stay up way past his normal bedtime trying to think of questions. John and Peter just exchanged glances, and John rolled his eyes as if to say, "I think we have just unleashed a monster, but at least he will now be more positive." John was again the first to be dropped off.

Because it was only around five o'clock, John decided to call Jane and ask her out for dinner. A quick call to the office just missed her, as she was already on her way home. Since it would take a good hour for her to get home if the traffic was good, John decided to meet her at her place and take her out to dinner from there. He quickly showered and shaved. He realized that he had plenty of time, so he didn't hurry getting dressed. On the way over to Jane's place, John was trying to decide if he should say any more to her about Burt's plan, because he knew she was going to ask. He also wondered if it was her who Burt had lunch with again. He felt that to gain her confidence he should not tell her everything about the plan but instead tease her a bit by giving her little pieces of it at a time. That way, he could get to see her more often also. He also felt because he and Peter had two candidates and Burt just had one, the chance of him winning the bonus had increased.

He pulled up outside Jane's apartment and rang her doorbell. There was no answer, but that was hardly unpredictable, as barely an hour had passed since Jane had left her office. He decided just to wait for her in his car. Thirty minutes later, there was still no sign of Jane.

Boy, the traffic must be bad, thought John as he tuned his radio to the traffic station.

There were no traffic jams on the route that Jane would be taking. After an hour's wait, John began to wonder where the hell she could have gone. *Maybe shopping*, he mused. *No, not on a Monday night.*

He decided to return home just in case there was a message on his answering machine. As he was driving back home, he realized that there probably wouldn't be a message because there would be no reason for her to call him unless she wanted to know about the latest developments of the plan. All these thoughts were racing through John's mind at the same time, and then he came upon the inevitable conclusion. She was out with Burt again.

"No, that's not it," John said to himself. "Boy, am I getting paranoid or what?"

Of course, the first thing he did when he got home was to check his answering machine. There were no messages.

That's funny, thought John. *I felt sure she would want to know about today's meeting. Maybe she is getting the information from Burt ... No, she wouldn't do that. Besides, Burt wouldn't tell her. Wait a minute ... what if Burt is trying to get the inside track to Jane by telling her the whole plan himself? That bastard would do just that too.*

John decided to give Burt a call at home, although he wondered what he should say if Burt actually answered the phone. John decided that if Burt answered, he would hang up, and if Nora or one of the servants answered, he would disguise his voice and ask if he could speak to Burt. Then, if he was home, John would hang up before Burt answered. John waited anxiously as he dialed Burt's number. He could hear the phone ringing and wondered exactly what he would say. It was Nora who answered the phone. John asked if Burt was there and when Nora said he had gone to Domino's for a business dinner. John promptly hung up.

So it was Domino's, huh? thought John.

He then called Jane's number just on the off chance that she wasn't the one out to dinner with Burt.

Only Jane's answering machine spoke to him. John left no message. He decided to go to Domino's. He had taken Jane there just once. It was quite a nice restaurant but far too pricey for John. He stopped himself before walking out the door.

I need an excuse to go to a restaurant like this. I can't just waltz in by myself, John thought to himself. *I'll have to get someone to go with. Who the hell can I get to go with me at this late stage?*

As he thought quickly, the only person to jump into his mind was an ex-girlfriend named Julie. She had been crazy about him when they had a whirlwind romance about eighteen months earlier. She had wanted to get serious, but he hadn't felt the same way. John looked up her phone number and quickly called her. He had no idea what he was going to say to her but decided to wing it. Luckily, she was home. John could charm people on the phone, and Julie was a willing listener. Julie was interested that he had called and agreed that they should go out for dinner sometime. When John suggested that they go out tonight, Julie said she had just put some meatloaf in the microwave. John suggested she put it in the freezer to have tomorrow night. Julie was overwhelmed but said she would have to have some time to get ready. John said he would be over in forty minutes and hung up.

It was just after eight o'clock when John arrived at

Julie's apartment. When he rang the doorbell, he was a little nervous and felt a little guilty because he was using her. He and Julie had not parted on the best of terms before, and Jane had been the cause. When the door opened, Julie stood before him. He had forgotten how beautiful she was.

When Julie's eyes met his for the first time in such a long while, her heart began to double its beat. The feelings she had for him had not diminished in any way. John tried to remember the feelings he once had for Julie as she stood before him. She was a shade under five foot three, had shoulder-length brown hair, and wore contact lenses. She was a little on the thin side but looked great in bikini all the same. He gave her a little hug and kiss.

"I'm ready," she said with a big smile.

As they traveled down in the elevator, Julie asked him what the occasion was.

"No special occasion," said John. "I was about to go out to dinner by myself when, all of a sudden, your face just popped into my head, and I thought maybe you would like to go to dinner."

Julie was flattered. "You assumed a lot," she said. "What if I wasn't home or was involved with someone?"

"Then it would have been my loss," John replied.

"Are you still going out with that girl Jane?" Julie asked with an inquisitive tone to her voice.

"I just see her at the office," said John. "We haven't gone out together in ages."

John was a good, believable liar but again felt guilty. He didn't really feel comfortable lying to her—just when it was absolutely necessary, and this was such a case. He did have the foresight to call ahead for a table, and seeing that it was not a weekend, he was lucky enough to get one. As they entered the restaurant, he tried not to make it look like he was searching for someone. As his eyes quickly darted from table to table, he came across his quarry.

A funny sort of feeling came over him when he saw Jane at the same table as Burt. They were in deep conversation over their appetizers. The restaurant was a large one, so John figured that the chances of Jane or Burt seeing him there were slim, unless he wanted them to. The maître d' seated them, and their table was dangerously close to Jane and Burt. As women always liked to be seated facing the door, it was to John's advantage that he sit facing Jane, although he was hidden from her sight by both Burt and Julie. Because of their heavy conversation, Jane had not seen John come in. As they panned the menu, John asked Julie what she fancied.

Julie just smiled and said, "I'm looking at him."

John felt flattered and said, "Well, we had better not start anything here."

During a lull in Burt's conversation, Jane decided to go to the ladies' room. Now the journey to the ladies' room would take Jane just two tables away from John and Julie. John pretended to be reading the menu but lowered it enough for Jane to see him

Jane caught sight of him. He saw her almost at the same time, and he could see her eyes move from his to Julie, who had her back to Jane. Jane glared at John as he looked at her without any emotion on his face. He then went back to studying the menu. Jane walked past without any acknowledgment. Her reaction caused John to assume that she was jealous; he figured he would be getting a phone call when he got home and knew he better have a bloody good reason for being out with Julie. When Jane came out of the washroom, Julie could not see her. As Jane walked back to her table, she turned and glared at John again.

I'm going to be in deep shit now, he thought. *Gee, this is exciting. I'm killing two birds with one stone. I found out that Jane did go out with Burt and discovered that she is jealous because I am here with Julie.*

The one thing John had overlooked, though, was what he was going to do with Julie after dinner. As the evening wore on, John could see Jane looking at him from time to time—quite often, actually. John was beginning to enjoy this. All through the main course, Julie talked about the old times when the two of them were together. All too soon, Jane and Burt got up to leave. Their exit did not take them near John's table, but Jane could see them clearly and turned to take one last look at John, who pretended not to notice. After their dessert, Julie announced that she was stuffed and invited John back to her place for a nightcap.

John had been in this situation the first time they ever went out together and knew what to expect.

"Well, just a quick one," he said. "I have a very important meeting early in the morning."

At Julie's apartment, John knew he was going to have to be firm with her. After the drink, John said he had to be leaving.

"You know, you really don't have to go home tonight," said Julie.

"I really do," replied John. "Can't we have a relationship without us getting too serious?"

"That depends on exactly what you want." She had a way of saying things that could make all excuses disappear. John felt that he had bitten off more than he could chew and was in a desperate situation.

"Look, I really like you, Julie," John said, putting his arms around her. "I just don't want to get too serious. I told you that before."

Julie kissed him gently. "I know, I know," replied Julie, ignoring him with little pout-like kisses. "It's just that I thought that since you had called me and taken me out to dinner, you may have changed your mind about me."

This really made John feel like a heel, and he didn't know how to answer her.

Julie continued. "It's just that I thought I had gotten over you. Now that you have come back into my life, I realize the feelings have not gone away. Oh, John, I just love you so much."

John didn't know how to respond to this admission by Julie, but he knew that he shouldn't get in any deeper. "Look, Julie, I really like you a lot, but I'm not looking for a permanent relationship at the moment. I would just like to go out with you from time to time," said John.

"Well, I may not be available when you call," said Julie as she played with her hair and pouted again.

"Then I would just be out of luck," he answered.

John tried not to notice how beautiful she was and thought that he must be out of his mind to pass her up. If it wasn't for his feelings for Jane, then he would have stayed the night. He realized he had better get out of there as soon as he could. He again put his arms around Julie's slim waist and pulled her against him. Her lips found his in a longing embrace that neither of them wanted to stop. Julie moved her body against his and began a soft squirming motion with her hips and thrust hard against him. It was John who reluctantly broke off the kiss. Thoughts of a passionate evening with Julie began racing through his mind, and he had to use all his willpower as Julie's gyrations moving against him were beginning to break down his resistance. He said his good-bye and promised he would call her again in the very near future.

All the way home he felt like a heel for the way he used Julie.

I'll send her a dozen roses tomorrow. That should make her feel happy, John thought to himself. *What woman can resist flowers, especially a dozen red roses? I know it is a cop-out, but it's about the only thing I can do without getting in too deep with her.*

It was after ten o'clock when John returned home. He played his answering machine. There were two phone calls between nine thirty and ten o'clock but no message was left. John knew it was Jane, and he also knew she would call again.

He didn't have to wait long before the phone rang. He knew that it was going to be Jane, so he answered with a, "Hello."

"Oh, so you didn't know it was going to be me," inquired Jane in a sarcastic manner.

"Oh, hi, Jane," said John wearing a big smile. "What can I do for you at this late hour?"

"You know exactly why I am calling."

"I have no idea," replied John.

"Liar!" yelled Jane. "I hope you had a nice dinner."

"I would have had a much better dinner if I was with the one I would have liked to have been with," John said.

"Liar," repeated Jane.

"Then why are you calling me?" asked John in an innocent tone.

"I was just wondering why you would take that girl out

71

to dinner when we had an understanding that we would not date other people."

"Of course, you were there by yourself I suppose," retorted John.

"You know damn well that was business."

"All I know is that I called the woman I love just after five o'clock today and was told that she had left the office. So I went around to her place because I desperately wanted to take her out to dinner. I waited for over an hour, and she didn't show up. I had to call Burt on a different matter and was told he was at a business dinner at Domino's. I realized it was probably you he was dining with, so I called the only person who I knew would go out to dinner with me at a moment's notice. I just wanted to see you desperately today, and I didn't care what the circumstances were. That's the truth."

Jane was flabbergasted at this confession from John, and she didn't really know what to say. Her tone of voice quickly changed as she said, "You just had to see me?"

"Yes," replied John.

Jane's tone changed back again as she said, "Well, you didn't get to see very much of me, did you?"

"I could rectify that now," he replied, "if it's okay with you."

Jane was torn about what to do at this stage. She was really mad at him, but she was also flattered at the confession of his love for her. She also wanted to find out more about his relationship with Julie, so she agreed he could come over.

John had an overnight bag packed very quickly and rushed over to Jane's apartment. She greeted him at the door with her arms folded.

"Now, the first thing I would like to know is what exactly is your relationship with Julie?" Jane asked as she took him by the hand and guided him to the couch.

John was prepared for this third degree, as he knew that Jane was almost as jealous of Julie as Julie was of her.

"Oh, we're just friends," said John. "Tonight is the first time I have seen her since I started going out with you."

The third degree continued when Jane asked, "Why would she go out with you tonight on such short notice?"

"She is madly in love with me, and I can't help that. The feeling is not mutual, and I made sure she knew that."

"Are you going to take her out again?" Jane continued.

"Not as a date. Maybe just as friends, but certainly not as a date."

"Did you tell her why you took her out tonight then?"

"I couldn't do that to her, Jane. I'm not a sadist," replied John.

"I guess you're right. I wouldn't want to be used like that and know about it," said Jane. "She didn't see me, did she?"

John replied that she hadn't.

"It is sort of romantic what you did tonight," admitted Jane as her tone changed to a more understanding one.

It was now John's turn to do the attacking. "That reminds me," he said. "How come you were out to dinner with Burt?"

"He called me at two o'clock and said there were some business matters he had to tell me about and asked if it would be all right to discuss them over dinner."

"What business did he want to discuss that couldn't wait until tomorrow?"

"Now you know that I can't tell you that," replied Jane. "It was not the urgency so much as the confidentiality.

Burt didn't want anyone to know that I was finding out through my sources some delicate information on people who worked for him."

"How many people?" John said.

Jane couldn't understand why he asked that question, but complied with an answer. "Five," she said.

John knew immediately that Burt was using Jane to try to find out about the five candidates.

"You know, it's funny that every time Burt meets with his top executives to discuss this stupid plan of his he has to call you or take you out to dinner. Why can't he speak to you during office hours? Why must he see you on my time?" said John.

"I do believe that you are jealous," said Jane.

"Well, that makes two of us who were jealous tonight, doesn't it?"

"Touché," replied Jane as she put her arms around her lover. "You know, I really do love you."

"And I really love you too," came the reply. "So why can't we make some sort of definite commitment to each other? It doesn't have to be marriage just yet, but we could live together for a while just—"

Jane put a finger to John's lips and said, "Darling, we've been over this time and time again, and I'm not ready for a serious relationship right now."

"Well, what do you call what we have right now?" said John. "I'm in love with you, and you're in love with me. How much more serious can we get?"

"The commitment part is what I don't want at the moment," said Jane.

John looked hurt.

"Oh, don't be like that, darling. You know that you are the only man for me," said Jane.

"Then I don't understand why we can't make a commitment to each other. Nobody but us needs know," pleaded John.

"They would know if our address was the same," said Jane.

"Well, what would it matter if someone did know? It would just be someone in personnel, and that person would not mention anything," said John.

"Burt would know," Jane stated.

"Oh, so that's it," yelled John in an irritated tone of voice.

"No, that's not it," said Jane. "You're twisting things again."

"I'm just trying to understand what is really going on here, darling," said John.

"Look, why can't we leave things the way they are for the present?" replied Jane.

"For how long?" asked John. "A month, six months, a year, five years? You tell me. How long do we have to remain apart like this?"

"I don't know," said Jane.

"Well, I don't think I can accept the situation the way it is, and the way it looks like it is going to stay," said John in an angered tone.

"Well, that's up to you, John; it's your decision," said Jane, not wanting to be blamed for this confrontation.

"I love you, Jane, and I want to be with you. I would like to marry you, but I can't go on under these circumstances that you have put me under."

"Like I said, John, it is up you."

Without really thinking about the consequences and the misery he would endure, John simply said, "No, Jane, I cannot accept these conditions. Either we both make some sort of commitment, or we part."

There was a small pause. Jane was not prepared for John to be so blunt.

"What sort of commitment do you want?" she asked. "You know that I do love you."

"Either the promise of marriage or living together within the next six months. God, Jane, I'm not asking for the earth—just you," he uttered.

With a tear in her eye, Jane simply said, "I'm sorry, John, but I can't promise you that."

John picked up his overnight bag, went over to Jane, gave her a little kiss on the lips, and said, "Well, I suppose that this is it then. There is no point in us going on like this. I'll always love you, Jane."

He then left, making a point not to turn around and look at her. His final word to her was good-bye. All Jane's instincts were to chase after him and tell him that she wanted him back, but as the tears rolled down her cheek in a torrent, she held back from opening the door. She went over to the window and watched him get into his car and drive off, again, without looking back.

Was it over? Jane thought to herself. *No, it can't be over. We still love each other, and that won't change. No, it is not over; it's just put on the shelf for a little while. Yes, that's it. We'll get back together shortly.*

Who was she kidding? She had had her chance to make some sort of personal commitment, and she blew it. She cried herself to sleep that night, and in the morning, she put on her best business attire. She couldn't wait to get to work to see if John could look her in the eye and admit that he really meant what he said last night.

When she got to work, she strode into John's office, but he wasn't there. She asked his secretary where he was and was told that he, Peter, and Bill had flown to San Francisco for a high-level meeting.

"That's funny," said Jane. "He didn't say anything about San Francisco."

"He didn't know until this morning," replied the secretary. "Mr. Donaldson called him early this morning about it."

Jane couldn't bear the waiting to see John. The day normally went too quickly for her, but today it really dragged. She lunched by herself, and when she got back to her office she checked if there were any messages. There were three. A big smile came on her face, but it quickly went away when none of the messages were from John. Throughout the day, she checked her messages again. But none were from John.

At her apartment, Jane didn't feel like cooking. She didn't feel like eating either. She made herself a nice cup of tea and curled up on the sofa in front of the TV. She wondered what time John would be home but decided not to call him in case he thought she was trying to back down from last night's conversation. At nine o'clock, she threw a ready-made pizza into the microwave. She wondered what John must be going through, so she decided to call him after all. Only the answering machine spoke to her.

Damn it. Where can he be? she mused to herself. *Surely he is not out with Julie again.*

As Jane flipped through the TV channels, she came across the local news channel. It was the weather report that caught Jane's eye, especially the part that said the San Francisco airport had been fogged in solid and no flights had left since three o'clock.

"So he's fogged in," Jane said to herself.

Thoughts began to run through Jane's head. *The least he could do would be to call me and tell me he wouldn't be home till later. Then again, why should he? He broke off our relationship. Or at least I think he did. If that's the case, then he won't be calling me ever again.*

It was very hard for Jane to accept that their relationship was definitely at an end—just like that. *Maybe a few days away from each other would be the best*, Jane thought. *I'll give him three days, and then I'm sure he will beg me to continue our relationship, just the way it has always been.*

While they were in San Francisco, the three vice presidents came up with a list of possible test questions. They submitted them to Burt at his home.

CHAPTER 5

The selection process of the candidate was professed to be one of the most thorough procedures that one would have to endure.

The five candidates were from different companies and had no knowledge of each other. When they arrived at the office at 10:25 Thursday morning, they had no idea what they would be auditioning for. They were led one by one into a meeting room and forced to sit facing Burt, Bill, Peter, and John. Burt had approved about 80 percent of the questions that his vice presidents had submitted and had added some of his own.

The five candidates were of varying ages, backgrounds, and personalities. The first test each of them was to endure was the test of numbers. Burt used a standard test for memorizing numbers that many firms give to their employees. It can tell whether a person transposes numbers and how fast they are at remembering what numbers have been flashed onto a screen. It wasn't a really hard test, but they would be competing against each other and an acceptable standard. Any candidates who couldn't meet the standard would be eliminated. It took barely an hour for the first two to be eliminated.

The next step was a memory test. It had nothing to do with numbers, and the three vice presidents wondered why it was included as a test. Burt explained that one of the major attributes the candidate had to have was an exceptional memory. Admittedly, it would be for numbers, but Burt wanted to make absolutely sure that the successful candidate could really memorize. Of the remaining candidates, three more were eliminated by the memory test.

This ended the first day of testing, and there were just two acceptable candidates left. Burt was a little disappointed that he was only going to have two people to choose from. Burt and his three cohorts discussed the results of the tests, and all could see that one of the candidates was quickly emerging as the front runner.

"It may be a little early to select the one candidate just yet," said Burt.

The others hesitated a little but eventually agreed.

"Then how do we get down to just the one?" asked Bill.

"We will each have a chance to interview both candidates in private tomorrow," said Burt.

Two meeting rooms were used for the interviews. Peter and John did the first two interviews, and then Bill and Burt did the next. The candidates were then interviewed by the other two, so each had been interviewed by all four men.

Burt and his three vice presidents all got together to make a final decision. Even still, there would be a final interview by Burt himself, which would take the form of a dinner for Burt and the final candidate when the whole plan would be outlined. Burt asked Bill to give his opinions on which of the two he considered as the best candidate and the reasons why. The other two were also asked for their opinions. Burt found that they all agreed with his own findings.

Burt announced to the unsuccessful candidate that they had made their choice, and then he thanked him and gave him a check for five thousand dollars before sending him on his way.

As for the successful candidate, named Jason, Burt called him into his office and mentioned that he would be taken out to dinner at one of the finest restaurants in San Francisco the following night and a fantastic offer would be given to him.

Jason was advised that he had been booked into the Columbus Hotel near Fisherman's Wharf. He would be picked up at his hotel at seven o'clock the following night to go to the dinner. He was also told that of all the people they interviewed, he should feel proud that he was the only one they felt could handle the job. Jason asked Burt if he could give him a bit of a hint as to what the job entailed. Burt knew he would be inquisitive but only told him that it would be the most fantastic offer he would ever have the opportunity in which to participate. He added that all would be revealed to him at dinner.

The trio of vice presidents waited for Burt to return to his office where they had all been summoned. Burt announced that he would be taking the successful candidate to dinner, and if Jason agreed to the plan the bonus would be paid to John immediately. The three vice presidents had made an agreement that no matter who won the bonus, they would split it fairly. John got sixty thousand dollars, and the other two received twenty thousand each.

The successful candidate left the building with an added swing to his step. He hailed a cab with a lot more confidence than he had previously. He couldn't wait to call his wife and tell her the good news. As the cab pulled up in front of his hotel, Jason's mind was filled with only the thoughts of what the job entailed. He decided against calling his wife until later, after Burt had given him that fantastic offer. As he entered his suite, he danced around like a little boy and kept chanting, "I did it; I did it," as his dance turned into a skipping motion.

The candidate, whose full name was Jason Chard, was a very sensitive and, at times, emotional man. He was just shy of his thirty-fifth birthday but looked more like twenty-five, as he kept himself pretty fit. He and his wife, Debbie, were both Australian citizens and had been married for just two years.

San Francisco at any other time would be an exciting city to look around in, but the way Jason felt waiting to know what job he was to be offered, the city itself was an anticlimax. That evening, Jason didn't get much sleep, as his mind was full of thoughts about the job. He so much wanted to call his wife but didn't know what he would say to her. He finally decided that it would be better to call her after he found out what the job entailed.

Jason slept late, and it was almost noon before he eventually got out of bed. He decided to take a half-day tour of San Francisco, thinking that the day would seem to go faster that way. He was wrong, as the day seemed to drag even more.

He still had a couple of hours to kill, and his mind was full of the various jobs he could be offered. His present job was that of a senior computer analyst in one of Burt's finance companies near Los Angeles.

It must be something really good since the losers got a

check for five thousand dollars each, he thought to himself. *The least I would get should be double that.* Jason tended to go a bit overboard when it came to fantasizing and was often let down when things didn't pan out just the way he envisioned.

As he was getting dressed, he looked into the mirror and said out loud, "Who do you think you are kidding, Jason? It's probably just another job that is not really any more special than a hundred others."

By saying this, he knew that he couldn't be disappointed this time.

The time set for their dinner was eight o'clock, and Burt had sent another limousine to pick up Jason at seven to take him to the restaurant. This only made Jason think that the job was going to be a lot more important than he realized.

As he passed the foyer and entered the restaurant, a full bar and lounge area led to the large outdoor patio overlooking San Francisco Bay. The restaurant looked like a really ritzy place, one where Jason would never go himself. As he entered, the maître d' asked if he had a reservation.

"I'm dining with a Mr. Donaldson," came Jason's reply.

As he was taken to Burt's table, Jason savored the clean, classically elegant main dining room with ornate chandeliers from Murano, Italy, and paintings created by Thomas Cannon. Cozy booths lined the walls, while dark wood and vanilla-colored chairs serviced dining tables. Dark wood detailing unified the restaurant throughout. Soft lighting helped create a feeling of comfort and imbue the dining area with an aura of privacy and intimacy. Classical music wafted through the entire complex, and a single candle sat on each table. Burt hadn't arrived yet, so Jason just sat there and perused the menu. He decided to decline a drink until after Burt had come, as he wanted to keep all his faculties completely clear.

It was barely a ten-minute wait before Jason was joined by his host. Burt apologized for his lateness out of habit rather than any real reason. He called the waiter and ordered a gin on the rocks. He asked Jason what he would like, and when he ordered a rum and Coke, Burt showed a very subtle hint of disapproval at his choice. Jason was very adept at sensing what people thought, mainly from their body language, and the disapproval signs did not go unnoticed.

Jason had already decided what he wanted from the menu. He was not a very adventurous person, basically a meat-and-potatoes sort of guy. While they waited for the waiter to return with their drinks, Burt engaged Jason in general small talk.

"They serve very good seafood here," said Burt.

Seafood was the one thing that Jason really detested. He liked fish okay, but as for the rest, such as crab, lobster, shrimp, and the like, he couldn't stand it.

"I have sampled the seafood for the three days I spent here, so I thought I would try the steak this time," came Jason's reply.

The waiter came with the drinks, and the two diners ordered their meals. Both would start with the soup. It was French onion, one of Jason's favorites. He used to make it at home and often had people ask him for the recipe. When he gave them the recipe, he would give them instructions on exactly how to eat it so they didn't end up with all the onions at the bottom of the bowl. For the main course, Burt chose the lobster. Jason went for the steak, and when he ordered it well done, he observed the look of disapproval from Burt.

As they sipped on their drinks, Burt opened the conversation.

"I suppose you are wondering what it is that you have been selected for," said Burt with a little smile creeping over his face but retaining a sense of seriousness in his voice.

"Well, yes I have," replied Jason.

"There is one thing I must insist upon first," said Burt, "and that is complete confidentiality here. What I am going to suggest to you, you must swear that you will never, and I mean *never*, tell another living soul. Do I have your word on that?"

Jason was more than a little surprised at this request and hesitated to find the right words. "Well, yes, I promise I will not tell anyone of this, whatever this is," he said.

"Good," said Burt. "What I am about to tell you will seem more than a little out of the ordinary and will only be known by a select few people. I am going to tell you of a scheme I have devised to save money on my taxes. You have gone through a very rigorous procedure to be selected as a participant in this scheme, and the only request that I make of you is that if you choose not to participate, you will be paid for your time and returned to your current job. However, if you do choose to be part of the scheme, then you make more money in a very short time than you have ever dreamed of making in ten years."

This last comment by Burt really got Jason's attention, and he leaned a little closer to Burt.

"I bet that got your attention, didn't it?" said Burt with a genuine smile this time.

Jason nodded his agreement. Just at that moment, the soup arrived. Jason would have chosen to forget the soup and have Burt continue with his story, but Burt was hungry and the soup would get cold.

"I'm sure you are wondering what this all about and how you can make so much money," said Burt as he took the first sip of his soup.

"Well, I must say that you have me very intrigued," said Jason.

Burt indicated, as he nearly burnt his tongue on the hot soup, that they should suspend the heavy conversation until after they had done away with the soup.

Jason always thought it was a special art to eat French onion soup. A really good bowl was when the cheese melted right to the side of the bowl so you could pry it loose with a spoon. After he had managed to free most of the cheese from the side of bowl, Jason then used his spoon to cut a hole through the cheese that had hardened on the top. This way, it was possible to dig down and gather some onions, bread, and soup all at once. The only problem Jason had with the soup was the soft part of the cheese that tended to hang in great lengths and refused to break. Over the years, he had practiced quickly turning his spoon, trapping what was already on the spoon, and then continuing to turn it until there was a fair sized wad of cheese adhering to his spoon. This also had the effect of drawing the cheese out to a thin elastic piece that could be broken fairly easily. This way, he managed to eat the whole of the contents of the bowl without having to touch it with hands or use a knife to cut the cheese like other people often did. When he had made the soup at home for some special guest, he often ended up showing them exactly how to eat it. Being a perfectionist, he always rated French onion soup that he ate at a restaurant. This one was pretty good, and he rated it about a six. He used his own, which, of course, was a ten, as a yardstick. One way he said that you could tell if it was a really good French onion soup was if your nose began to run when you were about a quarter of the way through. So far this evening there was barely a sniffle from either of them.

While they waited for the main course, Burt asked Jason some more of his background. Jason was basically a shy sort of person, but once he got started on a favorite topic, it was hard to shut him up. Luckily for Burt, Jason's background was not one of his favorite topics.

"Getting back to our previous topic," said Burt as he wiped some cheese remnants of the soup from his mouth. "I will outline the scheme to you, and you can let me know whether you are in."

"Just one question before you start," said Jason. "Just on the off chance that I do not agree to participate, for whatever reason, would you have to go through this whole procedure again, or will you just give the option to one of the others whom you have interviewed?"

Burt was not prepared for this question but answered as best he could. "We would just pick one of the others whom we have already seen."

"To continue the story," said Burt, "I will tell you exactly what is going to happen using the actual people involved. You are going to go to my casino and win more than $10 million in one evening by using preset numbers. You will then return to your native Australia and wait for approximately six weeks. After six weeks passes, you will send me a telegram telling me exactly where you are. I will go to Australia. You will give me back $9 million and keep the rest. The least amount of money you will receive would be

$1 million. Now, I know you have a million questions, but I am going to insist that you give me your answer tonight. I know that one of the questions will be whether this is illegal. I have already spoken with my lawyers, and as far as they are concerned, it sounds a little like embezzlement, but after checking all the laws in Nevada, there is nothing to cover this situation. The major factor is that the money is all mine to begin with. Well, what do you think?"

Jason sat there just staring at Burt. His mind was racing along at a very fast pace. The only thing he was really concentrating on was the fact that he could make in excess of a million dollars. "There is quite a lot you are asking me to absorb, sir," said Jason in as polite a manner as he could. "As long as it is all perfectly legal, I would be willing to listen to the details."

"Before I divulge any details, I need to know that you are definitely going to participate. This is because I don't want to tell you everything about it and then you decide that you don't want any part of it," said Burt.

"There are a couple of things I need to know before I make any decision."

"Like what?" said Burt, wanting to get on with it.

"Like if it is perfectly legal, why all the secrecy?" questioned Jason.

"As far as the legality of it all, I have already had my experts look through the law books," said Burt. "Under the laws of this state, there is nothing to cover it. I want it to be kept secret because it is not something that a man in my position would like bandied around. This is such a unique way to make a lot of money that I don't want others copying what we are trying to achieve here. That would just draw unwanted attention to the casino. Besides, you would make more than a million dollars for one night's work, and no one is going to get hurt."

"The only other thing I need to know is how do I win $10 million?" said Jason.

"Another good question," said Burt. "There will be one croupier who will rig one of the tables. You will be given a set of numbers to play, and as long as you play those numbers correctly, you can't lose."

"What about the other people who are playing at the same table as I am and betting that legitimate numbers will come up? With the table rigged, they would be cheated out of a fair chance," said Jason.

Burt was not ready for this question but gave a very professional answer by saying that the other people playing at the same table would all be members of the casino staff who would be given chips so they would not be playing with their own money. To make their emotions look authentic when they won, they would be allowed to keep any winnings. This, of course, was utter nonsense, but it sounded plausible to Jason.

"I'm almost in," said Jason, "but I would like to ask just one more question. How do you know that once I've won the money and returned to Australia I will tell you where I am?"

"One of the prerequisites would be that you sign a document saying you will give the money back. Of course, you could sign the document and still keep all the money. Another thing you should know is that I have some friends in Australia who are, shall we say, not the type of people you would want to cross. Besides, from all the checking we have done on you, it would be abhorrent for you to go back on your word."

Jason knew that was true.

"Besides, there is one other thing I haven't told you yet," Burt said. "That is, if this scheme is successful, then it would only be the first of many in which you would participate. So instead of just $1 million, you could win get between $10 and $20 million to keep for yourself if we ran this thing a few more times."

This was, of course, not likely to happen, because Burt knew that it was only going to be a one-time event. It did have the effect of giving Jason hope that there could be a lot more money coming his way in the future. It was also the hold Burt had over Jason to return the money—the promise of more riches.

"So you want my answer tonight?" Jason said with a slight smile just as the main course came. As the waiter fastened a bib around Burt's neck so he wouldn't get the lobster all over his shirt, Jason began to speak. "Okay, I'm in. Where do I sign?"

These words were what Burt desperately wanted to hear more than anything else. He refrained from reacting accordingly so as not to give Jason the upper hand.

"We'll just finish this dinner, and then you can sign," said Burt with contentment written all over his face.

Jason looked at his steak with a very disapproving eye. It wasn't done exactly to his liking, but tonight he would endure a less-than-perfect steak, because tonight the only important thing was the adventure on which he was about to embark.

As Burt battled with his lobster, Jason tried to avert his eyes as much as he could. However, his ears took over as they couldn't help but hear when Burt ripped off a piece of the lobster's leg and cracked it between the calipers that had been provided. Jason tried to keep his mind on his own meal and forget the way in which Burt was attacking and devouring the hapless lobster, but it wasn't easy.

As the last piece of lobster was gobbled up by Burt, a good part of his steak was still untouched. He had reached a point where the continual cracking, dunking, and slurping of lobster had taken away most of his once-hearty appetite.

"Something wrong with the steak?" said Burt with his mouth still containing some of the lobster, which almost leaked out from the side of his mouth as he spoke.

"Oh, no," said Jason "It was just too much for me." He sat back in his chair, indicating that he couldn't eat another bite.

"Any dessert then?" asked Burt.

"Maybe some strawberry ice cream," Jason replied. "It's about all I could handle at present."

The waiter came to clear away their plates and take their dessert orders. Burt waited until the waiter was well clear before he got back to the topic at hand.

"So you are willing to take on this job?" he asked.

"Well, I'll give it a shot."

"I'm afraid that you will have to give it more than just a shot," stated Burt with some authority in his voice. "Because there is so much riding on your performance, nothing less than near perfection is a must."

Jason looked straight at Burt, trying to read his face for some little character flaw. "What I meant by giving it a shot was that I would put 100 percent effort into the task," said Jason, trying to get back in favor with Burt.

"Good," said Burt. "I'm glad you see the importance of your role. Now, I will just get you to read this agreement and sign it in front of a witness."

With that, Burt pulled out an official-looking document from his briefcase. He asked Jason to read it over very thoroughly and to ask him any questions if there was anything he didn't understand or disagreed with. Jason read the document twice and indicated that he was satisfied with it as it stood. Burt called over the maître d' to witness the signatures.

With those formalities having been attended to, Burt described, in great detail, the part Jason was to play. Jason listened very carefully and saw it as an adventure, something in which he could try his acting skills, not that he had any. His only claim to fame was to be an extra in a made-for-TV movie, but he had dreams.

After Burt had put the finishing touches to his story, he asked Jason for his comments. The young man took a sip of his rum and Coke, which seemed to last forever, leaned back in his chair, and delayed replying just enough. "I think I would get great enjoyment playing this part," said Jason, trying to impart a feeling of confidence. "I suppose that the major question I have is how soon will all this take place?"

"Do you think you could memorize all the figures, in their correct sequence, within a week?" asked Burt.

"A week? A week will be plenty of time," Jason agreed.

"You did mention," said Jason, "that if this plan was executed correctly, there could possibly be more work for me in this line."

"Oh, I don't think I said *could* be more, but rather *would* be more. Yes, if this plan were to turn out successfully, then it would be used again but for much bigger stakes, and you would be the one who would be chosen. Your share would be far greater also," stated Burt.

Jason had dollar signs in his eyes.

"Well, enough about the future," said Burt, bringing them back to the task at hand. Burt handed Jason an envelope containing all the instructions and the set of figures that would be used. Also included were two tickets from Los Angeles to Las Vegas for Jason and his wife, first class of course. Burt said he would not see Jason until he received a telegram from him in Australia in a couple of months. Burt informed Jason that he must never tell anyone about the plan, even after it was over—not even his wife. Jason agreed.

The two men then shook hands, and Burt said that the whole success of the scheme depended on how successfully he could play his part.

"Don't worry about me, sir," said Jason. "As long as the croupier has the table set correctly, you can depend on me."

With that, the two men parted company.

Jason was still stunned with the thought of $1 million in his mind. All the way back to his hotel, the only thing he could think about was what he could do with $1 million. When Jason arrived back at his hotel suite, he thought it best that he call his wife. First he had to make up a good story. He decided to tell her that he had been chosen in a company lottery to win a free week's holiday in Las Vegas for the two of them. All expenses paid, of course, and the possibility of a new executive job. He thought that adding the latter phrase would give credence to the trip to Las Vegas.

There was one last thing that remained to be finalized, and that was the selection of the croupier. Burt had already approached the most logical croupier, a man by the name of Carl. He had been hired directly by Burt two years earlier. Burt had explained the unique offer to him that morning, and Carl appeared very interested. However, Burt did leave out a few important details, just in case Carl did not want to participate in the plan. Carl was to give him an answer around eleven o'clock that night at Burt's house.

As it was now after ten, Burt headed back home to wait for Carl. True to his word, at precisely eleven o'clock, Carl showed up at Burt's house. The two men went into the den. Carl asked Burt a couple of questions concerning some legalities, and after being satisfied with Burt's answers, he agreed to rig the tables and play his role. Burt then explained the plan to Carl—at least, as much of it that he needed to know. He would be paid one hundred thousand dollars for his part and was told that Jason would get the same amount. Burt knew the two men would not get a chance to exchange stories, so he could tell Carl this lie.

When Carl left, Burt was satisfied that the two main roles in his plan had now been filled. The only other thing that needed to be done now that they had a date to start was the memo to be sent to the casino manager to allow unlimited bets for the current month.

Burt went over to his computer and started to compose the memo. He decided to make it short and to the point. He explained in the memo that he was going to try to entice people to spend more at the casino by opening up the no-limit rule for just one month to see how effective it would be. Burt felt that would do the trick when the investigation into the loss was started. Burt headed this memo "For your eyes only." This was something that he had learned when he was a clerk in the navy.

CHAPTER 6

Debbie, Jason's wife, was very excited about going to Las Vegas. Jason was excited too, but he had a few doubts about everything going off okay. Jason was busy with his calculator as Debbie stared out the window of the plane or read one of the many women's magazines that she had brought with her. It was her turn for the window seat on the way to Las Vegas, and Jason would get it on the way back. This is something they had done every time they traveled, but it always seemed that Jason would grab the window seat first. Debbie would invariably be stuck in the middle, normally next to an obnoxious person who wanted to chat about nothing in particular or who would fall asleep on her shoulder. Jason's excuse was that Debbie would always go to sleep, and it was a waste to let her have the window seat when she wasn't going to take advantage of it. This time was different, though, as Jason was not interested in looking out the window, for he had a definite task to do. He started to make calculations by using his calculator. Besides, they were traveling first class, and there were only two seats in their row. And on top of that, the flight was just a short one.

Debbie decided to relish in the fact that she had the window seat this time and tried to make the most of it by looking out of the window as much as she could. She marveled at the way the clouds looked so fluffy and pure white, as if she could just step out and be supported by them. She hadn't realized how thick they were.

On occasion, Jason would stop playing with his calculator and utter something quite uninteresting to Debbie who would just nod in agreement, not knowing or caring what she was agreeing with.

Jason loved flying, but it was such a short flight that there was not much time to get in to a good book. Jason was partial to crosswords when he traveled by plane or long train trips. He was good at them too. Not a buff, mind you, just an interested crosswordie. His main forte was trivia, and on one trip, he actually had Debbie read a trivia book and ask him questions. His answers weren't always correct, but a good portion of them were. He was very adept at general knowledge and was a whiz at the game of Trivial Pursuit. On this flight, Debbie was pleased that her husband was immersed in his calculations and wouldn't bother her with some of the absolutely useless trivia that he would normally impart on her.

Jason soon tired of his calculator and put on the headphones. He liked to listen to the comedy channel. His favorite was British comedy, such as the Monty Python group and the Dad's Army series. On this particular trip, one of the Monty Python classics was included. It was one where a group of rich men were sitting around and trying to outdo each other as to how poor they used to be. Jason and Debbie's younger brother used to do this at the dinner table sometimes, and they would both end up in stitches. Debbie could hear Jason chuckling to himself every now and again, and she just looked over at her husband and smiled without him knowing.

As the plane touched down at the Las Vegas airport, Jason looked at Debbie with a smile that could always brighten up her day and said, "We're here."

There was a courtesy car provided by the company waiting for them when their plane landed. It was not really a car but a limousine. Debbie had only ridden in a limousine once before. A previous boyfriend had hired one. This one was huge, painted sparkling white, and had a bar and TV inside.

"Someday, we will drive in one of these all the time," Jason said to Debbie as he inspected the whole of the interior.

"Of course we will," came Debbie's sarcastic reply.

Jason was a wonderful person, but sometimes he let his dreams get a little too big, and they were never fulfilled. The couple was invited to enjoy the amenities. Jason poured a drink for each of them, and they both munched on potato chips. They were swiftly whisked off to the Sands Hotel in the heart of Las Vegas.

Jason stood outside the front of the hotel for a minute and mused to himself, *In a few days, I will bring this casino to its knees.*

The Sands was a very impressive hotel—one of the largest in Las Vegas and also one of the nicest. It had twenty floors and was well respected for quality. It had become a five-star hotel after Burt had purchased it ten years earlier and made quite a lot of restoration and improvements. Jason wondered what the casino looked like, but he resisted any temptation to jump the gun.

While Jason checked them in to the hotel, Debbie took a quick sneak peek at the casino. She had never been in a casino before and just stood at the doorway taking in the atmosphere. Jason took her by the hand and guided her toward the elevator. The elevator ride to the twentieth floor was very smooth and slow. It gave Jason some time to reflect on the upcoming events.

All the thoughts of the big con were now being cemented into his brain. He managed to disguise the feelings that were just now trying to explode from his body. As the elevator arrived at their floor, Jason was jolted back to the present. He had been told that they would have one of the nicest suites in the hotel, not a penthouse but one just as good. Jason wondered what the suite was going to be like. Debbie had no idea they would be on the executive-type floor.

In Las Vegas, luxury is the keyword, and nothing is spared. Their hotel room was no exception. As they entered the room, Debbie's eyes grew wide with approval. She knew they were getting the red-carpet treatment. There were two queen-sized beds, a large TV, video machine, large fridge stocked with soft drinks, and a small bar stocked with mini bottles of various liqueurs. There was only one room, but it was like everything else—huge.

Debbie checked out the bathroom. She was fanatical about cleanliness in the bathroom. It wouldn't be fair to say that she was paranoid about catching anything from the toilet seat, but she always checked to make sure that the little sanitized strip was over the toilet. When Debbie emerged from the bathroom, Jason could tell that it had received her seal of approval by the look of contentment on her face. It seemed to him that women always thought the bathroom and closet space were more important than, say, the TV.

Debbie bounced on the bed to see if it was hard enough

in the middle. It was perfect. Jason turned on the TV to make sure that it worked. That was the first thing he would do when he went into a new hotel room. He also checked out the bar—not that he was a drinker, but he knew that he was going to be celebrating in a few days, so he may as well be prepared by making sure he had his favorite Kahlua on hand. His favorite drink was brown cow—Kahlua and milk. He had never been drunk, and the closest he had ever come was to be tipsy on five brown cows one night.

Just then, their bags arrived. One suitcase and an overnight bag for Jason and two suitcases and a very large overnight bag for Debbie. Of course, half of Jason's suitcase held some of Debbie's stuff also. This was normally the case when they traveled, but Jason didn't mind, because he did like Debbie to look good. Jason tipped the porter generously. Being a non-American, he always found it difficult to decide how much he should tip, and because he didn't want to be embarrassed by someone complaining about the tip, he usually tipped too much.

Since most of the afternoon was gone, Jason suggested they both take a shower and then wander down to the dining room. Debbie wanted them to shower together. It had been quite a while since they had done that. Jason took Debbie in his arms and gave her one of those kisses that he usually reserved for very special and intimate moments. One of the reasons Debbie fell in love with her husband was because of the way he could kiss. Only one other person had ever come close, and he was long gone.

Jason then moved his lips down to her neck, and with his lips slightly parted, he gently kissed her neck in a special place in a very special way. While his lips lingered on her neck, his hands began to undo the buttons on her blouse.

Her head went back, and his lips moved down to the lace on the top of her bra. By this stage, they were both becoming aroused. Debbie often thought that Jason should have his lips insured because he could do so much with them. He loosened the snap of her bra but was careful not to let the bra drop. He used his tongue to slowly drift down from the lace inside the bra and down to her nipple. Jason felt this was the area where he was most adept as he softly placed his lips around her left nipple and pursed them together ever so slightly, increasing the pressure just enough to send a small chill down Debbie's spine. His tongue also began caressing the tip of her nipple while his lips had it imprisoned.

Fires of passion began to well up inside Debbie. John inched her skirt up to her thighs and slowly moved his hands to her upper thighs, caressing them with a gentle, circular motion. He was greeted with a little sigh when he reached her panties and a bigger sigh when his fingers probed inside those panties. By this time, Debbie was really panting with delight, and Jason was reaching the height of his sexual excitement. All thoughts of the shower had disappeared as Jason carried his wife to the closer of the two beds. As he gently placed her on the bed, his lips found hers, and both their hands searched each other's bodies.

As they lay on the bed, Jason expertly began to remove Debbie's clothing, except her panties. With their lips still together, Jason managed to undress himself. He kept up the sexual caressing by slowly taking off Debbie's panties. He always enjoyed this part; as he got them down to her ankles and as she raised her knees in the most seductive way, his eyes gazed upon one of the most beautiful sights he had ever seen. Both knew that ecstasy would come very quickly, as they were both already nearing their peak.

As they began to make love, all thoughts of the casino were completely erased from Jason's mind. Even when Debbie screamed with delight at the end, all of his thoughts were only on the events that were currently taking place. When they had finished making love, Jason was not one of those men who would roll over and go to sleep. He would always hold Debbie in his arms, tell her how much he really loved her, and kiss her lovingly. She would always respond by snuggling up to him and knowing that she was safe and secure in his strong arms. She would then close her eyes and go to sleep. Jason would always wait until she was asleep before he would close his eyes.

Forty minutes slid by since they had gone to sleep. This was no major problem, seeing that they had no deadline to meet. Debbie arose first and woke up Jason. As they had decided beforehand, it was a joint shower that they jumped into. They enjoyed soaping each other down, but it was a bit of an anticlimax after what had already gone on. Dressing didn't take nearly as long as undressing, and they were soon on their way to dinner.

As they were going down in the elevator, Jason decided he would put his own private plan into operation. He told Debbie he had devised a system to win at roulette that simply couldn't miss.

Debbie had heard of his can't-miss schemes before, and none of them had ever worked out. This was his first venture into actual gambling, but she felt that it had as much of a chance as all his other schemes. However, not wanting to hurt his feelings, she tried to show some interest.

The dining room was befitting the rest of the hotel with about forty or so tables mainly set up for two. They were ushered to a cozy little table near a large window, and Debbie gazed out at the rest of the city as the sun slowly disappeared below the horizon. She was always big on sunsets and was in awe of their beauty. When they were in Australia, they lived near the beach, and Debbie would take Jason down to the shore and walk along the sand, marveling at the golden sunsets. To her, there could be no prettier sight. Jason ordered a drink for each of them as they perused the menu.

Seeing as all the food and drink was included, Jason had decided earlier to order the most expensive thing on the menu, but after checking out all the dishes, he decided on a large T-bone steak instead. They started with the soup—cream of leek. It wasn't one of Jason's favorites, but it was okay. Debbie could always tell when he didn't really care for a particular soup, because he would not let his lips touch it. Instead, he would use his teeth to extract it from the spoon. Debbie was the opposite, she liked unusual soups and was more adventurous than her husband. Debbie had also decided on the T-bone. Both liked their steak well done, and Debbie couldn't even look at a steak that had blood coming out of it. When they had ordered the steaks well done, the waiter gave a disapproving look but said nothing. Both noticed the look, and when he had gone, they laughed about it.

When the steaks arrived, they were cooked to perfection. Brown all the way through with just a touch of black on the outside. The steaks were very large, and as usual, Debbie could only manage to eat barely half of hers, and Jason volunteered to eat the rest for her. He could never understand how she could claim she was too full to eat anything else, because when the waiter returned to ask if they wanted dessert, Debbie could always find space for it.

There was live entertainment in the dining room in the form of a pianist who belted out a little bit of the rock classics mixed in with some of the older music. When a romantic tune was played, Debbie reached over and grabbed Jason's hand and gave it little squeeze.

During a break in the piano concerto, Jason tried to give Debbie a little insight into his new gambling system, fully knowing that she wouldn't understand a word of it. Jason did admit that it wasn't perfect yet but told her he would try it out tonight and see if he had to make any adjustments. Debbie had planned to play her own games in the casino and didn't really want to be bothered with what Jason was going to do.

After dinner, they went back to their suite. Jason wanted to work on his system for about an hour, and then they would venture down to the casino. This suited Debbie, because she could always use a few minutes to touch up her makeup and her hair. Debbie was always very meticulous about her appearance and always took as much time as was necessary to look just right. Jason went through his gyrations with his trusty calculator, and after about forty minutes, he declared that he was ready. Debbie wasn't quite ready yet, so Jason had to wait a few minutes more. He decided to check out the movies on the movie channel. One was a soft porn classic, he smiled to himself because he didn't need stuff like this when he had a wife like Debbie. As he searched through the other movies, trying to find something he hadn't seen, Debbie announced that she was ready. When she emerged from the bathroom, Jason's eyes took in all of her body, and his mind rushed back to a few hours earlier.

"Well, do I look okay?" she said.

"You'll do," came the reply. With that answer, Jason received a very black look. He immediately went over to her, put his arms around her, and told her that she looked absolutely fantastic. He tried to give her a big kiss, but Debbie stopped him because it would smudge her lipstick. They once again headed for the elevator.

"You sure I look okay?" asked Debbie again as they waited for the elevator, just for reassurance.

"You look great," replied Jason again, wondering why she had to be told every ten minutes.

After all, we're just going down to the casino to mingle with strangers, he thought to himself.

"How do I look then?" Jason amusingly asked with his arms held wide.

She gave him the onceover and said, "Did you shave?"

"Of course I did," replied Jason.

"Oh," said Debbie in a way that she knew he hated, because she liked to tease him a bit.

They waited for the elevator in stone-cold silence after that. They both could be upset so easily when it came to their appearance. As they stood there trying their best to avert each other's eyes, the urge to look became greater and greater, and when Jason began to smile, he caught Debbie's eye. She returned the smile, and they both hugged each other, kissed, and confessed that they were just being silly. This scene had been played out many times before under similar circumstances.

As the elevator neared the casino floor, butterflies were beginning to well up inside Jason's stomach. This was just going to be a trial run of sorts, so he wondered what it was going to be like on the actual night.

As they entered the casino, the noise became very

audible, and the smoke formed a large haze over the whole room, something Jason was not too pleased about.

"Boy, it sure is smoky in here," he stated. "I hope my eyes don't run."

Jason was a hostile antismoker. He would never beat up on a smoker but held to the philosophy that "all smokers should be lined up against the wall and shot." He was only joking, of course, but as with most little jokes of his, there was an element of truth to it.

A feeling of excitement came over both of them as they began to wander past the various games. For Debbie, it was because it was a totally new experience, and for Jason, it was to be the beginning of the greatest thrill of his life. Jason had given Debbie fifty dollars to go and play the slot machines, while he headed for the roulette tables. He always insisted on looking after the money and was tightfisted with it on many occasions. He didn't have to worry about money this time, though, because he had received one thousand dollars as spending money from Burt for this trip.

"What do I do when I run out of money?" Debbie asked.

"Come and see me, and I'll give you another fifty," was his reply.

"Why don't you give me the whole hundred now?" she said.

"It will last longer this way," he said.

Debbie pouted.

"Look, I'm going to be playing with the same amount as you," he said. "We have to save enough to play the next few nights as well."

To keep the utmost secrecy, Burt had made sure that only three people knew exactly what was to happen: Jason, the croupier, and, of course, Burt himself. As Debbie went off to seek her fortune, Jason decided to wander around the main room to check everything that was on offer. The prearranged time for the initial trial run was between nine and nine fifteen. Since it was barely eight o'clock, Jason had plenty of time to just look around. After about an hour, he began to wonder how Debbie was doing, so he slowly made his way toward the acres of slot machines.

It wouldn't be correct to say Debbie was remotely addicted, but she did like the thrill of playing the machines. Jason found her as she was busily shoving quarters into two machines at once. He watched her for a while without her knowing and wasn't surprised when she moved on to another two slot machines after losing at least ten dollars. She hadn't seen Jason watching her, and he melted back into the crowd and headed toward the roulette tables. It could never seem logical to him that some people could throw their hard-earned money away so easily. He was a mathematical fanatic and had calculated the odds of anyone winning money on those machines or on the various other games of chance that were offered. He'd come to the conclusion that they had two chances: slim and none.

Of course, in his case, it was going to be different. Boy, was it going to be different. He was by now really looking forward to this trial run.

Jason picked out the table at which he was to play by recognizing the croupier's name tag. The croupier, Carl, was a young man in his early twenties. He was short and had a very neat appearance and a moustache. With a name like Carl, Jason had surmised that he was probably of German or Austrian heritage. The recognition of each took place in total silence and without any telltale look that would give them away.

If things didn't go just right, as soon as the hundred dollars that Jason had taken with him was gone, then he would be through for the night. The evening at the roulette table began with two losses of ten dollars each. However, it wasn't long before he was in front. By eleven thirty, he was more than eight hundred dollars in front, and it was time to quit. Debbie had watched him for a while and had gone off to lose her second fifty dollars. Jason caught up with her when she was on a winning streak, so he patiently waited until she had lost it all. She went over to him, put her arms around him, and gave him a little kiss.

"Okay, I'm done," she said.

As they started to walk toward the elevators, Debbie asked Jason how he had done.

He just smiled and said, "Guess." He was always getting her to guess things.

When he told her how much he had won, she couldn't understand why he wasn't excited. When they got back to their suite, Jason said that he had to make a few adjustments to his system and got out his calculator and notebook.

"Why do you have to change your system when you already have a winning one?" she inquired.

"I am still not quite satisfied with the return on money ratio," he replied with just enough double-talk that he knew would confuse her.

Debbie just shrugged and prepared herself for bed. It was in the early hours of the morning when Jason finally finished his so-called calculations. He had gotten so caught up in the pretense that he had actually come up with some figures that looked plausible. As he turned to say something to Debbie, he noticed that she was already tucked away in bed. He looked at his watch and was surprised how quickly the time had flown. He gently climbed into bed and tried his best not to awaken her. She stirred a little and automatically snuggled into his side as he gave her a little kiss.

The next day was spent sightseeing. Although the casinos are the major attractions of Las Vegas, there were other interesting sights within the city. Even though most of the scenic attractions were a few hours away, including Hoover Dam and the Grand Canyon, Jason wanted to stay within the city limits. This meant going to the malls. This was not something Jason relished, but to keep Debbie happy, he would endure it this once.

When it came time for the casino visit, Debbie decided to try her hand at blackjack first and then go and see how Jason was doing. The dealer was at a different table this night, and the recognition signals again passed unnoticed by others. By the end of the evening, Jason had won more than three thousand dollars. Debbie had joined him when he was six hundred dollars in front, and again, she seemed to get more of a kick out of his winning than he did. Debbie wanted him to continue while he was still winning, but Jason pointed out that according to his system, he should stop now and that was what he was going to do. When they got back to the suite, Debbie asked her husband why he wasn't really excited over the win. Jason replied that he didn't think that three thousand dollars was a lot.

"Well, it's a lot more than you won last night," said Debbie.

"These two nights have just been trial runs for me to make any necessary adjustments," came the reply. His main comment was that he now realized where his system was failing, and with a little more work on his calculations, he hoped to have it perfect for the next day. She knew it was useless to argue with him about leaving the system as it was, so she just went over, sat on the couch, and turned on the TV.

That evening, Jason spent a rather sleepless night as thoughts of $1 million danced in his head.

Thursday arrived, and Jason awoke with an excited feeling inside of him. He woke Debbie with a sensual kiss, and as she started to move her body against him, he interrupted her. "No time for that now. We have a fantastic day ahead of us."

Boy, that's unusual for him, thought Debbie. *He never passes up lovemaking.*

Jason suggested they go downstairs and have a leisurely breakfast. Now, this was not something Debbie would normally interrupt her sleep for, but when he added that they would then go out and do some shopping with the thirty-eight hundred dollars he'd won, it was a different story. Jason really hated shopping with Debbie, because she would drag him through all the women's shops, but it was one way to get her out of the hotel and make her look forward to getting some sunshine and fresh air. Debbie got ready in near-record time, and Jason suggested they go out to a restaurant downtown and then go shopping from there.

"How much can I spend?" asked Debbie eagerly.

"How much would you like to spend?" came back the reply.

"How about a thousand?" Debbie asked, expecting a reply that would cut that in half.

"How about two thousand?" Jason replied.

Debbie couldn't believe it and gave her husband a really big hug. She wanted them to eat at the closest place so she could get the shopping started as soon as possible.

"This looks like a nice place," she said about the first restaurant they came to.

Jason knew what her motives were, so he felt generous because of the coming events of the evening and agreed to her selection. Jason tried to have a relaxing breakfast, but Debbie was eager to hit the shops and tried to hurry him up. Jason would have none of it and asked her to have a little patience. After all, it was her who always said that he ate too fast. When Jason finally finished the meal, including the two cups of tea that he had ordered, Debbie said, "Now can we go?"

Jason smiled and said, "Okay, let's go. Do you know where to go?"

"I have heard of some shops in the main street that are supposed to have really good clothes. So I would like to try them first," she answered.

When Jason heard the word *first*, he wondered how much of this torture he would have to endure, but he had promised himself that he wouldn't complain. The rest of the day slid by slowly as Debbie tried on about two million dresses, or so it seemed. They had agreed to finish shopping around four o'clock to give them enough time to get back to the hotel, shower, dine, and be ready at the roulette table before seven.

Six thirty came soon enough, and the butterflies in Jason's stomach began to dance as they seemed to take on dinosaur proportions. He turned to Debbie and asked that she stay with him at the roulette table. He explained that with the new calculations he had made, he was going to win big. He wanted her by his side, at least in the beginning. Debbie felt flattered that her husband wanted her close to his side. It was unlike Jason to ask her to stay for most of the time; he really preferred to do his own thing and not have her around when it came to gambling.

"Are you sure?" she asked.

"I'm sure," he replied.

"I was just going to have a few games of blackjack," she said in an inquiring way.

"Not tonight, Deb," he said. "If you want a couple of games, then you can wait until I have racked up some big money first."

He did make one stipulation, though. He made her promise that under no circumstances was she to interfere with his decisions on what to play, even though they may seem idiotic. She reluctantly agreed, although he knew that as the money rose, she would not be able to hold her tongue.

"Oh, come now, darling. You know I don't tell you how to bet," Debbie protested.

"Not normally, but in this case, my system calls for rather unusual types of bets with large sums of money, and I know what you are like."

"How large are these bets going to be? You are not going to do anything stupid, are you?" said Debbie.

"See, that's what I mean," replied Jason. "You are already worrying about it, and I haven't even started yet. I have only brought five hundred dollars with me, so once that is gone, then we're out of here. I have a feeling things are going to seem unbelievable at the end of the evening."

Debbie was skeptical but agreed to keep quiet.

"The key to my system," he whispered to Debbie, "is to wait until a sixteen comes up and then begin the betting."

"Why a sixteen?" Debbie asked.

"It's just the way I have it planned," said Jason.

"How much have you planned to win?" asked Debbie.

"Can you keep a secret?" he said to her and leaned over closer to continue. "I don't know."

"You must have some idea," she said.

"Well, yes, I have some idea, but it would depend on how far they will let me go."

Debbie looked puzzled and said, "Why? How can they stop you?"

"They can close the wheel," answered Jason.

"Can't your system work any table?" Debbie said.

Jason knew that this conversation was going nowhere. He answered that he would have to start again at a new table, and the explanation was quite technical. Debbie knew that when he didn't want to have to explain anything to her, he said that it was technical, so she decided to let the matter drop. The ante Jason was willing to spend was one thousand dollars, but he wanted Debbie to believe it was five hundred. He bought chips in various denominations. Now it was time to put on the show of his life.

As the clock registered twelve minutes to seven, he took Debbie by the hand and went to find the right table. There were sixteen roulette tables operating, so Jason systematically went down each aisle searching for that familiar face. After the first twelve tables were passed, Debbie asked what table he was looking for.

In a minor panic, he blurted out, "The one with the least people."

Debbie accepted this as a logical answer and trundled off beside him.

"There are only five people at this table," said Debbie as she pointed to one they were about to pass.

As Jason checked out the croupier, he said, "Still too many."

"Well, I don't think that you are going to find one with fewer people," she said.

"Yes, I will," he replied without even looking at her.

With only four more tables to go, Jason was beginning to worry. Many thoughts were flashing through his mind. Did he get the right night at the right time? When he looked at the faces of the dealers at the last few tables, he broke out into a cold sweat, as they were all unfamiliar. Panic gripped him like a vice. It was six minutes to seven now. Jason's mind was working overtime, and he sent Debbie to get a couple of drinks so he could look some more. His eyes searched the whole casino, but the faces became just a blur. He began a panicked rush up and down the roulette aisles but still could not see his contact. The dollar signs in his eyes began to fade along with the dreams he had for the money. Before Debbie got back, he decided to search the whole casino in case his contact was not on the roulette tables. He began to curse to himself over and over, "Where the hell is he?"

As Jason darted between the various tables, he came across a special section right in the middle of the casino that he had not noticed before. This section was reserved for those gamblers who were deemed high rollers. It contained a roulette table and a blackjack table. As Jason's eyes searched this section, his heart jumped up into his mouth as the familiar face of the croupier appeared at the roulette table. Jason looked at his watch. It was three minutes to seven. He quickly raced back to where Debbie would be waiting, and luckily, she was still there. He grabbed her hand and raced to the elite section. She did her best not to let the drinks spill as Jason dragged her along.

"What's the big hurry?" she said as they almost sprinted along.

"Time is money," Jason found himself blurting out and then wondered why he said that.

The big clock at the casino struck seven just as he took a seat at the roulette wheel.

"There are more than five people at this table," said Debbie.

"Yes, but the bets can be bigger," he replied.

She pretended to understand that logic with a simple, "Oh." Debbie began to look around the table and leaned close to Jason. "Boy, the people at this table must be rich. Did you see all that jewelry on the women?"

Debbie felt out of place without having a diamond or pearl necklace like all the other women who were standing behind their husbands, boyfriends, or whatever. *Maybe their sugar daddies*, she mused.

Jason knew that she was checking out all the jewelry and leaned back and said, "Darling, by tomorrow, I will have enough to buy you jewelry like any in this room."

She just squeezed his hand. He bought another five hundred dollars in chips and smiled to Debbie who took up a position behind him. He leaned back again and reminded her of her promise not to advise him on his bets.

He waited patiently for the sixteen to come. It was just two plays later when the starting signal came up. Again, there was a recognition between Jason and the croupier that went unnoticed by anyone else. At this table, the minimum bet was one hundred dollars.

Jason placed chips worth one hundred dollars on number six. The wheel was spun, and all eyes were glued to the little white ball as it went round and round, seeming to continue on forever. No eyes were more intent than Jason's. As the white ball dropped into the number-six slot, Debbie let out a shriek.

"How much did we win?" she whispered to Jason.

"Three and a half thousand," he answered.

Debbie couldn't believe it and threw her arms around her husband.

"You are going to put some of that aside, aren't you?" Debbie asked.

Jason just put a finger to his lips and reached out to put chips worth one thousand dollars on the split of number twenty-two and twenty-three.

"What does that mean?" Debbie said.

"It means that if either of those numbers comes up, we will win seventeen thousand dollars," stated Jason.

"I sure hope you know what you are doing," said Debbie. "I can't watch this." She looked away.

This time, it seemed to take forever as the little white ball moved steadily around the wheel, seeming to search out one of the two magic numbers that Jason had his money on. There were groans all around the table as the ball finally dropped. At this stage, Debbie turned around to see where the ball had landed and couldn't believe her eyes when she saw that it had nestled into the number-twenty-two groove. Jason had a smile on his face but remained quite calm for a man who had just made over seventeen thousand dollars on one turn of a wheel.

Debbie showed her excitement by letting out a little squeal and hugged him again. Jason was beginning to believe in his own luck but knew it was because of the plan. He decided to follow it to the letter, although it would be very easy to stray a little from it and to bet more.

The next bet called for five thousand dollars to be placed on the corner bet of numbers nineteen, twenty, twenty-two, and twenty-three. By this time, Debbie was beginning to get more involved in the game and held back from querying any of her husband's bets. It was Debbie's eyes that were the widest as she watched the little white ball make another never-ending sojourn around the wheel. As the ball dropped into the number nineteen slot, Debbie almost pulled Jason's arm off with excitement.

She looked at the huge stacks of chips that were beginning to pile up in front of her husband and began to feel really proud. She wanted to tell all those watching, especially those snobs done up in their designer gowns and wearing outlandishly rich jewelry, that the man making them all go ooh and ah was her husband. Again, she asked how much he had won. This time, Jason chose not to tell her; otherwise, she would be asking him the same question every time.

He just said, "I'm not exactly sure, but it's a lot."

Debbie knew that this was his way of saying, "I'll tell you later."

The next move in the plan was to put ten thousand on four splits, which would net seventeen to one odds. The splits selected were numbers nine and twelve, twenty-three and twenty-four, twenty-nine and thirty, and the last one of thirty-four and thirty-five. Debbie couldn't hold her tongue any longer and questioned Jason putting on such a large sum of money.

Jason gave her an icy stare and just said very quietly, "Watch the ball."

The tension of watching that bloody little thing deciding the fate of their riches was almost too much for Debbie, but she complied with her husband's wishes all the same. Jason's eyes were only one of many pairs that were watching the rolling orb, as he quickly calculated that a win here would make him $200,500 up. The ball finally finished its long roll, dropping on cue into the number-thirty-four slot.

Jason didn't look at Debbie as the croupier pushed the large amount of chips toward him. A quick tug on his jacket told him that she was still there, shaking with delight. He dared not tell her how much they had won, fearing that she would pass out. By this time, quite a crowd was beginning to form around the table, and others were beginning to follow Jason's example. The next step was to net a cool $350,000 by placing three $10,000 bets on selected numbers, which would give a return of thirty-five to one. The numbers chosen were eighteen, twenty-four, and thirty. Five others at the table duplicated Jason's bet but used one thousand dollars instead of ten thousand. The croupier looked a little concerned at this, because it was one thing that they didn't count on. If the other people's bets got too big, something would have to be done, such as a purposeful loss of small amounts on a couple of successive occasions.

Again, all eyes were glued on the white ball as the croupier with great ease and dexterity flung it around the wheel. By this time, Debbie was nestled right up against Jason with her hand clasped in his for extra luck.

The noise from the table was attracting more people as the newcomers were trying to find out what all the excitement was about.

The people who had bet the same as Jason tried to inch closer to him in the hope that some of his luck would rub off on them. The ball seemed to take a week before it suddenly dropped into slot eighteen. Another win. The crowd shrieked and screamed, but none louder than Debbie who again begged Jason to put some of the money away and just play with a few thousand dollars, not knowing exactly how much they had won already. Debbie asked him how much he had won, but as usual, he remained mute about it and just put a finger to his lips. He could see that this was upsetting to her, because everyone else around the table had calculated Jason's winnings.

He leaned back and motioned for her to come closer and whispered in her ear. "Half a million dollars."

She was staggered at this amount and hugged him tightly. She had never been prouder of him. With the total winnings now over half a million dollars, Jason realized that he had this crowd eating out of his hand. He decided to put on a little theatrics by holding his next bet to the last few seconds. He then put down three bets of one thousand dollars on splits of one and two, thirteen and fourteen, and the last one of twenty-two and twenty-three. The croupier, who was working strictly within the rules and to the plan, advised Jason that this was over the limit. Only the casino manager could authorize such a bet. All bets were frozen on the table, and no one else was allowed to place any more bets. An attendant was dispatched to the casino manager's office. Burt had given the casino manager orders for the current month there were to be no limits to bets on roulette. The reason given for such a drastic step was that it was to be a pilot project to try to win as much money as they could from the high rollers.

While the wheel was stopped waiting for the manager to rule on the bets, a buzz went around the crowd. Many people came up to Jason and shook him by the hand. Debbie begged him to stop while he was still ahead, adding that they had already won enough money. Jason reminded her that she had promised to keep quiet about the betting.

"I know I did, darling," she said, "but I didn't think it would get to be this much."

Jason was hardly listening to all the chatter that was going on around him, but he did know that it was all about him. Everyone who shook his hand said something like, "We're all with you."

Even as Debbie was putting in her two cents, Jason's concentration was on the manager's approval. He knew Burt had issued the order to allow unlimited bets, but it was still up to the manager to actually say yes.

Debbie thrust a drink into Jason's hand as they waited for the approval. As he surveyed the crowd, Jason knew all eyes were going to be on him when the wheel started again. *Boy, I'm sure that a lot of these people will have a really good story to tell their children or grandchildren in years to come,* Jason thought, again letting his own importance run away with him.

The attendant quickly raced back with a piece of paper in his hand and the word *approved* written above his signature. You could almost feel the tension in the air as the whole crowd held their breath waiting for the answer to be divulged.

Debbie couldn't decide what she really wanted the answer to be. On one hand, she wanted her husband to quit and to at least keep what he had already won. On the other hand, if he was so confident about the continuance of his winning streak, then maybe he should place some more bets as long as he kept some money back.

When the croupier read the note, he looked at Jason and said, "The bet has been approved."

A great cheer went up from the crowd again. Debbie's decision had already been made for her, so she decided to trust in fate—the spin of the wheel.

The wheel was started again. Many of the crowd thought that Jason had really screwed up this time with such large bets. Debbie, who was trying to follow what all the fuss was about, suddenly realized that the chips she thought were worth one thousand dollars were actually worth ten thousand. Her husband had just bet thirty thousand dollars on one spin.

Debbie protested to Jason that he should just stick to betting one thousand dollars at a time, but the protest fell on deaf ears. The ball was well on its tenth lap of the wheel and due to die soon. Debbie couldn't watch and put her hands over her eyes like she used to do when watching scary movies, with her fingers parted slightly so she could peer between the gaps. A loud cheer of joy erupted from the crowd when the ball dropped into the number-fourteen slot—one and a half million dollars on one turn of the wheel. Debbie didn't know whether to scream or cry. She chose the former. Debbie again wanted to know how much he had won. Jason liked to play little games with her, so he asked her how much she thought he had won.

"Oh, I don't know," she said in a pleading voice. "Maybe six hundred thousand?"

Jason just said, "More than that."

He then turned back to the game. Remembering the next phase of the plan was the four-bet play, Jason surveyed the numbers, pretending to study them. He finally put a one-hundred-dollar chip on each of the numbers seven, nine, twenty, and thirty-three, fully knowing that the number twenty would come up. Since no copycat gambler was betting more than a hundred dollars, the problem that they thought may arise has not. Thoughts of what he was going to do with his share totaling approximately $1 million were beginning to loom very big in his mind, as he stared at the ball going around the wheel but not really seeing it.

The shrieks of joy from the crowd and the tugging at his jacket from his wife snapped him back to reality as the ball dropped into the number-twenty slot. News of Jason's phenomenal luck had filtered back to the casino manager, and when he was told that his winnings were now more than $5 million, he made a hurried call to Burt. However, Burt was away and could not be reached. It was now up to him to make the decisions.

The only recourse he had left was to have the table closed down. The only way to close down a table was to do it in person, so he raced out of his office and headed toward the table. Since the crowd was now packed in tightly around the table, the manager couldn't get through in time to stop Jason from placing his next bet. The number that was to win was twenty-five, so he put down one hundred thousand on numbers seventeen, twenty-five, thirty, and thirty-three just to give the feeling of authenticity. The casino manager made it to the table just as the ball was dropped. His eyes were anxious as they were glued to the ball, and when he heard the cheer from the crowd, he knew that the casino had lost again. The manager went over to the croupier and asked him how much Jason had won.

"Just over $8 million," came the reply.

The manager reeled at this answer and then declared that the table was now closed. The crowd booed vehemently, and Debbie pleaded with Jason to leave while he was still ahead, fearing that if he continued, all the money would be lost. Of course, she had no idea how much money Jason had already won. Jason would not be shaken and was determined to see the plan through to its end. This was not part of the plan; the closing of a table was the last resort open to a casino manager and was usually done because of suspected cheating. Seeing that no one would be able to detect any cheating in this case, Jason could challenge the closure. Burt had not planned for the closing of the table, so Jason had to do this part off the cuff and improvise.

Jason knew the crowd was 100 percent behind him, so he decided to use this to his advantage. He called for quiet from the crowd, or rather his audience, and the noise fell to a hush; all ears and eyes were strained toward him. He raised his voice so that all could hear him and told the manager that if the table was closed, he would just move to another and win there. However, if he allowed it to remain open for one more play, then he would quit and no longer bet at the casino for a year. The manager had always hated making tough decisions; his health had not been too good lately, and he worried about what Burt would say or do to him if this young upstart were to win again. Beads of sweat started to form on the tip of the manager's nose, and the hairs of his pencil-thin moustache began to stand up on end as if they were frozen. At first, his voice was rather weak and squeaky. You could almost see his heart beating beneath his starched, white, neatly pressed shirt. His once-neat white handkerchief should have been dripping wet with the amount of sweat that it had soaked up from his brow.

"Is there a problem with that?" said Jason almost haughtily. He could play the snob when he wanted to and often pretended to be wealthier than he actually was. In fact, he wasn't wealthy at all. He and Debbie owed money to various finance companies and barely managed to pay the minimum payment each month. Jason stared straight at the manager, almost defying him to say no.

The manager was aware of the tremendous pressure that had been placed upon him. All his senses told him to close the wheel. Debbie was squeezing Jason's hand and urging him not to do anything foolish. The crowd was silent, and all waited for the answer with great anticipation. The manager weighed up the odds of this man winning on just one game; they must be astronomical. Oh, why did he have to become a casino boss? If he closed the table now, the house would still be out of pocket by $8 million.

No, he thought to himself. *It is too much of a gamble.* The boss then announced that the table would remain closed. Again, the crowd booed and hissed, some calling the manager a cheat and a coward. Jason again held up his hands and asked for quiet from his faithful hoard.

"What if I put half of my winnings down on four numbers, and we have a six-to-one bet? This would mean that I would either walk away with $12 million or $4 million."

The croupier looked at Jason, not sure whether he had gone out of the bounds of the system but decided it was probably the best thing to do under the circumstances.

All eyes were now on the casino manager. The pressure was now really on him. He needed time to think about this and asked for a ten-minute break while he reconsidered. He took the croupier aside, and they both went to the manager's office and contemplated the odds. The croupier was careful not to give his opinion even when asked, because he didn't want to be implicated at all.

Back at the table, the crowd moved in ever closer to Jason, and the fact that newcomers were arriving all the time pushed them together like sardines.

"This could be a record for this casino," said one member of the crowd.

Debbie was trying to figure out what was actually being decided and leaned down to ask her husband what the outcome could be either way.

"Well, darling," he said, "we have at present $8 million in hand. If the table remains closed, we walk away with that sum, but if they reopen the table, we will walk away with $12 million."

"What if you lose?" asked Debbie.

"If that were to happen, we would still have $4 million to keep," replied Jason. "I have enormous faith in my system, and I know I am going to win."

As soon as Debbie heard the amount of $8 million, she swayed a little and felt that she was about to faint. She stood on very wobbly legs and said in a disbelieving voice, "You did say $8 million dollars, didn't you?"

Jason just nodded with a smile. Just then, a flashbulb went off in Jason's face and a microphone was thrust up to him.

Oh no, he thought. *The press have arrived.*

"What do you think the manager will decide?" said a rather pretty female reporter.

"I can't second-guess what he will decide, but if you had the chance of saving $8 million or losing $4 million, what would you do?" replied Jason.

This answer threw the reporter. She didn't really have time to form an answer, so she moved on to the next question.

"What do you think your chances of winning the final bet are?" she asked.

"I have great confidence in my luck at present," he replied. "Otherwise, I wouldn't bother to bet."

"With such a large amount of money at stake here, aren't you nervous?"

"You bet I'm nervous," said Jason. "I have never been this nervous in my life. It is also so exciting. Look around the room here. These people are all on my side. They all want me, a total stranger, to win. Can you possibly imagine how that feels?"

The reporter saw how Debbie was all over Jason and figured that she must be his wife or girlfriend. Her attention moved to her. "Are you the wife?" said the reporter, thrusting the microphone into Debbie's face.

"Yes, I am," Debbie answered with a smile from ear to ear.

"What do you think of your husband's big winnings so far?"

"So far, he's doing great."

"I take it that you don't feel as confident in this final bet."

"I am always 100 percent behind my husband, and I know that he is confident, so that's all that really counts."

"What do you plan to do with all this money?" said the reporter.

"I haven't even thought about that," Debbie replied. "Besides, I will leave that decision to Jason."

The reporter continued her questioning of Debbie. "Tell me some background of your husband."

"Like what?" came Debbie's reply.

"Well, for starters, is he a big gambler?"

"Oh no," Debbie replied. "He rarely gambles, but he

is a mathematical genius and has developed a system that appears to working."

"A gambling system?" questioned the reporter.

"I don't know too much about it," Debbie volunteered, "but he has been working on it for quite some time, and he now thinks he has perfected it."

"I didn't think that there was such a thing as a perfect system," stated the reporter.

"Neither did I," replied Debbie, "but it appears we were both wrong."

The reporter then began to ask questions about their personal life together. Debbie was happy to tell her everything she wanted to know. Debbie did tend to go on and on about things and took forever to finish a story, according to Jason.

After this rundown, the reporter's attention turned back to Jason.

"I hear that you have been working with a system," she asked.

Jason looked at Debbie with a blank look that indicated that he was not pleased that she had mentioned his system. "I do have a system, yes," replied Jason.

"Is it one that you have devised yourself?"

"Yes," came Jason's curt reply.

"I suppose that such a system, if it worked, would be worth an awful lot of money," she noted, sounding more interested.

"I suppose so, but it's not for sale," he replied.

"Not at any price?" questioned the reporter.

"Not at any price," replied Jason. "Besides, there are too many variables to calculate."

The reporter wished them both good luck and moved on to get some interviews with the crowd.

Various members of the crowd, in turn, gave Jason their opinion as to what he should do. Nearly all were in favor of him continuing. Since the chance to work a crowd that was so much behind you doesn't come very often, Jason thought that he should get them involved and probably create a type of mass hysteria that could force the manager's hand to his advantage. Jason stood up, put his hands up, and asked for quiet. He was very adept at this by now.

"I would like to thank you patient people for being behind me to fight for the little customer against a big establishment. I would also hope you agree with my decision to carry on, because it is not just me who will win here tonight, but it will be all of you."

This had the effect of stirring the crowd to even louder noise as they began to chant. "Leave the table open."

Jason again held up his hands and asked for quiet. "Do you think that I am doing the right thing in having one last bet that could give me a total of $12 million for the night?" he yelled.

The whole crowd shouted: "Yes."

Some added other things as well, but it seemed like the whole crowd was on his side. Jason wanted to make the most of this situation, and maybe he could use it to get the manager to reopen the table. He held up his hands again, and by now, all knew that this meant that he was going to talk.

"Do you think that the table should remain open for this one last bet?"

The whole crowd in unison said: "Yes."

They again began the now familiar chant: "Leave the table open."

The chanting got so loud that the whole casino was enveloped in the noise. The manager knew that he had to make up his mind quickly. He decided to reopen the table.

As he returned to the table with the croupier, all eyes were upon him. "Due to these unusual circumstances, I am reopening the table only for this gentleman and only for one play at the terms he discussed."

This brought a loud cheer of approval from the crowd. The croupier took his accustomed place behind the table but was ushered away by the manager. For this important turn of the wheel, it was going to be him who would win it or lose it. Jason looked a little scared by this change in plans, but after looking at the croupier and not getting any worried looks, he felt reassured.

The wheel had been set up already, so it didn't matter now who the croupier was. With almost the whole casino coming to a standstill, as word had quickly gone around that there was a $4 million bet about to be won, Jason surveyed the table, pretending to weigh his options. With the delicacy of a crystal glass maker, Jason selected the numbers thirteen, twenty-six, twenty-nine, and thirty-three, knowing full well that thirteen was going to come up. As he moved his mountain of chips onto these four numbers, the crowd sighed. They had never seen anyone put such a large number of chips on each of four numbers before. The people in the back strained their necks to try to get a better view of the proceedings. It was quite a sight to see elegant ladies done up in their finery standing on the plush casino chairs just to get a glimpse of the wheel.

By this time, Debbie had given up trying to persuade

her husband to quit, for she too had been caught up in the whole euphoria that surrounded this table. She put her arms around her husband and gave him a good-luck kiss.

He took her hand, held it, and whispered in her ear, "Are you excited?"

She squeezed his hand tighter and said, "I'm so excited I dare not look."

"What numbers did he bet?" was asked around the room.

The numbers were relayed to those who couldn't see. And then the call was made: "No more bets."

Debbie's heart raced now, and she knew full well the importance of this roll of the wheel. She held her husband's hand and gave him another kiss for good luck. Jason asked her to put her arms around him and hold him tightly. She did and felt good about it. To her, it was a signal to the other women in the casino that he was her man.

The wheel was started, and with the dexterity of a surgeon, the manager flicked the little white ball—the one that had done so much damage—around the wheel to make its last journey for the night. The noise that the ball makes was not noticeable before, but now it loomed very loud to Jason. It seemed like a dull hum and was similar but less intense than the noise a bowling ball makes as it travels the distance of the lane.

There was always the chance that there could have been a slipup with the numbering system, and for just the second time tonight, Jason had doubts. Debbie held his hand so tightly now that the flow of blood was almost cut off. A few members of the crowd began to call out one of the four numbers, and soon others joined in, calling out the number they thought would win. Jason looked around the crowd in amazement and couldn't believe the power he had provoked. They were all caught up in the struggle of the little guy against the house—one struggle they had all succumbed to at least once and a majority many times before.

It was as if they, not Jason, were choosing this bet, and if one of the numbers came up, they would all share in the win—not in money, of course, but in the defeat of the house. As usual, the ball took forever to make its slow roll around the wheel. Jason wondered if there was any relation between the speed of the ball and the amount of money that was bet; perhaps the larger the amount bet, the slower the ball went. This was just a fleeting thought that flashed through Jason's mind as his eyes were glued to the ball. As the ball was nearing its arc, the crescendo of the crowd grew. With a low-pitched ping, the ball eventually dropped into the number-thirteen slot. The crowd screamed with delight, but it was Debbie who screamed the loudest as she squeezed Jason, almost choking him. Strangers slapped Jason on the back and wanted to shake his hand. He was a little dumfounded that everything worked out so well in the end, and he just sat there, oblivious to it all. His eyes were still glued on the little white ball, making sure it didn't jump out of the slot.

The casino manager also had his eyes on the ball, his pencil-thin moustache twitching just a little as he looked on in disbelief.

"We're rich! We're rich!" Debbie screamed in Jason's ear and shook him.

It was at this point that a cold shiver came over Jason. In an effort to make himself look good in Debbie's eyes, he had played his game too well. He had convinced her that it was his system alone; of the $12 million that he had won, it would be $12 million that she would be expecting to keep. How was he going to explain to her that it would only be about $1 million that they would actually receive? He had to think of something very quickly. His train of thought was interrupted by the casino manager asking him to come to his office with all his chips.

As they fought their way through the crowd of well-wishers, few words were exchanged between the two. Jason told Debbie that he wouldn't be long as he disappeared into the office with the manager and a security guard.

The manager motioned for Jason to sit down.

"This is the biggest loss the casino has ever had to one person in a single day," stated the manager in a manner that was just short of accusing Jason of cheating.

Jason sat quietly as the security guard counted the chips. The total was a shade over $12 million. The manager reminded Jason that he had promised to stay away from the casino for at least a year, and Jason answered that it would probably be a lot longer than that before he ever returned. A special bank check was drawn for $8.5 million, as tax was deducted. The manager instructed the security guard to accompany Jason to the cashier to have the check countersigned. They shook hands, and Jason left with the guard.

The manager called the cashier to give permission for the countersigning of the check. Debbie was waiting for her husband outside the office, and her eyes went wide when he emerged. She excitedly asked exactly how much they had won. The thought that he would now have to confess to her that the plan was not his and it was all a setup loomed up in his mind, and concern showed on his face.

"There is something I have to tell you, Debbie, and I

don't know exactly how to say it," said Jason as they walked away from the manager's office.

Debbie looked puzzled as she accompanied her husband and the security guard to the cashier's office where the check was countersigned. Jason put the check in his wallet and made sure that it was safe.

"What is it you have to tell me?" inquired Debbie. "The money is good, isn't it?"

"Sure the money's good," Jason replied.

Just at that moment a loud bang echoed through the building; security guards raced from everywhere. No one seemed to know exactly where the noise came from. Jason heard one of the security guards say that it sounded like a pistol shot as he ran past.

Mass confusion gripped the entire crowd as casino officials started to race around in a panic. Requests by the casino patrons to find out what had happened were met with blank statements. The crowd was soon inundated with rumors of what they thought had taken place. One person, and there's always one, said that the manager had been murdered. Others jumped on the bandwagon and claimed to have seen a man running from the manager's office just after the gunshot was heard. Jason could see how easy it was for rumors to start, and like a locomotive after it has started, it was very hard to stop and easier to pick up speed. Others confessed to seeing this mystery man and said it out loud.

The manager's office was indeed the source of the gunshot. Two security guards had been the first to arrive at the scene, but finding the door locked, they tried to break down the door with their shoulders but without luck. They then picked up one of the large, ornate ashtrays and continually smashed it against the door until it eventually opened.

The sight that met them was the most ghastly either of them had seen. The manager was sitting in his chair facing the door but with the back of his head blown off. The back wall was covered in blood with pieces of his head and brains stuck in it. There was a gun still clutched in his right hand. One of the security guards threw up at the sight of the mess. The other guard quickly closed the door and sent for the assistant manager. Some members of the crowd who had gathered outside the office were trying to find out what had happened by asking the security guard, but he was tight-lipped and just waited for the assistant manager.

When the assistant manager arrived, he arranged to have the aisle leading to the manager's office sealed off and called for the police. It wasn't long before the police arrived—a mere three minutes, because a passing patrol car had heard the call. When the two patrolmen saw the body of the manager, they asked to see the two guards who found the body. As they were waiting, one of the patrolmen asked if the manager had left a note.

"You mean like a suicide note?" asked the assistant manager.

"Yes," said the patrolman.

"I don't know," came the reply. "We called you as soon as it happened, and we haven't disturbed a thing."

The other patrolman called his superior. The two security guards arrived, and one averted his eyes as much as he could so he didn't have to look at the mess again.

"My superior will have to ask you some questions when he arrives," said the patrolman.

The superior was an Inspector Harry Luger. He had

been a cop in New York but moved to Nevada for his health. He really enjoyed his job and was happiest when he was investigating murder. Although this seemed to be a suicide, Luger would have to determine that first. He was flanked by his assistant, Timothy Cummings, a young man in his late twenties who had only recently made detective. The patrolman related to Luger what had happened after the gunshot was heard.

"Are these the ones who found the body?" inquired Luger, pointing to the two security guards.

"Yes, sir," was the reply.

"Any note?" said Luger.

"Not that we have found yet," replied the patrolman.

"Well, don't look too hard. We will shortly be having the experts here to look around, and we don't want you messing the place up with unwanted fingerprints," said Luger with a snarl.

It took about ten minutes for the crowd to learn what had happened, mainly through rumor. When it was suggested that the manager had taken his own life, a horrible feeling came over Jason. He looked at Debbie with an anguished look on his face.

He simply said, "This was not supposed to happen. No one was supposed to get hurt."

Debbie didn't understand what he was talking about and couldn't understand why he was taking it so hard.

Luger decided to question people in the assistant manager's office so that the forensic boys could do their job. Jason was summoned as one of the last people to see the manager alive.

"What's going on?" Debbie said as Jason was asked to accompany one of the patrolmen.

"I don't know yet," he replied.

Jason was guided into the assistant manager's office.

"I understand that you are the one who won this huge amount of money tonight," Luger said to Jason in a way that made Jason feel guilty even though he hadn't done anything.

"Yes," was Jason's reply.

"Do you know that the manager has shot and killed himself because of this loss?" continued Luger.

Jason's mouth opened wide in shock. The only thing he could say was, "I know he has killed himself, but I don't know the reason."

"You act surprised," said Luger.

"I am," said Jason. "When we left him, he didn't seem too pleased about having to part with the money, but I didn't think he was suicidal."

Luger could see Jason was telling the truth, because the security guard who was with him when he received the money corroborated this story.

"You and the security guard were the last people to see the deceased alive," stated Luger.

"He was definitely alive when we left him," answered Jason.

"What I can't understand, though, is why would he commit suicide just because someone won big at the casino? After all, the money wasn't his," said Luger, thinking out loud.

"No, but he had the final say in the loss," replied Jason.

"What do you mean final say?" queried Luger.

"He wanted to close the table, but I made him an offer that would put the pressure on him to make the correct decision," said Jason.

"Let me get this straight," said Luger. "The manager wanted to close the table but decided to leave it open?"

"Just for one final bet at reduced terms," replied Jason.

"What are reduced terms?" asked Luger.

"A six-to-one bet instead of the customary seventeen-to-one," Jason replied.

"So if he had decided to close the table, you wouldn't have won all that money?" said Luger, trying his best to understand what actually happened that may have led to the suicide.

"Not exactly," came the reply. "To that point, I had already won $8 million, and I stood the risk of either winning another $4 million or losing $4 million."

"So it was his decision alone whether to keep the table open or not?" asked Luger.

Jason nodded.

"Well, that would be enough of a worry to commit suicide, I suppose," came Luger's reply. "To be responsible for a $4 million loss on one bet. Boy, that must have been hard to take."

"It must have been," came Jason's reply.

When Jason emerged from the office, Debbie was waiting anxiously for him. Jason's face was white, and he felt really sick.

"What happened?" she said.

The only thing Jason could say was, "This was not supposed to happen. No one was supposed to get hurt."

Debbie didn't understand what he was talking about. Jason was really upset at this latest event and partially blamed himself.

Debbie was still in the dark about what had happened

until Jason just looked at her with a very sad face and repeated, "This was not supposed to happen."

"What wasn't supposed to happen?" Debbie asked as she took hold of her husband and refused to let him move until he told her.

"He's dead," said Jason with just a blank, staring expression on his face. "He killed himself."

"The manager?" said Debbie.

Jason just nodded. Debbie stood there with a look of utter shock sprawled across her face.

"Look, Deb. There's something I have to tell you," said Jason as he took her by the arm and headed toward the elevator.

Luger managed to piece together that the manager was despondent over the big loss to the casino because he was responsible for everything that happened there. Blaming himself, he'd then taken the pistol from the top drawer, put one bullet in the chamber, leaned back in his chair, placed the gun barrel in his mouth, and pulled the trigger. Luger had arrived at this conclusion because of the following points: The door was locked from the inside, and the door handle had only the manager's fingerprints on it. The gun also had only the manager's fingerprints on it. These facts were enough to convince Luger that the death was suicide. He was disappointed that he couldn't turn it into a murder case, though.

Debbie could tell that her husband was deeply troubled, even though he had just won $12 million. She also knew that he would tell her what was on his mind in his own way.

The elevator ride to the suite seemed to take a long time. Jason just kept repeating himself. "It wasn't supposed to happen." He looked at Debbie with pleading eyes.

After they entered their suite, Jason told her to sit down because there was something very important he had to tell her. First, she had to promise that no one was ever to know the truth, because a lot of people could be hurt by it. Debbie knew from his manner and the look on his face that he was about to say something he didn't really like having to say, and she wondered what it could possibly be.

Jason finally began. "Now, Deb, I am going to tell you a story—a true story, exactly how it happened—and I don't want you to say anything until I have finished, because it's a long story."

Debbie listened in disbelieving silence as Jason went through most of the plan for her. He didn't think that it was necessary to give her all the details and just explained how the wins were arranged and who was involved. He did, however, say they had to give $11 million back to Burt. He stressed that it was extremely imperative that no one else know how the big win was achieved. Otherwise, they would be in big trouble. He swore her to secrecy.

When Jason finished his story, Debbie was shocked and upset that someone had died as a result of the plan. The other thing that she had now realized was that instead of $12 million, they were only going to get $1 million. She realized that such a sum was hardly a mere pittance, but because she was expecting a lot more, it did put a bit of a damper on her excitement. Debbie was, by nature, a very greedy person. This fact had only come to the surface after they were married. Jason's salary went to pay for all their expenses, including rent, utilities, and the car payments, just to name a few. Debbie's salary, on the other hand, was used to buy clothes for her. She also enjoyed buying things for others and would spend quite a lot on Christmas gifts for relatives and friends.

"Do we have to give all the money back?" she questioned.

"Unfortunately, we do, darling," Jason replied. "And move back to Australia. We had a deal."

Debbie reluctantly agreed. She moved closer to her husband, put her arms around him, and told him how much she loved him. "You were just doing your job, darling," she said.

"I know, I know, but I feel like maybe if I hadn't pushed it at the end, he may still be alive."

"Then you would not have won," she said, "and the plan would have failed. The fact that the casino manager committed suicide over his decision to let you continue—and I emphasize *his* decision, not yours—is no reason to blame yourself. There is one question I would like to ask, though.

"What's that?" asked Jason. He sounded puzzled and had a faraway tone in his voice.

"Would you have told me the truth if the manager hadn't committed suicide?" she asked.

Jason wasn't prepared for this question and had to think about it for a split second. "I would have told you, but I think that this has just made it sooner than I had planned," he replied. "Look, Deb, I've never kept anything from you before, and I would honestly have told you, but it wouldn't have been for a while yet. You must realize, Deb, that I was sworn to secrecy."

CHAPTER 7

Back in their hotel suite Debbie assured her husband that the death of the casino manager was a mistake and all but convinced him that none of it could be attributed to him.

"I feel so responsible, though, because I was the one who put him in such a position that he took his own life," Jason said.

Debbie knew that he would keep this guilty feeling unless she could convince him that it was the manager's own mental instability that caused his death and not the casino's loss. Jason could not see this logic very easily, but Debbie worked from different angles to eventually convince him that maybe, just maybe, it wasn't his fault. Jason eventually capitulated that although his huge win may have had a bearing on the death, it was not the actual cause. Jason was often hard on himself but could use a rather perverse logic to talk himself out of blame when the need arose.

"Well, what do we do now?" asked Debbie.

Jason suggested that they just continue with the plan as though nothing had happened. After all, there was nothing they could do about the unfortunate death, and it may have happened sooner or later anyhow. Jason was trying to hide his true feelings regarding the matter. He had found out that the casino manager was a widower and had no family. The funeral arrangements would be taken care of by the casino.

Debbie now turned the conversation to thoughts of the money. Jason wondered how she would take the fact that the amount of money was to be $1 million and not $12 million. It didn't really matter to her if it was only $1 million; it was still far more than she and Jason would ever need.

With the evening's events slowly starting to take their toll on them, Jason and Debbie decided to go to bed. *After all*, thought Jason, *tomorrow we will go to the bank and exchange this check for a bank draft in Australian currency, and then we can head off to Australia.*

Jason didn't go to sleep straight away. Various thoughts danced through his mind. He could still see the face of the casino manager. Maybe he should have noticed that the man was capable of suicide; maybe he shouldn't have pushed him to make that final decision. This would torture him unless he could find someone else to blame for the death. Maybe Burt should be blamed. After all, it was his plan that actually caused the death.

Jason went over every step of the evening, from the very first bet to the last. He could still hear the cheers of the throng, which quickly turned into a crowd after he had begun his winning streak. The shrieks of the women casino groupies, as Jason preferred to call the many gorgeous women who literally hung around the gaming tables, could be heard now and then. They bet with other people's money and occasionally latched on to someone who was on a winning streak. Jason wondered why none of them grabbed onto him, but he quickly realized that Debbie had been all over him like a rash. The look on the face of everybody when he placed his final bet was as clear as if it were happening now. He could also see the final spin as all the faces watching were willing that little ball to fall into one of the four slots Jason had selected. Their eyes were glued to it. And, of course, he could also see the sadness and disappointment in the casino manager's eyes when the last ball finally dropped. The more he thought about the look on the manager's face after the ball had dropped into the winning slot, the more it looked like the face of a person who was in desperate trouble. The eyes were filled with an eerie blackness as they looked at Jason.

Jason tried to forget about the evening but found that was no easy feat. He finally got to sleep at five o'clock the following morning and awoke again at seven. Debbie was up by this time and was languishing in the shower. As he arose, Jason ambled over to the phone and ordered room service. He called to Debbie to ask what she would like for breakfast, but because the shower was still running, she couldn't hear him. Jason decided to order for both of them—two fried eggs done over hard, white toast, and tea with milk for each of them. Debbie hated her eggs to be runny. They had to be hard, or she would refuse to eat them. Jason was the same; they both had a fear of the yellow yolk running all over the plate. Although they liked the same food, they ate or drank it differently. Jason was a typical Australian and put his eggs on top of the toast. He also smothered everything in ketchup. Debbie would often look over at the ketchup and eggs on Jason's plate and make a face.

Jason went into the bathroom to freshen up and told Debbie that he had ordered breakfast and it would be up in about fifteen minutes. When breakfast arrived, Debbie was only a quarter of the way through drying her hair. This was a ritual that often took hours, according to Jason.

Debbie emerged from the bathroom in a white terry-towel dressing gown and a huge white towel wrapped around her head. She hadn't started on her makeup yet. Jason always thought she looked great first thing in the morning. He noticed that the dressing gown showed most of her legs and that she only had her panties on underneath. He was looking at her and imagining what was underneath. Debbie had many good points, but it was her beautiful face and figure that first attracted him. Whenever she walked into a room, all eyes would turn toward her. The men's eyes would be full of thoughts of fantasy and the women's eyes full of jealousy and envy.

Debbie was still excited about last night's big win. Before she sat down for breakfast, she gave her husband a nice big kiss.

"What was that for?" asked Jason.

"Oh, just for winning last night," she replied.

"It was a foregone conclusion," said Jason. "I didn't really do anything."

"Oh, yes you did," said Debbie. "If it wasn't for you, some idiot could have blown the whole lot. You acted out your part to perfection. I'm proud of my little hubby."

Jason hated it when she called him her little hubby but always forgave her because she was very sincere in her praise for him.

"What happens now?" she said.

Jason mentioned that he was going to fill her in on all the details that he hadn't mentioned last night. He briefly explained that they had to go to the bank to arrange for an $8.5-million letter of credit that he could cash in Australia.

The next step would be to book a flight to Sydney, establish themselves, and wire Burt after six weeks. After Burt arrived in Sydney, they would give him back $7.5 million and keep the rest for themselves.

At ten o'clock that morning, Jason and Debbie headed for the largest bank in Las Vegas. Jason chose the largest because it would have an overseas department and would make things easier. Also, cashing such a large check may pose problems at a smaller bank.

Jason presented the overseas teller with the $8.5-million check and asked for a letter of credit payable in Australian currency. The teller was a young yuppyish man, probably in his early twenties. He gave the impression that he thought he was more important than he really was and tried to put on airs when he spoke. Jason sized him up as probably having gone to England once, after which he decided to try to speak like the English in a la-de-da voice. He looked at the check and then at Jason's face. His eyes lit up and his mouth gaped wide.

"I read about you in the paper this morning," said the teller in an excited tone and called some of his colleagues to see "the man who beat the casino," as Jason was now being dubbed.

Jason had forgotten that the win would probably be front-page news and felt a little embarrassed. Some of the staff asked him for an autograph, which he gladly gave. After all, to them, he was a real hero. No one had ever taken a Las Vegas casino for so much money in one hit before.

Debbie leaned over to her husband and whispered in his ear. "You're loving every minute of this, aren't you?"

Jason gave no reply but just smiled a cheeky smile.

The customers standing in line behind Jason also began

to ask for his autograph, and soon all the people in the bank were clamoring for it. Some of them thought he was a movie star. Debbie had to drag him away, with someone else's pen still in his hand.

With their business now concluded and the letter of credit safely in Jason's hand, the next stop was a travel agency. The travel agent also recognized Jason from the photograph in the paper. Unlike the scene at the bank, there were no lineups for his autograph.

The travel agent, a very pretty dark-haired woman in her early twenties, simply smiled and said, "What plans do you have for all the money you won?"

Jason replied, "I think my wife has the major plans for it."

At that point, Debbie stepped forward and smiled at the agent sarcastically. The smile was returned by the agent.

Jason booked a flight leaving that night for San Francisco and then on to Sydney a couple of days later. Jason always liked to travel Qantas whenever he could, and with the letter of credit in his possession, he decided they would fly first class. Being Australian, Jason and Debbie would have no trouble in getting into the country. The rest of the day was spent just wandering around Las Vegas, being careful to avoid the casinos, which seemed to spring up in front of them and beckon them inside.

After running the gauntlet till one o'clock, Jason took Debbie to a nice-looking restaurant for lunch. It was not very expensive, as none of the restaurants in Las Vegas were. The menus weren't very large either, which was good because Jason didn't want to have a big lunch. When they arrived in San Francisco, he planned on taking Debbie for dinner at a favorite restaurant they had eaten at a few times before. The remainder of the day was spent shopping, mainly souvenirs for Jason and clothes for Debbie, although they didn't spend too much money.

When they were about to settle their hotel bill, the hotel manager came up to Jason to shake his hand.

"So you are the one who made the big killing at the casino last night," he said.

"Yes," replied Jason, beginning to tire of this recognition. "We hope you have enjoyed your stay at the Sands, and we will welcome you back anytime."

"Well, thank you," Jason replied. "And if we are ever back this way again, we will make sure we stay here. I don't think I will be doing any gambling."

They both laughed, and the manager wished them a safe journey.

The flight to San Francisco was at four o'clock that afternoon. Jason had reserved a table at the Hilton Hotel at Fisherman's Wharf for eight thirty.

It was just a short flight to San Francisco. Jason and Debbie checked into their hotel around six thirty and had enough time to have a quick shower before leaving for dinner. To save time, Jason suggested that they have a joint shower. However, this was not going to be a prolonged sex feast as was the case in Las Vegas. Debbie was already in the shower when Jason got in. He offered to soap down her back.

She agreed but said, "No funny business. We don't have enough time."

After the shower, Debbie put on one of her new dresses that she had bought in Las Vegas. She looked stunning. It was black and cut fairly low, not too low as to be revealing but just low enough to be provocative.

When they arrived at the restaurant, Jason could feel all the men's eyes on his wife as the maître d' ushered them to their table. Jason decided to order for both of them. After all, he knew what Debbie liked, and it was a very special occasion. The waiter introduced himself and asked if they would care for an appetizer. Jason never ordered appetizers for himself but asked Debbie if she would like one. She shook her head. Jason ordered a Bloody Mary for Debbie and a brown cow for himself. The waiter asked if they were ready to order, and Jason nodded. He politely asked Debbie if she wanted the soup.

"What is it?" she asked the waiter.

"Cream of asparagus," came the reply.

"We will both have the soup," said Jason, "followed by a small salad, one with Thousand Island dressing and the other with French. My wife will have the small T-bone steak, well done, with a baked potato and carrots. I will have the large cut ribs of beef, well done, with fries and carrots also."

While they were waiting for their drinks, the conversation began with a discussion on the money.

"How much do you think we will end up with in Australian dollars?" asked Debbie.

"With about a month's interest added on, we could be looking at about $1.15 million," Jason replied. Debbie's eyes grew wide. Jason stated that they should buy a big house in a nice area of Sydney.

After the meal, Jason and Debbie decided to take advantage of the dance floor. Jason wasn't the best dancer in the world but managed not to step on Debbie's feet. They decided to return to their suite early, as the following day they would be busy doing some last-minute shopping.

The flight to Australia was to leave at nine o'clock the following evening, so they had a good twenty-four hours to kill in San Francisco.

The flight to Sydney was to be nonstop. Thirteen and a half hours in the air was not something that Debbie relished.

"I thought that we would have to make a stop in Hawaii," she said.

Jason explained that the new 400-type 747s with the wingtips could go all the way without refueling.

The seats in first class were far superior to second class. They had added leg room, but the best advantage was that they were in a row of just two seats, so they didn't have to share with anyone else.

Debbie leaned over to her husband and said, "What would you like to do with the money, darling?"

Jason smiled and said, "Oh, I don't know, probably the usual—new house, new car, such as a Jaguar or BMW, a really good computer, and the fastest printer I could get."

"What about some new clothes?" Debbie asked. "I could pick them out for you."

Jason was one of those guys who could look great in anything but never bought anything new. This frustrated Debbie a lot, but now with all this money they would be getting, Jason could buy all the clothes he could ever want. However, clothes were not what motivated him. To him, clothes were just a necessity and not something he would spend a lot of time picking out. Debbie was just the opposite. To her, clothes were everything. She would spend hours at a mall searching through the clothing stores till she dropped.

"How about an exciting cruise?" Jason suggested. "We could spend a couple of weeks cruising the South Pacific."

"A romantic two weeks," replied Debbie.

"Of course," answered Jason. "It wouldn't be much of a cruise without a lot of romance in it."

With that, Debbie just put her head on Jason's shoulder and closed her eyes.

The flight was going well, and the service was excellent. The food, for airline food, was well above average, and so far, there were no crises.

However, just near Fiji the plane hit an air pocket. This was not just an ordinary air pocket but the granddaddy of all air pockets. As the plane began to drop, everyone on board started to get that ticklish feeling in the pit of their stomachs that was running up and then down again. It seemed to rise just below the throat and drop to the stomach. The tickling sensation was almost unbearable to some. Jason found it quite exhilarating. Jason looked at Debbie with a little smile. The look that Debbie returned was one not unlike total fear. She held onto his hand so tightly that it felt numb.

When the drop concluded and the plane again returned to its normal altitude, Jason turned to Debbie and said, "Wasn't that great? I wonder if it will happen again."

Debbie's eyes were still wide and her heart was beating wildly, as she was genuinely frightened. She began to cry. Jason hadn't realized how scared she really was, and when the tears came, it eventually dawned on him. He hugged her and used soothing words to let her know she was safe.

When Jason had his arms around her, she knew that everything was okay. Although Jason did find it exciting, he only liked it after it had stopped. As long as he knew that the drop was going to finish soon, he could enjoy the fun. It was the not knowing how long or how far they were going to drop that was the hard part. According to some of the passengers, the plane had dropped anywhere from five hundred feet to a mile. According to the record, the captain apologized for the drop of 150 feet. Of course, everyone knew the captain wouldn't admit how far the plane really fell.

About an hour outside of Sydney the captain announced that when the plane landed, officers from the Australian Fauna and Flora Department would board the plane and spray the entire inside of the cabin with a spray. This spray would eradicate all nasty little bugs that may be inside the aircraft but was harmless to humans. A few of the passengers started to ask questions as to the safety of the spray, but with the usual Aussie attitude, the attendants calmly explained again that the spray would not be harmful to anyone even if they had a respiratory problem.

The landing at Kinsford Smith Airport in Sydney was very smooth. The officers boarded the plane and began spraying. Some of the passengers ducked so the spray would not get on them. The officers just smiled, knowing that the spray would permeate throughout the cabin. A lady with an American accent sitting behind them said to Jason, "Is that it?"

"Yep," Jason replied.

"Are you sure that I'm not going to keel over in my bed tonight?" she jokingly said.

"No," replied Jason, "just don't go brushing your hair too much tonight, though."

She hoped he was joking.

The lineup at Customs and Immigration was long, and it seemed to take forever to get through. Jason always did the packing, and he managed to pack a suitcase to the limit. Debbie had to sit on the cases to enable him to close them.

She always dreaded going through customs in case they wanted to open the case, because she knew no one else would be able to stuff the clothes back into the suitcase except Jason. Luckily, they didn't have to open them.

Jason and Debbie headed to a nice little hotel that Debbie had booked from San Francisco. Jason kept on checking to be sure he still had the letter of credit with him. He checked and double-checked on things almost to the point of paranoia.

The first thing Jason wanted to do was to deposit the letter of credit. That way, he knew it was safe. Debbie asked if they would have to pay taxes on this money. "Only on the interest," Jason told Debbie, "but I suppose we had better figure out if there is any way we can get out of paying any taxes."

"I saw a movie once; I can't remember the name," said Debbie, "but there was a guy in the same predicament as we are. What he did to prevent from paying taxes was to convert his money into cash and put it in a safe-deposit box."

"That's a good idea in theory, but it would have to be a pretty big box to contain $12 million in cash," Jason said jokingly.

"Well, what if the money was in bearer bonds or whatever they are called?" asked Debbie.

Jason looked at his wife rather surprisingly. "How do you know about bearer bonds?" asked Jason.

"I don't know the first thing about them, but it was in the same movie," came the reply. "This guy also decided that the amount of money he wanted to hide was too large to convert to cash, so he bought bearer bonds with it in large denominations."

"That must have been quite a movie you saw, darling,"

said Jason. "It does sound like a good idea to use bearer bonds instead of cash."

"What exactly are bearer bonds?" asked Debbie.

"They are bonds in various amounts in the name of bearer instead of an actual person's name. The only trouble is that if you lose them, then whoever finds them can cash them."

"If we put them into a safe-deposit box, it would be highly unlikely we would lose them," noted Debbie.

Jason hated to admit it, but it seemed like his wife had come up with the perfect solution.

They went to one of the largest banks in downtown Sydney and rented a safe-box in both their names. The reason for this was just in case something happened to one of them, the other would be able to retrieve the money. Jason was not confident that Burt was not capable of pulling a double cross. Although he didn't really believe he would, it was just a precaution.

In the meantime, back in Nevada, Burt and Nora had conveniently been away in Florida when the casino had lost the $12 million and couldn't be reached. It was three days later when Burt decided to return to Las Vegas. No one knew when Burt was returning, and it wasn't until his chartered plane was an hour outside of Las Vegas that he called Bill, one of his vice presidents, to tell him he was returning and to have someone meet him at the airport. Bill was out of town, so Burt just left a message with his aid to make sure a car was sent to the airport.

Somehow the local newspapers and television stations found out that Burt's plane was about to land, and they all rushed out to the airport. As he alighted from the plane, microphones were thrust into Burt's face, and the TV cameras zoomed in so close you could almost see Burt's nose hairs.

Burt was surprised by the crowd of press people who were there to meet him but knew that there would be a lot of questions the press would want answered about the casino's loss. So he was prepared to answer as though he was genuinely surprised by the loss. He had rehearsed his reactions for the past few days, practicing his facial expressions of surprise and anger in front of the mirror until he felt that he had them down perfectly.

"What do you think about the $12 million loss?" one reporter blurted out.

"What $12 million loss?" yelled Burt.

"You mean you haven't heard about it?" stated another reporter.

"Heard what?" was Burt's reply.

At this, the whole entourage of reporters and cameramen knew they were on to a hot scoop. Burt and Nora, with the aid of some of the people who had come down to meet him, managed to force their way through the crowd of reporters and microphones and cameras, which were often used as assault rifles, to the waiting limousine.

"What the hell are these people talking about?" he inquired of his vice president.

"A young man won $12 million at your casino," the man explained. The $12-million figure threw him a little, because according to the calculations they had worked out, the final amount was to be a shade over $10 million. Burt pretended to get really mad and ordered an immediate investigation into the matter.

"What about the manager's death?" another reporter added.

This stopped Burt in his tracks. He turned to face the reporter with a genuine look of shock. "What death?" he bellowed.

"Your casino manager shot himself to death," came the reply.

Burt staggered for a second, and his face went white as if he was in a state of shock. A huge lump came into his throat, and he stammered a little as he tried to speak.

Bill's aid, Patrick, who had come to meet Burt, said, "Let's get the hell out of here. Now."

They helped Burt into the limousine and sped off.

"What's this about Roger's suicide?" said Burt in an agitated tone.

Patrick explained that because the manager had approved the huge bet, he must have felt that he was personally responsible for the loss and may not have been able to shoulder the guilt.

Burt felt responsible for Roger's death but could not acknowledge this fact to anyone. His mind was filled with thoughts of guilt. Roger had been a friend as well as an employee, and his death was felt very hard by Burt.

Patrick concluded recounting what had happened: "He went back to his office and gave the gambler a certified check for the $8.5 million. He then waited for the gambler to leave, reached into his top drawer, pulled out the revolver he kept there, placed it in his mouth, and pulled the trigger."

Burt winced at this graphic description and was genuinely upset at the turn of events that had taken place. Nora was visibly shaken and just sat there in a state of shock.

"What did the police say?" inquired Burt.

"Well, they have concluded that it was probably suicide.

Although the guy in charge, Inspector Luger, is from back East, and he has it in for rich people, especially casino owners. He was trying to find out if it may have possibly been murder."

"Murder?" yelled Burt. "How the hell could it possibly have been murder?"

"It's just this guy Luger. They say that he used to be in charge of homicide in a New York precinct and stepped on someone's feet too much. This someone was a personal friend of the mayor, and Luger wound up being reassigned out here. He tells people he is here for his health, but that's not the truth. Anyhow, the official verdict was suicide. Don't be surprised if Luger asks to see you."

Burt turned the conversation back to the gambling loss. He wanted to know all about the gambler and instructed Patrick to organize an inquiry into the win. He wanted to know his name, where he lived, and anything else they could find out about him.

"Did he just play at the one table or several?" Burt asked.

"Just the one table," came the reply.

"Who was the croupier at that table then?" Burt asked.

"It was Carl Hoffman, one of the better ones we have on staff," replied Patrick.

"I want to see him first thing in the morning, and he had better come up with some bloody good answers, or he is in a lot of trouble," stated Burt. "Did this gambler talk to anyone at the tables?"

"As far as we have been able to ascertain, the only person he really had a conversation with was his wife," replied Patrick. "And, of course, the croupier."

"Did anyone notice any passing of information between the two?" said Burt.

The aid replied, "As is customary, when a person is winning big, the internal security system does monitor all bets to make sure there is no sleight of hand."

"And?" said Burt.

"We could not detect any communication or wrongdoing by either party," replied Patrick.

"Was it taped?" asked Burt.

"Yes, sir," came the reply. "We have reviewed the tape and the bettor carried no book and did not communicate in any way with the croupier by signals or verbal commands. The only thing that was said were normal instructions or banter. The tape was started after one hundred thousand had been won."

"I would be more interested in the last bet," said Burt.

"That was what we looked at several times but could not find any evidence of wrongdoing. The manager wanted to close down the table, but the gambler made him an offer he couldn't refuse."

"What sort of offer?" asked Burt.

"Well, sir, up to that point, the gambler had won $8 million and wanted to make one final bet. When Roger wanted to close the table, the gambler said that if he was allowed to make one bet, he would put $1 million on each of four numbers, and if one of those numbers hit, he would get a seven-to-one return. This meant that if the gambler lost, he would walk away with only $4 million, but if he won, it would be a $12 million win."

"So Roger gambled that the guy was going to lose?" said Burt.

"Oh, there was one other stipulation to the bet,"

continued Patrick. "The gambler said that if the table was closed, he would just win at one of the others. However, if it was to remain open, he would make the one last bet and not set foot in the casino for at least a year."

Patrick waited for Burt to ask something else. Burt decided to wait until he viewed the tape himself. As the car pulled up in Burt's driveway, Burt turned to the aid and said, "Do you think that Roger could have had anything to do with it in any way?"

The aid thought for a moment and then replied, "From what we viewed on the tape, absolutely not."

With that, Burt and Nora went into the house.

Burt went into his study. Nora knew that the death was very upsetting for him, so she knew enough to let him be by himself for a while. The loss of $12 million would be enough to make him upset, but the loss of a life was a lot worse.

Burt arranged to have a hurried meeting with his three chief executives in the morning. When he arrived at the office the next morning, the three men were waiting for him in his office.

As he entered his office, Burt told his secretary that he was not to be disturbed for any reason whatsoever. Burt began the meeting by mentioning the unhappy death of the manager.

"This was an unfortunate thing to happen, but I am sure that it had nothing to do with the big win," Burt noted. "I have since found out that Roger was having some personal problems of late. The girl with whom he was living had recently left him, and this was getting him down."

"Inspector Luger thought that the casino loss was a contributing factor in Roger's death," interjected Peter.

"Yes, it was a factor but just one of many," said Burt. "Now for the plan. I think we can all feel proud that we picked the right person for the job. As for the plan, to date, it has gone off perfectly."

"If you can say that one death is a perfect result," chimed in Peter.

"Look, we may as well air any differences we have on this point right now," said Burt. "Otherwise, it will crop up every two minutes."

Peter wondered when Burt was going to get to this boiling point.

Burt went on. "It is agreed that Roger's death was in some way caused by the loss, but it was just one of a series of causes. I too feel bad about it, you know, but there is nothing we can do about it, and there was nothing we could have done to prevent it. Now, do you all agree with that, or are we going to argue some more about it?"

"Don't you even feel just a little remorse that you have lost a friend because of your plan?" Peter asked.

"Now come on, Peter. Of course I feel bad that Roger is gone. I don't think that the plan should take the whole responsibility for his death, though," said Burt.

"I just don't think we should be congratulating ourselves on the success of a plan that, rightly or wrongly, was a major factor in the death of a person. I'm sorry, Burt; I just don't see it the way you do," Peter answered.

"What about the rest of you?" Burt asked.

John was the first to speak up. "My personal opinion is that the suicide—and let's call it what it really is, a suicide—was the result of the mental state of Roger at that time. The casino loss was just, to pardon a pun, the final nail in the coffin. Let's put it this way: if your health was in bad shape, your girlfriend left you, you owed money, and you had just made the biggest gambling blunder of your life, I'm sure suicide would cross your mind. The only difference between Roger and the rest of us in the same circumstances is that we would not have gone through with the act, I hope. We will not know what else may have been tormenting Roger, but I feel sure that if it was just the loss of the money alone, it would not have caused anyone to commit suicide."

Bill was taken a little by surprise by the eloquent way in which John expressed his thoughts and simply said, "I agree with John."

"Let me make one final point before we lay this issue to rest," said Burt. "I think that we now agree there were several reasons why Roger took his own life, and yes, the plan was one of them."

Peter interrupted by saying that he didn't know Roger had health problems. Burt stated that according to Roger's doctor, he had a congenital heart problem and was also suffering from acute depression. Peter finally relented and agreed with the rest that the plan should not be held responsible for Roger's death.

"Now, to get on to the task at hand," said Burt. "The plan so far has worked very well. In approximately six weeks, Jason will contact me and tell me where he is so that I can go to Australia and retrieve my money."

"Sir, how sure are you that Jason will even contact you?" said John.

"Before he signed the agreement," said Burt, "I indicated that this plan was just the tip of the iceberg, and there would be more to come but for a lot more money. From my studies of human nature, the more people have, the more they want."

"Well, we will know in about two months' time," said John in a sort of disbelieving tone.

"At ten o'clock this morning, I will be interrogating the croupier," said Burt. "It will take about two hours and, of course, will be staged. I will do it alone, but I want a number of people to be listening near the door to give authenticity to it."

"It's almost ten now," said Bill.

Burt called the croupier into his office for an interrogation and was prepared to give the performance of his life. Burt had rehearsed what he was going to say and found that raising his voice at just the right moment would give those listening near the door something to talk about. Anyone within earshot could hear that this was not just an interrogation but more like an inquisition. The interrogation lasted more than an hour and a half, and Burt wanted to get his pound of flesh. The croupier had answered all the questions in a seemingly honest manner. When the smoke cleared, the door opened, and the croupier exited Burt's office. He had a hangdog look on his face and dared not look at any of the other staff. He still had his job, and he was now one hundred thousand dollars richer. Burt had instructed him not to spend any of the money in the United States and noted that it would be better to wait until this all died down before spending it.

Burt called his three vice presidents into the office again. "Now for the gambler," said Burt. "Is he still around?"

Bill stated that Jason had left Las Vegas the day after the big win and was probably in Australia by now. Burt concluded the meeting, saying that all in all, the hardest part of the plan had been successful.

"I suppose I had better have a look at the tape with

the security people," said Burt, "just in case there was something that they missed."

The chief of security accompanied Burt to the security office, and the tape of Jason's betting escapade was viewed. After looking at the tape very closely, Burt was proud that the two men who he had picked had played their roles so well.

Burt also held a meeting with all the staff of the casino and announced that there was to be a memorial service for the casino manager in the next few days, and they were all invited to attend. He also said that the authorities would probably speak to some of the staff members about the events leading up to the unfortunate event. He commended them all for having to work after such a trying episode and tried not to lay any blame of the big loss on the manager, although all who were present could sense that Burt felt that the manager erred in allowing such a bet to take place.

The funeral for the casino manager was held the following day. Burt and most of the casino staff were in attendance. Burt had the casino closed for the duration of the funeral, about three hours. There were no family members there. Burt volunteered to give the eulogy. It was a short speech dwelling on all the positive aspects of the manager's life and leaving the negative ones dormant. As to the cause of death, Burt left it unannounced.

By the time all the investigations were completed, almost two months had passed since the big loss. The conclusions were that the manager had taken his own life after becoming deeply depressed. However, the loss of the money was only the final nail in the coffin, so to speak. It appeared that the investigation into the manager's personal life had uncovered a few problems that would send even the sanest of men to contemplate taking his own life.

The IRS also wanted to conduct their own investigation into the proceedings that night, because Burt was claiming a loss of income of $12 million. They commented that it was unusual for someone to win so much money in one night. Seeing that the person who approved everything was dead and another had left the country, their main investigation now centered on Burt and the croupier. The croupier had already had some practice at his speech after Burt's interrogation, so he gave a near-perfect second version to the IRS people.

Burt also gave a good performance, mainly because he had not been in Las Vegas at the time the loss occurred. The IRS wondered if that was a coincidence. Burt stated that he often went to Florida for a vacation without leaving any notice of his exact whereabouts. This seemed to lead the investigation away from Burt. The IRS admitted that they didn't have much to go on, especially since neither the police nor the Nevada Gaming Commission were laying any charges against Burt after their own investigations. The bottom line to all this was that Burt would be able to deduct the loss from the year's income.

Although the investigation of the suicide had been completed, Inspector Luger was one of those people who could never believe in the obvious. Luger was not a tall, strapping policeman like is often depicted in the movies. Actually, he was about the exact opposite of that image. He was on the short side and didn't believe in fitness. In his late forties, he was a twenty-five-year man who had spent most of his time back East.

Luger was a typical unhappy cop. His wife had left him

after twelve years of wedded bliss. Luger was one of those officers who always had a chip on his shoulder. He likely had forgotten the real reason why the chip was there in the first place. He was constantly in debt and hated people who had wealth, probably because he could never manage to accumulate any of it himself. He enjoyed investigating cases that could put the blame on the wealthy, such as casino owners.

When he was given the suicide case, he was determined to prove that it was murder. However, all the preliminary investigations proved that it was, indeed, suicide. Luger felt that he had somehow been cheated out of a really good case. So when he came to meet Burt, his opinion of him was not one of respect. Luger had not achieved a high level of education, and Burt quickly summed him up as a borderline moron and adjusted his way of tackling him accordingly.

Luger asked Burt if he thought, from the facts that were investigated, that the manager had taken his own life.

"Imagine if you will, Inspector, that you were the casino manager and you had just approved a bet that would make a win the biggest payout in the history of roulette. A win that would cause a great deal of anguish to your boss, not to mention a huge loss of income for him. The reason why he approved such a large bet, we will never know. Maybe he believed that a win was impossible.

"I know the crowd would have booed him if he had closed the table, but he was a professional and could handle things like that. The fact that he felt that he was solely responsible for the loss must have played very heavy on his mind. This, mixed with the personal problems he had and his failing health, made his state of mind a little precarious. I feel sure you have investigated the case very thoroughly, and whatever conclusions you have come up with are good enough for me," Burt said in his best butter-up fashion.

Inspector Luger had not often had praise like that before and wholeheartedly agreed that the verdict of suicide was indeed the correct one. When Luger left Burt's home, he had an unusual respect for the casino owner, and his chip had tilted a little. Burt, on the other hand, knew that he had met an idiot the first time he shook his hand, and that opinion had not changed by the time he had left.

CHAPTER 8

Burt waited very impatiently for notification from Jason. He didn't know exactly when, but the time they had agreed to wait had long passed. Almost four weeks after the visit by Inspector Luger, Burt received the all-important telegram. It was not delivered to Burt's office but to his home, as was agreed. It simply read: "No. 585 Collins St. Sydney between Nov 6 and 16."

Burt was very pleased, to say the least, that Jason had finally come through.

He needed to gloat a little. He knew what the other three people who knew about the whole plan were thinking—that Jason had taken Burt for a ride and would keep the whole amount for himself.

Boy, are they going to be surprised, thought Burt to himself.

A meeting was called by Burt with his three executives. He had told them before that he would keep them up to date with any news he received about Jason or the money. The three men listened to what Burt had to say, and Peter was a little surprised that Jason had actually replied. He didn't think that he was as honest as he appeared, especially with $8.5 million in his pocket.

"So what do you plan to do?" asked John.

"I will be flying to Sydney in the next day or two," said Burt.

"Make sure that you book into one of the better hotels down there," John added.

"Don't worry," said Burt. "I was advised that the Menzies was about the best one there."

Within two days, Burt had arranged a flight to Australia. The reason he had given Nora was that he wanted to look into an opportunity to invest in a sheep or cattle station in the outback.

Nora wasn't pleased that she was not going to accompany her husband to such an exotic place. Burt had not anticipated Nora's interest in going and had to come up with a good reason for her to stay behind. He rambled on about the dangers of the outback, how he would be sleeping in huts or tents, and how it was not going to be a sightseeing trip. The final excuse he had to use was the you-can-go-next-time one. He stated that if he did decide to buy, then there would be many trips Down Under. They could spend the time to see the sights. Nora could see that he had his mind already made up and gave up pressing the issue any further.

Burt told his three senior vice presidents where he was going. He promised them that for their role in finding the right candidate, they would each receive a bonus of twenty thousand dollars. They would receive it as soon as he received the $7.5 million. This was so out of character for Burt that the vice presidents were each in a state of shock. Of course, John knew that this bonus was a bribe to stop them from saying anything about the plan.

The flight to Sydney was very long and tiring. The enormity of the achievement actually hit home. *This year*

I could make more money than I would have made in the next four years, thought Burt. The reduction in tax due to the loss would be a bonus.

Burt, being alone, whiled away the time by thinking of the money or, more correctly, about the execution of the plan. Because the whole idea was his own, he felt that he should get most of the credit. Jason and Carl were merely pawns playing to his preset instructions. The fact that it had come off as well as it did was, to say the least, miraculous. Of course, there was the manager's suicide, which was the only thing to put a blemish on the whole affair.

Burt was quite amazed that no one had caught on to the plan. He attributed that to good planning and good execution by all concerned.

Being a notoriously bad sleeper on planes, Burt tried to get some rest. As soon as he closed his eyes, he could see Jason waiting for him with all the money in his hand.

As the flight was nearing its end, Burt's heart began to race with anticipation. He hoped he wouldn't get too excited since he'd had a double heart bypass operation four years earlier. He didn't want to go to the big casino in the sky just yet.

When Burt arrived in Sydney, he checked into the Menzies Hotel. He had a nice, relaxing shower and looked forward to sampling the Aussie-style foods. After the shower, he felt like a human being again. More than fifteen hours in the air gives you a feeling of uncleanliness.

Next, Burt decided to try the restaurant in the hotel, because it was known for its good seafood. He didn't speak that much at the restaurant so as not to draw too much attention to himself, being an American. Burt was very impressed with the food. For an appetizer, he managed to get through a huge helping of prawns. For the main course, Burt thought that he would try the lamb. He wasn't normally partial to the lamb he had eaten in the past, but the lamb down here was supposed to be the best. He chose the leg of lamb. What he received was a huge piece of meat surrounded by small, round baked potatoes that were very crisp. It also came with green beans with almond pieces added for more flavor and baby carrots. The waiter asked Burt if he wanted mint sauce.

"Is that like mint jelly?" asked Burt.

"Similar," replied the waiter, "but this is the real stuff, and it's fresh."

When Burt saw all the food on his plate, he wondered how he was ever going to get through it. He did manage to eat most of it. The mint sauce was just the thing to bring out the excellent flavor of the lamb. Burt passed on the dessert and finished off with a black coffee.

Burt thought to himself, *Well, they don't make coffee as good as back in the States, but at least it was digestible.*

Burt decided to make it an early night, as tomorrow was to be his big day. As he made his way to the elevator, he realized how much food he had eaten. His pants seemed a bit tight, so he discreetly let his belt out by two notches.

The next morning Burt hired a taxi at the hotel. The cab driver was a burly, well-tanned man who liked to talk and must have spent most of his life down at the beach.

As soon as Burt opened his mouth, the cabby said, "So you're a Yank."

Burt just nodded.

"Which part of the States are you from?" inquired the cabby.

"Nevada," was Burt's lone reply.

"Where the casinos are," the cabby said.

"Yes," replied Burt, who was not the slightest bit interested in conversation.

"Just arrived here, have we?" the cab driver said.

"Yes," said Burt, becoming very weary of the conversation.

The cab driver was experienced enough to know when a fare was interested in talking or not. The rest of the journey continued in total silence. As they turned onto Collins Street, Burt's heartbeat doubled with anticipation. As the cab made its journey down the street, it became painfully obvious there was no such address as 585. They pulled up where 585 would be and just stared at the vacant space.

"Are you sure this is the right address?" asked the cab driver.

"It's the one I was given," said Burt in a tone that made him feel like he was never going to see his money again.

Burt rechecked the telegram and then gave it to the driver to check.

"Yep," said the driver. "This is the right address … Unless," he continued, "it should have been Collins Street in Wooloomooloo."

"Where's Wooloomooloo?" asked Burt.

"It's an inner suburb of Sydney," came the reply.

Burt instructed the driver to rush right over there.

"It's on the other side of town, and it may not be the right address anyhow," said the driver.

Burt insisted they take that chance.

"Okay, it's your money," said the driver.

It took more than fifty minutes to get to Wooloomooloo. As they drove down Collins Street, they could see that it was just a small street. Since the numbers began at one, the chances of them getting to 585 were highly unlikely. As they made it to the end of the street, Burt's worst fears came true—no such address.

"Are you sure this is the right street?" said Burt, trying desperately to believe that it was just a mistake.

"Look, mate, I've taken you to the only two Collins Streets in Sydney," said the cabby. "If that's not good enough for you, then you had better get another cab."

"Just take me back to the hotel," said Burt. He was in no mood to be congenial.

The ride back was in total silence. Burt's mind was going a mile a minute. It had not occurred to him that Jason would have doubled-crossed him, especially after the way he was picked and the rigid examination that was done on him. He felt sure that Jason had fallen for the added incentive of the promise of further plans that could net him a lot more money.

Could I have been that bad in judging a person's character? thought Burt. *Maybe the huge amount of money was just too much for him. I could go on all night trying to figure out the reasons why he has done this. It will just all come back to the same thing, and the money will still be in his hands.*

All these thoughts were racing through Burt's mind like a freight train.

I'll kill the bastard, was Burt's first thought.

When he arrived back at the hotel, there was a message from his secretary. Burt made the phone call to his secretary, but his mind was still focused on his disappointment. The secretary told him there was another telegram.

"What did it say?" he asked.

"I don't know. I didn't open it," said the secretary.

"Well, open the bloody thing," bellowed Burt.

The few seconds it took for the secretary to answer seemed like minutes to Burt.

"It's from Australia," she said.

"Well, what does it say?" yelled Burt impatiently.

"It says: 'Sorry about the mistake in the address. Stop. It should have been Collins Place not Street.' Does that make any sense to you, sir?" said the secretary.

"You bet it does," said Burt, and he hung up.

Burt shouted for joy when he put the phone down. He raced outside and grabbed the first cab he saw, jumping in front of an elderly couple who had just opened the door of the cab.

"How many Collins Places are there in Sydney?" asked Burt.

"Just one," came the reply.

"Then take me to No. 585 Collins Place," said Burt.

"It's a good forty-five-minute drive from here," said the cab driver, giving Burt some idea of how much it was going to cost him.

"That's okay," said Burt.

He was feeling in a much better mood this time and chatted freely to the cab driver as they made their way to Collins Place. Burt knew that Sydney was a big city, but he didn't realize how big it really was. Everything seemed so far from the center of the city—well, every place that Burt wanted to go anyhow. It was a sprawling town, similar to Los Angeles, but without the smog.

The cab driver didn't talk that much. Burt thought that he probably didn't like the way Burt jumped in front of the old couple to get into the taxi.

The faith that Burt had in Jason had now been restored. Although he still hadn't received the money yet, at least

Jason had sent a second telegram. If he wanted to keep the money for himself, he would not have bothered, Burt mused to himself.

As the driver turned onto Collins Place, a lump formed in Burt's throat. He anxiously counted off the house numbers. When they came to No. 160, there was an intersection. The street changed to Peter Place, and the numbers started at No. 1 again.

"I think you must have the wrong address," said the cab driver.

"That's not possible," said Burt. "It must be here somewhere. Turn around, and we'll look again."

"Okay," said the driver. "It's your money."

They cruised up and down the street, looking desperately for No. 585. Burt finally realized that he had been made to look like a fool for the second time. Burt felt betrayed.

It's him against me, thought Burt. *He thinks he has me on a string like a bloody puppet, but he has another thing coming. I don't give up that easily.*

The drive back to the hotel was as quiet as the previous one. This time, Burt had murder on his mind. Jason wanted to play a game with him. There could be no mistake in addresses this time.

Back at his hotel, Burt walked past the front desk and headed for the elevators. The concierge called out to him there was a message for him. Not wanting to run the risk of more agony, Burt calmly went over to the front desk. The message again was from his secretary who wanted Burt to call as soon as he got in.

It must be Jason sending another bloody telegram, he thought to himself. *I am not going to fall for it again.*

Burt knew that he had been fooled, and the only thing

on his mind at the moment was how to destroy Jason. That was all he could think about, and he was going to spend the rest of his life tracking this cretin down. It wasn't just the money now but a point of honor. He chose not to play the little game Jason wanted and decided not to call his secretary.

It took a while for Burt to get to sleep, as thoughts of the money and Jason merged. He tossed and turned, trying to find a comfortable position, but there was none. Burt's mind was full of the pictures of Jason. He could see him counting the money and laughing.

He is laughing at me. Burt knew this to be true.

Burt finally managed to erase the pictures of Jason from his mind at three o'clock in the morning and entered sleep. Burt was awakened at five with a phone call from his secretary.

"I'm sorry to disturb you at this early hour, sir," said the secretary.

"Do you know what bloody time it is here?" yelled Burt with the anger of anyone being awakened from a deep sleep too early.

"I believe it to be about five in the morning your time, sir," was the reply.

"Right. Five o'clock!" yelled Burt. "And I don't want to hear what is in another telegram from Australia."

"There is no telegram," the secretary said.

"Well, what is so important that you had to call me for this emergency?" said Burt.

"The police were here looking for you," she replied.

"Looking for me?" he exclaimed in a new state of panic. "What for?"

"Well, they were looking into the murder of Roger," said the secretary.

"Murder? What do you mean murder?" yelled Burt as he was beginning to get hysterical. "The case was closed as a suicide. What is this about a murder?"

"The only thing I know is that the police have received a letter that the manager was murdered by someone who was hired by you. The police have asked me to call you and to make sure that you get back here as soon as you can. They also mentioned that if you didn't get back here soon, then they would contact the Sydney police."

"Look, you can tell Inspector Luger that I will be flying back immediately to find out what the hell this is all about."

Burt was livid when he got off the phone. *That stupid bloody inspector. I knew that he didn't like me, but murder?* This thought went through Burt's mind.

Burt racked his brain trying to come up with some reason why anyone would try to implicate him in murder.

Boy, I didn't think things could get worse, Burt thought to himself. *Well, I was wrong—a murder indictment now. I wonder what is in the letter.*

The flight from Sydney to Los Angeles was one where Burt did a lot of thinking. He retraced all his steps, and there was no way anyone could tie him to the murder. If it was murder, which it wasn't. After all, he had been in Florida when the manager died. Suddenly, it dawned on him. It was Jason.

Yes, that's it, he thought. *That's why I got the runaround from the telegrams. Jason wanted me to be arrested, so I won't find him and get the money back. Surely the American justice system would not fail so grievously now.*

Burt began to wonder what evidence the police had.

In Las Vegas, the plane was met by the three senior vice presidents. They knew that Burt would be fit to be tied. When they saw him, they weren't disappointed. They also knew that when Burt was in one of these moods, it was better to let him do most of the talking.

Burt opened with, "What the hell is all this nonsense about Roger being murdered? And, what's worse, how come I have been implicated?"

Burt immediately told Peter to call Luger and arrange for him to meet them at Burt's home in ninety minutes. Peter called on the car phone and made the arrangements.

At police headquarters, Inspector Luger called two of his better officers in to see him.

"That old codger Donaldson has returned to the scene of the crime," he told them. "We have been invited to interview him at his house."

"You know, sir, the evidence we have is pretty flimsy," said one of the officers.

"It's good enough for me to reopen the case," Luger snapped back. "I don't want Burt to get out of this one."

"Don't we have to prove that it was murder first?" asked the officer.

"Of course it was murder," said Luger. "It is perfectly logical to me."

"You said that it was suicide before," said the officer.

"Well, I was wrong then. Besides, we didn't have the evidence before. Now we have this letter," said Luger. He kissed the letter as if it were a godsend.

"We can't arrest someone on the basis of an anonymous letter," said the officer.

"I know that. Do you think I am stupid or something?" said Luger. He was beginning to tire of this third-degree from one of his junior officers. "By showing the letter to Burt, it could force him to drop his guard and try to cover his tracks. When he does that, we've got him."

With that last remark, Luger showed that it was time they had to be leaving for Burt's house.

When the police arrived, Burt was still perplexed. Luger apologized for forcing Burt to cut his trip short but assured him it was necessary.

"Exactly what is this new information that you have?" said Burt.

"It's a letter we received two days ago," said Luger.

"Do you have the letter with you?"

Luger produced the letter and gave it to Burt to examine. The main part of the letter stated that Burt had arranged for someone to win $10 million at his casino, leave the country, and give Burt back $9 million. As Burt read the letter, he knew that it had to be written by Jason. He would be the only one who could possibly gain anything from all this. The letter went on to mention that the casino manager had learned of the plan and wanted a cut. He had threatened to blackmail Burt, so Burt arranged for him to be killed.

"Is this what you call proof?" asked Burt. "I have never read anything more preposterous in all my life. The letter is not even signed. Do you have the envelope that this letter came in?"

Inspector Luger produced the envelope. Burt was a bit surprised. The letter had been sent from San Francisco.

"How well did you know the man who won all the money at your casino?" said Luger.

"I didn't know him at all," said Burt.

"Are you sure about that?" said Luger with a smirk on his face.

"Of course I'm sure," came the reply.

"Then why did you get two telegrams from a Jason Chard from Australia?" asked the Inspector. "We have copies of the telegrams that were sent to you by the gambler. Do you still deny that you knew him?"

Burt was in a bit of a tight spot here, although he knew that he could outwit Luger even if he had a Polaroid photograph of him standing over a body with a gun in his hand.

"These telegrams were an invitation for me to go and visit him in his own country and to thank me for being the owner of the casino that had earned him so much money. Sort of I've seen your place; now come down and see mine."

"Then why did you pay for the trip yourself?" said Luger.

"I always pay my own way," said Burt. "That's the way I have always done it and the way I will continue to do it."

"And what did this man in Sydney say to you?" asked Luger.

"Oh, we just chatted a little about his good fortune," said Burt.

"You didn't happen to bring any of the money back with you, did you?" Luger asked.

"Of course I didn't!" exclaimed Burt. "You are taking this letter too much to heart, Inspector."

"So you just chatted about his good fortune," said Luger.

"That's what I said," replied Burt, who was becoming rather annoyed with these questions.

"Did you ask him how he won all that money?" asked Luger.

"Well, yes. I did ask him that," said Burt. "My curiosity came to the fore. After you have lost $12 million to some foreigner, you tend to try to find out how he managed to achieve such a feat."

"And what was his reply?" asked Luger.

"He claimed that he had a system," said Burt.

"What sort of system?"

"One that wins," he replied cheekily. "Look, Inspector, I really don't think that this has anything to do with the death of the casino manager."

This bluff seemed to stall Luger. Burt quickly moved the subject back to the alleged murder.

"What proof do you have that there was a murder committed? I thought that the police had closed their investigation into this matter," said Burt.

"Well, apart from the letter, we don't have too much evidence, but there are some inconsistencies. The first one was why the manager approved of such a bet when it was clearly against the company policy. The second was that there is another door leading to the manager's office that could have been locked from the inside or the outside. A man was seen coming out of this room by several people around the time of the gunshot."

"This is a preposterous scenario you have given, Inspector. When there is a death and there are a lot of people around, there is always one person who will say he or she saw someone running away or spotted someone lurking near the scene and acting suspicious. This is human nature. Besides, even in the wildest possible case, you have nothing to tie me in with the death."

"Oh, but we do have the most important piece of evidence in any murder case," said Luger. "A motive."

"How can you have a motive when it hasn't been

established that there really was a murder?" Burt responded. "Besides, what motive did I have to kill Roger?"

"Until I received this letter, I didn't know of any either," said Luger, "but to protect this secret of winning the $12 million is a big motive."

"Now come on now, Inspector," said Burt. "You don't really believe that I could have pulled off such a plan right under the nose of all the security we have here, do you?"

Luger ignored this innocent plea and continued. "Most suicides leave a note, but there was no note found."

"Well, maybe he didn't have time to write a note. Maybe it was a spur-of-the-moment thing," protested Burt. "I am sure that not all suicides leave a note, since you said most and not all."

Luger agreed. "The other piece of evidence came out of the autopsy. The deceased had a heavy dose of the drug Ritalin in his system. This drug is used in some medical circles to calm a person down. It may have been given to the deceased to allow him to be manipulated into holding the gun. In this way, the assailant could stand in front of him and pull the trigger."

"That's the most ridiculous piece of nonsense I have ever heard," snapped back Burt. "He probably took the drug himself to calm his nerves from accepting such a large bet." Burt paused a moment and then asked, "Is this a prescription drug, Inspector?"

"I don't know," said Luger.

"Well, I suggest that you find that out first, Inspector," Burt shot back. "Because if it is and Roger had a prescription for it, then the use of the drug would have no bearing on Roger's death or, rather, on the way he died."

Luger looked a little embarrassed that he hadn't thought

of that point himself. The officer with Luger did his best to suppress a smile that would telegraph an "I told you so."

"I will admit," said Luger, "we don't have much hard evidence to go on at the moment, but when we do, we will be back. So don't go leaving town."

With that, Luger and his officer exited the house. The three executives who had accompanied Burt home could see that he would rather be left alone and decided to say good night. John offered their help in any way they could if the need arose.

"I should be able to beat this preposterous charge, but I would like to thank you guys for sticking by me," said Burt. "By the way, with this latest mess, I haven't told you of what happened in Australia."

"I'm sure that can wait till later," said Peter. "You are probably pretty tired at the moment."

"You're right. I am very tired," said Burt. "It was a long flight."

The three men traveled back to Las Vegas in Burt's limousine. They knew that the murder rap was false. Without knowing what was in the letter, they had to piece together their own scenario.

As soon as they entered the limousine, Bill started the conversation. "From Burt's reaction, it sounds like he didn't get the money back."

"That's obvious," said Peter, who at times could be quite short with Bill.

"Well, we may as well wait until Burt fills us in on what went on in Sydney," said John. "Otherwise, we will be trying to put our own interpretations on things."

"I know that he didn't get the money back. Otherwise,

he would have been in a much better mood, even with a murder investigation hanging over his head," said Bill.

"We all know that he worships money, Bill," said Peter, "and it sounds like he suspects Jason for sending the letter."

"Well, we will know tomorrow when Burt fills us in," said John, wanting this conversation to end before Bill and Peter started to argue about it.

"The thing we have to concentrate on now is this ridiculous murder charge," continued John. "I think Burt is not really worried about that, because he knows that the inspector is stupid and has nothing concrete on him."

Things were not going very well for Burt. It was bad enough there was a man, halfway around the world, who had $7.5 million of his money, but now there was this idiot masquerading as a police inspector who was trying to pin a murder rap on him.

With Burt stuck in Las Vegas, he couldn't return to Australia to pursue Jason and the money. There was no one else he could trust to go there for him and try to look for Jason. Burt didn't know what to do.

Burt's next move was to find some unsuspecting person he could shift the inspector's suspicions onto. He felt that the best bet would be to kill two birds with one stone and shift the blame onto Jason in Australia. After all, he was the one who won all the money, and he had sent the telegram. Burt began preparing a good presentation to offer Inspector Luger.

He made an appointment with the inspector and presented a very good case against Jason. Every time Luger asked a question that seemed to implicate Burt, he was answered with an equal one to blame Jason. At the very least, he put a great deal of doubt in Luger's mind about the case.

The anonymous letter that Luger had based most of his case on began to seem more and more incredible. Such a plot as the letter had suggested was a bit far-fetched, although there were a few loose ends, like the telegram Burt received just before he left for Australia. This may have been a coincidence. Burt had to make the inspector more suspicious of Jason.

"Have you possibly thought that the casino manager and Jason were in this together, Inspector?" asked Burt.

"What do you mean?" said Luger.

"Well, what if Jason did have a really good system, but it relied on one large bet to make it work. The only person at the casino who could approve such a bet was the manager. He also spun the wheel for that bet," said Burt.

"Then why would the manager need to be killed?" asked Luger, not sure what he believed any more.

"Just picture it," said Burt. "Jason had just won more than $12 million, and they were probably going to split the money fifty-fifty or sixty-forty or whatever. Now, Jason or Roger may have demanded a bigger cut, and they probably had a falling out. However, if you truly believe that it was murder, then I'm sure you realize who the logical person was who employed the murderer."

"Jason," exclaimed Luger.

"If you say so," said Burt, trying to give all the credit or discredit to Luger for solving the crime.

"So now you agree with me that it was a murder and not a suicide?" said Luger with a feeling of pride in his voice.

"Well, not exactly," said Burt. "All I am saying is that if—and I stress the *if*—if Roger was murdered, then the one who had the most to gain under this situation would be Jason."

"Well, I suppose we should have this guy picked up on suspicion of murder," said Luger.

"He's in Australia," said Burt.

"Oh, well we'll just have to get the Australian police to pick him up then."

"How will they find him?" said Burt.

"Oh, they should have no trouble there. Besides, you already have his address," said Luger.

Again, Burt found himself in trouble. "No, I'm afraid I don't. He didn't live there; it was just an address that he had used for a few months. He was leaving there shortly after I left," said Burt.

"Well, he may have given a forwarding address," said Luger.

Burt's mind was now filled with different thoughts. If the Australian police found Jason before he did, then the truth may come out, and the money would be lost forever. Also, if the police went to the address that Burt had given, then it would come out that he had never seen Jason. This would just make Luger get back on his case.

Burt quickly summed up the situation. If he hired some private detectives in Australia, they should be able to find Jason within a reasonable length of time. This meant that Burt would now have to reconvince Luger that the death was a suicide. He could use the stupidity of the inspector to his advantage.

"Of course," said Burt, hesitating just enough to get Luger's whole attention, "we may have the murder theory way out of proportion."

"What do you mean?" said Luger.

"If the death was a suicide, I don't think your superiors would take too kindly to your involving the Australian police for nothing."

"Are you saying that you now think it wasn't murder?" questioned Luger.

"Yes," said Burt. "I am agreeing with your first conclusion that it was, indeed, suicide, Inspector."

"I am confused," said Luger. "But what about the letter?"

"Come on now, Inspector," said Burt. "The letter was obviously written by Jason to discredit me—like winning in my casino and then thumbing his nose at me. He should have known that you wouldn't fall for something that easily, Inspector."

Luger had again been outwitted by a much superior intellect. With the final verdict on the death finally determined to be suicide, Inspector Luger and his officer left Burt's house. Burt couldn't help but notice the smile the officer had on his face as if he knew that the inspector had been completely manipulated.

Burt's next step was to hire some Australian private detectives. He called his secretary to start the ball rolling. Within a few days, four detectives were hard at work trying to track down Jason and Debbie.

The first news of Jason was received just two weeks after the detectives started to search. It was a small lead, but it was a lead. Unfortunately, the lead fizzled out to nothing. In the coming weeks, the detectives came up with numerous leads, but none came to anything. It seemed as if Jason was playing a game with Burt.

With Burt's spirits quickly beginning to diminish, he could see his $7.5 million going the way of the dodo bird.

At the office, Burt had another meeting with his chief executives. He had intentionally put this meeting off as long as he possibly could. It was now time to confront them and admit that they were right, and he had been wrong.

Burt hated to admit that he was wrong, especially to those who were in his employ. He would be able to tell by their eyes that they were thinking to themselves, "I told you so."

There was no smile on Burt's face when he met with the three men. The once-confident expression had been replaced by worry. His head hung a little lower than usual, and his eyes did not burn right through them. He began by stating that the latest news of Jason was not good news.

"It looks as if the plan has come to an unhappy end. Not that I have given up yet—far from it," Burt stated. "It's just that Jason has the upper hand. He calls the shots, and I will have to just wait until he is ready to contact me."

"You think he will contact you then, sir?" asked Peter.

"I believe so," said Burt, trying to convince himself, as well as the others in the room.

"I don't really see why he would," said Bill. "After all, he has the money. Why would he want to give it back?"

"I think he would," John said, to the surprise of everyone. "You had mentioned before that you had made him an offer that would be very hard to pass up when he signed the agreement."

"That's right," said Burt, "and I feel that is the main reason why Jason will still contact me. However, I will admit that, at this stage, I must now say that the whole operation has been a failure. You were right at the outset to tell me that I was embarking on a foolish idea. I was a man looking for a dream. What I got was a headache. Oh, don't get me wrong, I haven't given up on Jason yet. I am just not as confident as I once was."

The visitors all tried to show some encouragement for Burt. It was John who was behind him all the way. This was unusual, because Burt always felt that there was a lot of tension between the two of them, just over Jane.

When they left the office, the three executives tried very hard to suppress their pleasure at seeing Burt in this predicament. They headed straight for Bill's office for an impromptu meeting.

It was Bill who began. "I knew it wasn't going to be as easy as he thought it would be."

"We all knew that," agreed Peter. "I just think that we shouldn't gloat about it. After all, we did help select Jason." Peter then turned his remarks to John. "What did you find out about this guy when you went over his personnel file?"

"Well, there was nothing to show that he was the type of person who would go back on his word. I suppose the thought of getting to keep $12 million instead of $1 million would tend to sway someone just a little."

"What about his wife?" Peter then asked.

"She was a real looker," said John, "but she seemed a bit on the dumb side according to the report I received on her."

"Boy, you sure did a thorough job of investigation," said Bill.

"Oh, there was one other thing about her that I failed to mention before," said John. "I once dated her for two months."

Bill and Peter just stared at each other.

"Not that any of that made me select Jason. It was just a coincidence," said John. "Seeing that Jason was the best candidate I could come up with, I had to make sure there was nothing in his background that could spoil it. He was squeaky clean."

"If you want my opinion," chimed in Bill, "Burt should cut his losses and stop wasting his money by employing these Aussie detectives. He should write the loss off to experience."

"It's a really big amount to write off to experience," replied John.

"Well, it doesn't really matter what we think he should do," said Peter. "Burt will continue to look for Jason until he finds him or the money or until he realizes it is costing far too much."

As time went on, Burt chose not to wallow in self-pity but continued his duties at the office. He received constant reports from his operatives in Australia, but the future didn't look too bright.

People could see he was upset and believed it to be the combination of his casino's loss and the death of Roger. Nora was very supportive and tried to switch his attention to his business interests in Australia. Burt knew that she was just trying to take his mind off his problems, not knowing the extent of them. He told her that his business interests in Australia had not yet been finalized. and it would take at least one more trip Down Under before they were.

As Burt was in his office, Nora phoned him to say there was a telegram for him from Australia. He knew that it was not from his detectives, because they used faxes not telegrams.

"I'm sure that it is something confidential, so I will come home as soon as I can," said Burt.

The telegram was indeed from Jason. It read: "Let's stop the search and split money 50/50. If agreeable, put ad in personal column of L.A. Times under heading 'Lonely Casino. Burt agrees in two days' time.'" Burt was at first happy and then furious. He quickly summed up that half of $8.5 million was better than none.

Burt immediately had the detective search called off. An ad was placed in the *LA Times* as instructed, and the wait began. It was three long weeks before Burt received another telegram—another way Jason was staying on top at Burt's expense.

The telegram gave explicit instructions for Burt and Jason to meet in five days at a specific time.

A meeting was quickly arranged by Burt with the three chief executives. He had two reasons for calling the meeting. The first was to tell them that he would be returning to Sydney to pick up his money—well, half of it anyway. The second reason was to retract his previous statement that they were right and he was wrong about Jason.

Just before the three executives entered Burt's office, Bill asked the other two if they had any idea what the meeting was about.

"I'm sure it's got something to do with Jason," said Peter, who always seemed to grasp things a little faster than the other two.

"He's probably received another telegram from him," John added.

Burt's secretary told them to go straight in. Burt eagerly motioned them to their seats and got the meeting under way. He divulged the contents of the two telegrams and waited for their comments.

This time, it was Peter who spoke first. "Are you sure you can trust him this time?"

"I hope so," replied Burt. "Unfortunately, I have no choice if I want to see any of the money again."

"I don't know about this, Burt," said John. "It sounds like you are leaving yourself wide open here."

"Wide open for what?" asked Burt.

"Well, for anything, I suppose," John replied. "You don't really know what this guy will do now that he has the money. You are the only one who stands between his keeping the money and losing it."

"I know that I am taking a bit of a risk, but at least I now know where I can lay my hands on the money," said Burt.

"Well, we all wish you luck, Burt," said Bill. "I hope you get all your money back. Well, half of it at least."

Burt told them that he would be leaving the following afternoon so he could have plenty of time to take any necessary precautions.

As the three executives left Burt's office, John turned to Burt and said, "If I were you, Burt, I would get myself a gun when I got there."

Burt just nodded.

Bill asked the other two what they thought Burt meant by taking the necessary precautions.

"Oh, probably a body guard," said Peter.

"Or maybe a gun," said John.

CHAPTER 9

Jane was trying to be civil to John, but he was determined to avoid her as much as possible. He knew she was trying to make up, but he was very determined. *After all, she was the one who didn't want to make a commitment,* he thought to himself. *Just let her try to make up. I'll show her.*

The day after Burt's last meeting with his three executives, John was in his office when Jane burst in unannounced and closed the door behind her. John had a fair idea what was on her mind.

She strode over to John's desk and leaned on it with both hands. "Okay, John, this has gone far enough," she said. "If you want to act like a little schoolboy who can't get his own way every time, then you can consider our friendship ended."

Jane was in no mood for John to be coy with her. He knew that his charm would not be enough to sway her this time.

"Look, Jane," he said, "if you would calm down a minute—"

"Don't say it, John. Don't tell me not to get my tits in a tangle. You know I hate that expression," she replied in a very agitated state.

"All I was going to say was let's discuss this calmly," replied John.

"Okay, okay, I'm calm," said Jane as she sat down.

"What is it that you want?" said John as innocently as he could.

"What is it that I want?" replied Jane in the same agitated state as before, jumping up from her chair. "What is it that I want? Well, that's just fine."

John managed to calm her down again. "Now," he said, "I thought that we had decided the relationship we had enjoyed was now over and—"

Jane cut him short. "But I didn't think you actually meant what you said that night."

"Well, I did," replied John with a touch of authority in his voice.

"So that's it then," said Jane with a very hurt look on her face. "All the time we have spent together, the things we have meant to each other, are all thrown out of the window, just like that?" She glared at John, defying him to defend his actions.

"I think you have this a little backward, Jane," John said, getting up from his chair and sitting on his desk in front of her. "That night I asked you point-blank if you wanted to make a commitment. To marry me or for us to live together, and it was you, not me, who chose not to."

"Just because I said that didn't mean we couldn't continue our relationship the way it was. I would eventually agree to marry you—you know that. It's just that at the moment, it is not the right time."

"That's just it, Jane," replied John. "Without a commitment, we have nothing."

"Nothing," she said staring right at John with a fixed look.

"I am not going to back down on this, Jane. I needed a commitment at that time, and you were not willing to give one. To me, that was the end of our relationship."

"I can't believe that you are saying this, John," said Jane. "You mean that you don't miss what we meant to each other?"

"Of course I miss it," replied John in a rather nonchalant tone, "but it doesn't mean that I will change my mind."

Jane couldn't believe that her lover was actually calling it quits. Apparently, he was not as in love with her as she thought. There was a long pause.

John cut in with, "Besides, you always have Burt to take you out to dinner." John realized he may have gone a little too far with this last remark and wished that he could retract it.

Jane stood up, stared John right in the eyes, and said, "You bastard." She then turned her back and stormed out of the office.

John's secretary came in just as John was sitting back down in his chair.

"Boy, she certainly was mad about something," said the secretary.

She was the only one at the office who had figured out that the two of them were seeing each other. After all, can you ever keep anything from your secretary?

"Oh, she'll calm down eventually," replied John.

"I don't know about that," the secretary remarked. "You know the old saying about a woman scorned."

John chose not to think about that.

Jane was determined not to give John the satisfaction of

seeing her apologize or try to make up. She purposely didn't see him at the office for the next three days. In those three days, though, Jane was going through her own personal hell. She hadn't realized just how in love she was with John.

After the three days, Jane dressed in one of her best business outfits and did her hair just the way John liked it. "This should make his mouth water," she said out loud as she admired herself in the full-length mirror in her bedroom before heading off to work.

As soon as she arrived at work, Jane calmly went into John's office and asked his secretary if he was in yet.

The secretary looked up at Jane, no doubt thinking of the episode a few days before, and answered as politely as she could.

"I'm afraid he is on vacation," she said.

"Vacation?" Jane said in disbelief. "How long will he be gone?"

"Four weeks," came the reply.

As if there was an echo in the room, Jane replied, "Four weeks."

She looked very surprised, and her eyes opened to the fullest. The secretary was a little afraid that Jane may have a tantrum judging by her reaction the other day.

"Would it be prying too much into his personal affairs to ask where he has gone?" Jane said in a much softer tone after realizing that she was almost screaming before.

"I'm sure he wouldn't mind you knowing that he has gone on a cruise to the Caribbean," the secretary responded.

"A cruise," said Jane, reverting back to her semihysterical voice. Jane then just turned and left. Back in her own office, Jane could not concentrate on any of her work.

"I can't believe he would go on a cruise just like that

without even telling me," she said as she paced the office. "The least he could have done was to ask me if I would like to go. I would have jumped at the chance to go on a cruise to the Caribbean. He knew that."

When Jane was alone, she would say what was on her mind out loud, and coworkers could often hear voices coming from her office when there was no one else there.

Just at that moment, a horrible thought came over Jane. *He better not have taken that Julie on the cruise*, she thought.

She would have liked to have been able to call Julie to see if she was home but didn't have her phone number and had no way of finding it.

"He can't do this to me," Jane continued as she talked to herself. "I hope he has a lousy time, and if he gets laid just once, then our relationship is definitely at an end."

For the rest of the day, Jane tried to put the thought of her lover on a cruise out of her mind. When she arrived home, she put some leftover lasagna in the microwave, curled up on her favorite sofa, and switched on the television. She stared at the program on TV without really seeing it. Her mind was on the ship with John. She could see him sitting at an elegant dinner table with several beautiful women.

Jane was torturing herself with these thoughts. She was jolted back to reality when the timer on her microwave told her that her meal was done. She couldn't eat anything at this stage and just left the lasagna where it was.

Tears began to form in Jane's eyes as she thought again about the man she loved on a cruise. She couldn't get John out of her mind, and she now realized what a fool she had been.

I could have had him all to myself, for the rest of our lives, she thought to herself.

"All I had to do was agree to marry him. Was that so hard for me to do? I do love him so much. Oh, what a fool I have been. I may have lost him forever now," Jane cried to herself.

Over the course of the evening, Jane's feelings ran the gamut from love to anger and then back to love again.

"I know," she said. "When he gets back, I will not act jealous or ask him what he has been up to or anything like that. I will just show him how much I really love him and tell him that I want to marry him. That should make him happy."

With those happy thoughts still floating in her head, Jane went to bed.

CHAPTER 10

Burt had arranged for a flight to Sydney as soon as the last telegram had arrived. The plane ride was similar to the previous one with one exception—the amount of the prize at the end.

Burt was still not 100 percent confident that Jason would keep his part of the bargain. *After all, he had tried to pin a murder rap on me*, thought Burt to himself. *Will I get the runaround again, or will it just be a one-shot deal?*

The weather in Sydney was a balmy thirty-four degrees, or ninety-two on the Fahrenheit scale, and the sun was shining. Burt knew this time that he would get the money. He had gone over and over in his mind that $4.25 million would still put him way in front.

He had three days in Sydney before the meeting. Burt thought about what John had said to him the other day. He decided to get some protection in case there was a double-cross and his life was in danger.

Burt found that in Australia, a handgun was very difficult to obtain. He strolled along the waterfront area of Sydney, hoping to get in touch with some of the Aussie underworld. It took a while, but he did find someone who could provide him with a handgun. However, it was going to cost him. The total was more than ten times what it would have cost him back in the United States. He didn't have time to haggle and didn't want to attract too much attention to himself, so he agreed to the price. Half the money had to be paid up front, and the balance was due in twenty-four hours when he would receive the gun. The gun seller said that he would meet Burt at the same spot at exactly ten o'clock the following night. Burt was a little worried about the timing, because it only gave him an hour in which to meet Jason.

It would be a long twenty-four hours waiting for the gun.

The Aussie rules on handguns were very stringent, and if he were caught in possession of a firearm, he would have a lot of explaining to do and probably end up in jail.

By this time, Burt was more than a little paranoid about Jason.

It seems so out of character for him to have become so greedy, Burt pondered. *I thought I had this guy figured out, but he has sure thrown me for a loop.*

The place where they were to meet was on the outskirts of Sydney proper. Burt checked a map to find out exactly where he was to go and was pleased to discover that the trip to meet Jason would take less than an hour. Burt thought that eleven o'clock at night was rather an odd time, but it was Jason who had all the cards to play. Burt was just a player in this game.

On the following evening, Burt picked up the gun and hailed a cab. It took just under an hour to get there. As the cab pulled up in front, the house was in complete darkness. It was an old house, one that would probably be torn down in the very near future.

"Well, at least there is such an address this time," Burt said to himself.

"It doesn't look like there's anyone at home," commented the cab driver. "Are you sure this is the place?"

"I'm sure," said Burt, "and there had better be someone home."

Burt asked the driver to wait because he didn't think that he would be too long. Burt took out his gun and checked it. The cabby saw the gun and looked worried.

"Don't worry. This is not for you," said Burt. "It's for that bastard in there. If he tries anything, he will be going to the big casino in the sky."

"Hey look, mister," returned the cabby. "I don't want to get mixed up in any murder."

"This is just for protection," answered Burt. "I have no intention of using it. Don't worry."

"I bet that's what they all say," said the cabby under his breath.

When Burt walked up to the front door, he hesitated about going in. He went to a window and peered in. The house was in total darkness, and he could see absolutely nothing. He became a little fearful at this stage and wondered what he was getting into.

Well, I'm not going to get any of my money back by standing out here, Burt thought to himself. As he reached for the door handle, a lump came to Burt's throat. He had already figured out that Jason would be the prime suspect if anything were to happen to him, and he felt Jason was smarter than that. As the door opened, Burt peered in and tried to look around. It was as if all light had been prevented from getting in.

"Hello?" called Burt nervously.

"Burt," came a voice.

"Yes?" replied Burt.

A loud bang rang out. The noise echoed right through Burt's head. There was a quick flash of bright white light and then nothing. Burt couldn't see a thing, so he just instinctively dropped to the floor, pulled out the gun, and fired wildly as the rush of adrenaline pumped through him. His heart was pounding excitedly. He had no idea where the shot had come from but decided that he was lucky not to have been hit and didn't want to press his luck. He quickly got up and bolted through the door, which he had left open.

The cab driver had taken off at the sound of the first gunshot and turned around as Burt rushed out of the house. However, he was not going to go back for him.

It's his problem, the cab driver thought to himself as he sped away. There was no way that he wanted to get involved with a shooting.

Now Burt was alone except for the person in the house. Burt wondered what the hell he had got himself into. He stopped running about one hundred yards from the house and turned around to see if he was being chased. There wasn't anyone following, and he didn't detect any movement at the house.

There must have been someone in the house, he thought to himself. *Should I go back to the house, or should I just keep walking and get out of here? What the hell am I thinking? Someone just tried to kill me!*

Burt stood still for a moment as he pondered going to the police with his story.

"What would I say to them?" Burt mumbled as he began to walk down the road, not knowing if he was going in the right direction. All these thoughts were racing through his mind, and his heart was beating a mile a minute. The thought of having a coronary also flashed into his mind as he realized that he had just run the one-hundred-yard dash at a very fast pace. You tend to run fast when you think someone is chasing you, especially when that person has a gun.

"I'm too old for this sort of thing," he said, shaking his head.

It was still before midnight as Burt made his way up the street in search of a cab. As he walked over a bridge and watched the water rushing beneath him, he suddenly realized that he still had the gun. He again turned to make sure no one was following him, and without thinking of the consequences, he tossed the gun over an embankment.

It was more than an hour later when he finally came to a main road and fancied his chances of getting a cab or at least finding a telephone box. Burt's luck changed a little as a cab came down the road with his vacant sign lit. As Burt got in the cab, he was breathing heavily.

"Going for a midnight run?" asked the cab driver in a joking manner.

Burt ignored the remark and just gave the name of his hotel. It was two thirty in the morning when Burt finally arrived back at the Menzies Hotel. He climbed into his bed. It felt so good to lie down on something nice and soft. Then he remembered the money.

That bastard doesn't want to give up without a fight.

He now realized that Jason was a much better adversary than he had originally thought.

Well, at least he is still in Sydney, thought Burt as he managed to close his eyes, oblivious that he may have just escaped being killed.

The next morning, Burt rose early. He had tossed and turned so much that he couldn't sleep. He still couldn't believe the events of the previous night. He wondered what he had gotten himself into and also wondered what Jason's next move was going to be.

Burt could never get going in the morning without a nice, relaxing shower. He slowly dragged his weary body into the bathroom and stepped into the shower. This helped rid his mind of the crazy events from the previous night. He took breakfast in the hotel and then decided to get some fresh air by going for a walk. On his walk, he tried to make some sense out of the mess of last night.

On his return to the hotel, the police were waiting for him. The cab driver had informed them of the trouble of last night. It took a while for Burt to realize that they were there to arrest him.

"What's the charge?" he asked.

"You shouldn't say anything until you have seen a solicitor," said the policeman.

"I just want to know what you are charging me with," Burt repeated.

"First-degree murder," came the reply.

Burt went into a temporary state of shock. "Murder?" he questioned. "Who was murdered?"

"I can't tell you that, because the deceased hasn't been identified yet," replied the police officer.

"I didn't kill anyone," said Burt.

"Well, suppose you explain it to my superior," said the officer.

On the way to the police station, Burt was trying to figure out how he could have hit anyone by firing one bullet wildly. The enormity of the trouble he found himself in still hadn't really dawned on him. His thoughts still went back to the money, and he tried to figure out how he could get it back now that he had been arrested for murder.

The superior was an Inspector James Dobie. There was no similarity between him and Inspector Luger. This was a real policeman—one who knew how to investigate, Burt surmised.

Dobie suggested that Burt contact his solicitor before any questions were asked.

"I am afraid I don't have one here," said Burt almost apologetically.

"I can suggest a few for you to get in touch with," Dobie replied.

Burt phoned about three solicitors before he could get one who would agree to come down to the station right away. He was prompt, as it was a scant twenty minutes before Burt was face-to-face with the man who was to be charged with the task of trying to get Burt off of this murder charge.

"The first thing I would like to know, Inspector," said Burt, "is who exactly did I supposedly shoot?"

"How did you know the deceased had been shot?" asked the inspector, putting Burt on the spot.

"I thought the policeman had said it," replied Burt.

The policeman who had arrested Burt stated that he hadn't mentioned the cause of death to Burt. Burt went on the defensive and again asked who it was that he was being accused of murdering.

"Well, the victim has not been officially identified. However, according to the only identification he had on him, his driver's license, his name was Jason Chard," said Inspector Dobie.

"Jason," exclaimed Burt with bewilderment written on his face.

"Do you know him?" asked the Inspector

"He was the one I was going there to meet," replied Burt.

"Well, suppose you describe in your own words what happened last night," said the Inspector. "I may caution you, however, that anything you say may be used against you. Maybe you want to confer with your solicitor before you say anything."

The solicitor advised Burt of his rights. Burt wanted to set the record straight and did not believe things were as bad as they were being made to appear.

Burt gave his version of the evening, leaving out the real reason why he was going there and replacing it with a simple business transaction. When he had finished his story, the inspector compared it with the statement that the cab driver had given. He excused himself to question the cab driver some more.

The most incriminating evidence against Burt was that he had said the gun "was meant for him in there," and Dobie wanted to make sure that the facts were exact.

"Did he say he was going to kill him?" the inspector asked the cab driver.

"No," said the cab driver. "He said exactly what I have stated there." He pointed to the part in his statement. "Oh, wait a minute, Inspector. There was one other thing he said. I can't remember it exactly, but just after he said, 'It's meant for him in there,' he said, 'If he tries anything he would be going to the brick casino in disguise,' whatever that means."

The Inspector added this phrase to the statement, and the cab driver signed it.

"Did you see who fired the shot?" asked the Inspector.

"Well, no," replied the cabby. "As soon as I heard the shot, I took off out of there so fast. I did manage to turn around as I whizzed away, and I saw the guy running out of the house."

"By 'the guy,' I take it you mean Mr. Donaldson, your fare?" said the inspector.

"Yes, sir," replied the cab driver. "He seemed such a nice guy too, even for a Yank. He was very nervous, though."

"During the cab ride to the house, what did he say?" asked the inspector.

"He chatted as most fares do but was quieter than most. He didn't seem like the type who could kill somebody," said the cabby.

"They never do," said the inspector. "One thing bothers me about this case, though. The suspect didn't use much common sense. I mean, if you were planning to kill somebody, you would hardly ask the cab driver to wait for you." The inspector thanked the cab driver for his statement and dismissed him.

While they were alone waiting for the inspector to return, the solicitor, a man by the name of Tom Brady, asked Burt whether there was anything that he had left out of his statement.

"Like what?" asked Burt rather impertinently.

"Well, like the reason why you were going to see a business associate at eleven o'clock at night to discuss business in an out-of-the-way house that was in complete darkness. It all seems a little odd," remarked Tom.

"I know that it doesn't look too good for me, but someone else fired at me first. I just took out the gun and fired. Christ, I couldn't hit the side of a barn even if I was standing next to it," Burt said.

"We should find out a little more of what the police have as evidence," the solicitor said.

"Why? What's the difference?" asked Burt, not familiar with the Australian way of police investigations.

"Well, for one thing, if what you say is true—"

Burt cut him short at this point. "What do you mean *if*?" said Burt. "I hope I at least have you on my side."

"Of course I'm on your side," said the solicitor. "What I meant was there seems to be some inconsistencies here."

"Like what?" said Burt moving a little closer, as if maybe there was a God after all.

At that moment, Inspector Dobie returned. The solicitor motioned to Burt that he would ask the questions of the inspector and he was to remain silent.

Burt was impressed with the way in which Tom conducted his questioning of the inspector. It was as if the inspector did not know he was even being questioned.

The inspector turned to Burt. "Now, you are not obliged to answer any of these questions if you don't want to," said Dobie.

"Well, I have nothing to hide," said Burt. "Besides, I have my lawyer here to advise me."

"The cab driver who drove you to the murder scene has given us some very incriminating evidence we can use against you."

"I did nothing," said Burt.

"The victim was shot at very close range," said Inspector Dobie.

"Honestly, Inspector, I am no murderer. I only took the

gun as protection. I had no intention of using it," protested Burt.

"You did fire it, didn't you?" said the Inspector.

"Well, yes, I did, but just once, and I'm sure I didn't hit anything. It was too dark in there to see anything," replied Burt.

"And you just happened to throw the major evidence, the gun, over an embankment on the way home?" said Dobie in a sarcastic fashion.

"Look, Inspector, I know that it sounds a little ridiculous, but—"

"I am afraid you will have to be held on a charge of first-degree murder until we find out any further information," said Dobie.

As he sat in his jail cell, Burt thought about the weird chain of events that had started with just a simple idea to save some money. Now he could end up behind bars for the rest of his life—in a foreign country, no less.

Burt tried to think about who could have set him up. The only other person who was involved in the plan was the croupier, but he was back in the United States as far as Burt knew. Besides, the croupier would have nothing to gain by Jason's death. The only others who knew of the plan were the three vice presidents, but they were only in on the original planning, not the execution of it. Besides, they would have nothing to gain from the death of Jason.

Burt quickly realized that this was a unique frame-up. Nobody he knew could have done it. It seemed that the best—no, the only—defense Burt had was to find the real killer, and that could take forever. The thought of the $8.5 million had all but disappeared from Burt's mind. Having your life turned upside down made one think of things other than money, no matter how much.

My God, it's actually my life on the line here, Burt thought to himself. *I must be dreaming. This cannot be happening to me.*

The following morning, Burt was paid a visit from his solicitor. Before he could say anything, Burt requested that Tom contact his secretary back in Las Vegas and tell her what had happened.

"I have just spoken with Inspector Dobie, and I wanted to clear up one particular point that has been bothering me," stated the solicitor.

"What's that?" said Burt in an interested tone.

"It just struck me odd that you fired after you were shot at."

"What's odd about that?"

"So you didn't see what you were firing at?" said the solicitor.

"No, I just fired wildly into the air. Why?" said Burt, starting to take more of an interest.

"You do know how the deceased died?"

"Yes, he was shot," answered Burt, puzzled by this question.

"He was shot right between the eyes at very close range."

"Between the eyes?" exclaimed Burt. "I have never shot a handgun before, so how could I possibly have shot him right between the eyes when the house was in total darkness?"

"That's exactly my point," said the solicitor. "If you can remember exactly where you threw the gun, it may be retrieved. Look, I am going to speak to the inspector and get somebody to check out the murder scene to see if there is another bullet there. Then all we need to do is to find your gun to see if the bullet is from your gun and prove that the one who killed the deceased is from a different gun."

In the meantime, the news of Burt's arrest had reached Las Vegas. As a result, Inspector Luger decided to reopen the suicide-come-murder-come-suicide case of the casino manager and list it again as a possible murder with Burt as the only murder suspect.

Inspector Dobie allowed Burt to show him where he thought he had thrown his gun, and a police team began to comb the depths of the embankment. The area was covered with a thick undergrowth of various types of bushes and weeds.

"Are you sure that this is the place where you threw it?" asked the inspector.

"It was on a little bridge, and this is the only one in the area where I walked," replied Burt.

"You know, it was a bit of a stupid thing to throw the gun away," said the inspector.

"I know, I know, but you must realize, Inspector, that I wasn't exactly thinking very clearly at the time. After all, someone had just tried to kill me."

Another team of police also went to the murder scene to look for another bullet.

Because of Burt's position in business and his US residency, Inspector Dobie allowed him to be able to make several phone calls to Las Vegas, provided he pay for them himself.

The first person he called was Nora. It was just a short conversation to say that he was in good spirits and hoped the police would get to the bottom of the case soon. Then he could get out of jail and return to her. The next person he called was Jane. Because of the trouble Burt was in, Jane thought it best that they just keep their relationship on a purely business level from then on. Burt was taken aback by this and was annoyed at her coldness when he really needed some comforting words.

"Are you involved with somebody new?" asked Burt.

There was a hesitation in her voice as Jane began to answer. "No, no one new. Just somebody I was involved with once. I now realize how much he really means to me. That is, if he will take me back on any terms he wishes."

"Anyone I know?" said Burt.

"Good night," said Jane, and she hung up.

I don't know why I used to entertain her anyhow, thought Burt to himself. *She never came across when I casually mentioned it. I was probably wasting my time thinking there could be anything more than a casual dinner.*

No, I am probably better off without her. My God, she is beautiful, and I did like to have her with me when I went out to dinner. It made all the other men in the room envious of me. Burt smiled as he thought.

Inspector Dobie came to see Burt as he languished in his cell.

"Well, you have had a stroke of luck," said the inspector. "We have located a second bullet. It was embedded in the ceiling."

"Does that mean you believe my story, Inspector?" said Burt.

"We still have to find your gun," said the inspector.

"How long do you think that will take?" asked Burt.

"According to the search team, at least a couple of days."

"So I am going to have to rot here for another few days?" Burt exclaimed.

Inspector Dobie ignored the question and left.

As Burt sat in his jail cell, his thoughts turned to Jason. He tried to feel a little remorse that he was dead and could see that even though he hadn't pulled the trigger, he was partly to blame. He was the one who got Jason into this mess in the first place.

Burt still couldn't understand who would have shot Jason, though. Maybe it was a robbery. After all, Jason was probably flashing some of the money around that he had converted into cash or at least bragging about his big casino win. It was probably a simple robbery. Yes, that was the most likely reason.

Burt seemed a little happier now that he felt that he had pieced together what may have happened. He was still in a quandary, because he couldn't tell the police about the money. As Burt tried to think some more about his problem, he realized that he could tell the police about the money. At least he could tell them that Jason had won the money at his casino, and then his theory of what may have happened would sound a little more plausible.

The following morning, Inspector Dobie paid another visit to Jason. This time he was accompanied by Burt's solicitor.

Burt was pleased to see them, because he could now relate his robbery theory to the inspector. However, the news with which Burt was greeted could add another twist to the problems he has endured so far.

"The murdered man, although he had identification on him saying he was Jason Chard, is, in fact, not one Jason Chard," stated the inspector.

Burt's mouth gaped as he grasped for words.

"It's not Jason?" he said.

"No," replied the inspector. "A routine fingerprint check showed that he is actually a small-time thief named Brian Cox. He had been arrested once before, which is how we found out who he was."

"How come he was identified as Jason then?" asked Burt.

"He had a driver's license in the name of Jason Chard but with his own photo on it."

"You mean that the guy who I am being charged with murdering is someone who I have never even met?" said Burt, becoming a little hysterical. "How come Jason's wife wasn't asked to identify the body?"

"We couldn't find her," came the reply.

"Who was the person who identified the body then?" asked Burt, putting the inspector through the third degree.

"Look, I am supposed to be the one asking the questions," said the inspector. "I may as well tell you that it was a cousin of Jason's, and he has now disappeared."

"So what's your theory on the murder now?" asked Burt, full of confidence.

"Well, it looks more and more like you were set up to take the blame," said the inspector. "However, we can't release you just yet, because you were placed at the murder scene at the time of the murder."

"Oh, come now, Inspector. What bloody reason would I have for killing a man I don't even know?" shot back Burt.

"I must admit, there is a lot more to this case than we first thought," came the reply.

Burt was beginning to think the inspector was a distant relative of Inspector Luger. It was at this point that the solicitor, who had been extremely quiet, actually decided to say something.

"Isn't it obvious?" said the solicitor. "Jason wanted to fake his own death for whatever reason, so he had this guy get some fake identification in his own name and then killed him. He must have gone to a lot of trouble to get the ID, because you know as well as I do how hard it is to fake a New South Wales driver's license."

"I can supply a possible reason," volunteered Burt.

"Jason had won quite a lot of money at my casino in Las Vegas. He probably wanted to avoid paying Australian taxes on it, so he decided to fake his death."

"If that was the case, then the death duties that would have to be paid would be a lot more than the taxes," said the inspector.

"Only if the casino money was accounted for," said Burt. "I bet you didn't find a lot of money, did you, Inspector?"

"No, we didn't find any large sums. How much money did this guy win?" asked Dobie.

Burt watched their faces as he answered. "Twelve million dollars."

Both the solicitor and Dobie sat there staring at Burt with their mouths wide open.

"Twelve million dollars?" exclaimed Dobie in an unusually high voice. "I must admit, I would hate to have to pay taxes on that."

"How well did you know Jason?" asked the inspector.

"I didn't know him at all," replied Burt. "As I said, he had won all this money at my casino, and he had sent me a telegram to invite me down here to meet him."

"Is that usual?" questioned the inspector.

"No, it isn't," said Burt. "However, this was an unusual circumstance. The money Jason won was the most in a single win at my casino. I was curious to meet the man who had accomplished this feat,"

"So what's the next step here, Inspector?" said Burt, becoming eager to get out of jail.

"Well." Inspector Dobie grinned. "Until we find your gun or a better suspect, then you're it."

"Don't worry, Burt. We'll soon have you out of here," said the solicitor, trying to put his client a little at ease.

It didn't work. This new bit of news just tortured Burt even more. He now knew Jason was alive and was probably laughing at him as he began to spend the money.

Just wait until I get out of this hell hole, Burt said to himself. *Just wait. I will make sure, no matter how long it takes, that I track that bastard down and get all my money back.*

It was about a lot more than just the money now. Jason had played Burt for a fool by trying to pin a murder on him.

"Just think," Burt said out loud. "I was actually feeling sad when I thought he had been murdered. The little creep better be on his guard when I eventually meet up with him."

It was another two days before Burt had another visit from his solicitor. He again was accompanied by the inspector, and Burt began to think that the two were inseparable.

"Well, what news have you to give me today?" said Burt.

He hadn't noticed before, but neither men was smiling. They both had the same expression on their faces—the sort of expression you expect from a policeman when he has come to tell you that someone you love has been killed.

Inspector Dobie looked at the solicitor before he began to speak, probably waiting for some sign of approval.

"Burt," he began, "we have found what we believe is

the gun that you tossed over the embankment, but we need you to identify it before we are sure. You are, of course, not obliged to answer any of these questions if you so wish; however, if you do, anything you say may be held against you."

"I know the drill," answered Burt.

Burt's solicitor stated that he would advise him not to answer if he thought that it would damage his client's case and, unfortunately, such proof of the gun would do just that.

"I think I can answer for myself on this one, Tom," Burt replied.

With that, the inspector took out the gun from a plastic bag in his briefcase.

"That's it," said Burt very quickly.

"I want you to examine the gun very carefully," instructed the inspector. "We want you to make absolutely certain that this is the gun you purchased and fired one bullet from."

Burt took the gun out of the plastic bag and gave it a thorough investigation. "Yep," he repeated. "That is the gun that I fired."

"Are you absolutely sure?" said the Inspector.

"Of course I am," said Burt. "How many guns would you normally find at a particular embankment?" he said jokingly.

Neither Tom nor the inspector were smiling. In fact, the looks on their faces were even more solemn than before.

"What gives, you guys?" said Burt. "I thought you would be happy to get me out of here. Now that you've found the gun, you can prove that I didn't kill the guy at the house, can't you?"

The last sentence from Burt showed some genuine concern.

"Look, Burt," Dobie began, "the reason that I have asked your solicitor to be present is that we have some bad news for you."

"You don't mean that the gun was the one that killed him?" Burt uttered in an astonished tone.

"No, it wasn't the one that killed him," answered the inspector.

You could almost hear the sigh of relief from Burt. "Then why all the long faces?" he asked.

Dobie again looked at the solicitor for a sign to continue.

"There was something else we found at the house, though," said the inspector.

"Not another bullet?" said Burt, not taking this all that seriously.

"We found another body," said the inspector, trying to show little emotion.

"Who?" said Burt, this time showing a lot of concern.

"Jason Chard," was the Inspector's solitary reply.

"Jason?" Burt blurted out in disbelief. "Are you sure it is him this time?"

"We're sure," said Dobie.

"Then why should it be bad news for me?" said Burt with a puzzled look on his face. His main fear was that they had discovered the money.

"He was murdered with your gun," said the inspector.

At this point, the solicitor advised Burt not to say anything. Burt ignored this advice mainly because he hadn't heard a word after the inspector dropped the bombshell.

"My gun?" said Burt. "But there must be some mistake here, Inspector."

"There is no mistake. The bullet that we have recovered from Jason's body matches your gun exactly," said the inspector.

Burt was completely floored by this and just slumped in his chair. The solicitor advised Burt not to say anything more, and that he would try to post bail.

Burt just sat there with a stunned look on his face. Inspector Dobie turned his remarks to the solicitor and told him to advise his client what he was to be charged with and what the implications were. Dobie then left the two to discuss their next steps.

Tom asked Burt if he wanted a few minutes alone. Burt declined, as he wanted to find out what nightmare he had now stepped into.

Tom disclosed the information he had and what the police had uncovered. The only bright spot was that Burt was only being charged with the one murder. Burt sat there only partially conscious of what his solicitor was saying to him.

Burt maintained his innocence throughout and said that he had only been to the house that one time and only for a few minutes.

Bail was going to be a difficult thing to obtain because Burt was a foreigner in Australia. Because he was in the country on a visitor's visa, the police would not want him to skip town if he were to be released. Tom said he would try.

After Tom had finished relating the details that he knew to Burt, he asked if he could do anything for him.

"Just find the real killer," said Burt, still in a state of shock and not knowing the full extent of his implication.

Tom could see that Burt needed some time to think about

these charges, so he decided to leave him to his thoughts. As his solicitor rose to leave, Burt asked one question.

"What's the penalty for murder over here?" he said.

"Let's not even think about that," came the reply. "We have to be confident."

Chapter 11

As Burt sat in his cell like a common criminal, he had time to reflect on the events that had transpired since he'd arrived in Sydney. He went over and over everything he had done, everyone he had talked to. He even started to question whether the one shot he did fire may have possibly killed Jason but decided that would be too preposterous.

The next few hours were the worst Burt had ever experienced to date. The realization of what may happen to him was almost inconceivable. The shock had now turned to anger. What made it worse was that he didn't even know the person he was angry at. Oh, he knew it was the person who actually killed Jason, but he didn't know who that person could be. That was the most frustrating part. Burt began to feel sorry for himself. He began to feel that he had been used. The biggest question in his mind now was, why?

The following morning, Burt was relieved to see his solicitor coming. Unfortunately, the news he had to impart was not what Burt wanted to hear. Bail had been refused.

This was a setback but not a major one. Burt wouldn't be able to prove his innocence whether he was out on bail or in jail. He had to rely on his solicitor or the police to come up with the evidence. The solicitor told Burt that the investigation into the murder had not come up with any new developments that would improve Burt's case. He also advised that Inspector Dobie wanted to see both of them the following day to tell them exactly what evidence he had, probably hoping for a confession from Burt. He again advised Burt to say absolutely nothing at the meeting.

Burt had called Nora and told her of the latest developments. She couldn't believe it and decided to fly to Sydney to be with her husband when he needed her most.

Burt had to endure another sleepless night before he could find out exactly what he was up against. He knew that the money had to be the major reason for the death. Unfortunately, that would have little bearing on who the killer was. Burt had time, lots of time, to reflect on the scheme that he had devised, which had now blown up right in his face.

It was early in the morning when Burt was taken to the interrogation room. His solicitor, Tom Moody, was already there.

"Now, Mr. Donaldson," said Inspector Dobie, "I am going to tell you what we have managed to piece together. If you have any comments, then I would like you to keep them until the end. I am sure, though, that your solicitor has advised you against comment of any kind."

Dobie then began his oratory after first stating that the whole session was going to be recorded. It appeared that both men were killed on the same night, although the time of death was different. They were shot by different guns. Burt was not being charged with the murder of the imposter, but the gun Burt had purchased was the weapon that killed Jason. Burt could be placed at the murder scene at about the time of the murder, which added more suspicion to his guilt. Add these two factors to the knowledge that Burt had of the money, and there was a pretty good, although circumstantial case against him.

When the inspector had finished, Burt could see why he was the only suspect. The catch was, he knew he wasn't guilty.

Burt's solicitor spoke first. "This is only circumstantial evidence, you know, Inspector," he said. "I doubt whether it will stand up in a court of law. What have you done about finding the cousin who identified the first victim as Jason? It sounds a bit suspect to me."

"In answer to your question, we have put out an apprehension notice for the cousin. However, we have since found out that he was of no relation at all, and he spoke with an American accent."

Burt couldn't resist saying something. "It seems to me, Inspector, that this guy should be on your list of suspects." Burt continued, "Also, Jason's wife should be a chief suspect."

The inspector stated that the police had been looking for her since the first murder. It appeared that she had either fled without leaving a trace or come to an end similar to Jason.

"I suppose you suspect me of that too," yelled Burt, wondering what had happened to justice.

The inspector ignored the remark. "The most incriminating evidence, though, is the murder weapon that you have already identified as the gun you purchased and fired," he noted.

"Well, what if it was the murder weapon? Maybe the person who had it before me committed the murder before he sold me the gun," said Burt, clutching at straws.

"Do you realize how ridiculous that sounds?" answered the inspector.

"Well, it must be the answer," protested Burt amid constant haranguing from his solicitor to remain silent.

"I think that you should take your solicitor's advice," said Inspector Dobie.

"I can't just sit there and say nothing when my whole life could be dissolving in front of me," Burt shouted back.

Inspector Dobie then turned to the solicitor and advised him to tell his client how things were done Down Under. He then left the interrogation room.

Burt again found himself back in his cell with nothing but questions and very few answers. *Maybe I am going about this the wrong way*, he thought. *Maybe I should be looking at who would want me in trouble. Who would gain if I were locked away for life, or even worse?*

After many hours of racking his brain to come up with people who would benefit from such a case, he was still without any names.

Burt had discovered that they had abolished the death penalty in Australia a long time ago. He was still the chief candidate to be convicted of Jason's murder and would possibly face many years behind bars in a foreign country.

Burt could now understand what wrongly convicted men went through. He never had much sympathy for them before, thinking that if they were convicted, they must be guilty. Now that he was in the hot seat himself, it sure looked a whole lot different from the other side of the fence.

The police weren't sitting idly by either. They had come up with the person who had supplied the gun to Burt. This was at least a lead and could be either very helpful or very damaging to Burt's case.

The gun seller, Alan Calnan, stated that no one else owned the gun before he sold it to Burt. A routine check on Mr. Calnan's bank accounts showed an unusually large amount deposited in one of his personal accounts the day after Burt bought the gun. For someone who listed his occupation as a clerk, a lump-sum deposit of one hundred thousand dollars did not seem very logical.

Calnan was again questioned by Inspector Dobie. When he was asked about the money in his bank account, he began to squirm a little, not realizing to what extent the police would go. He asked to speak to a solicitor. The questioning was suspended for about an hour until Calnan's solicitor could be summoned. Dobie wondered where this line of questioning would eventually lead. He had a gut feeling that Calnan was lying. Once he got the truth out of him, maybe it would help find the real killer if it wasn't Burt.

When the solicitor arrived, he asked what his client was being charged with. The inspector explained that he was merely being questioned and no charge had been laid. "That is, no charge as of yet," stated Inspector Dobie.

The questioning began again. It was pointed out to Mr. Calnan that if no one else had owned the gun before he sold it to Burt and if Burt was not or could not have been the murderer, then the most likely suspect would be Calnan himself. Such a statement caused great alarm in Calnan. He asked if he could speak to his solicitor in private if he agreed to tell them exactly what had transpired prior to the night of the murder. Dobie knew that he was now getting somewhere and granted Calnan an hour to speak with his solicitor.

After the brief meeting, the questioning began for the third time, and Calnan started to relate his story to the police. It didn't take him long to make up his mind to cooperate.

"About four days before the murder, I was contacted by a friend of a friend, so to speak, who said that he had a gun he wanted to sell to one particular person. This person was to be booked into the Menzies Hotel within the next two days. I was to follow him wherever he went. At one point, he would want to buy a gun and would probably head for the waterfront to inquire about buying one. It would be at this point that I was to befriend him and tell him that I knew where I could lay my hands on a gun. We were then to meet the following day at the same place, and I would sell him the gun for one thousand dollars. He was to pay half of the money up front as a sign of good faith.

"My contact then went on to say that the gun would be left for me at a locker at the Sydney railway station. Exactly fifteen minutes before I was to meet this guy again, I was to get the key for the locker from the attendant after giving my name and identifying myself. Maybe he didn't trust me enough to have the gun any earlier. I was to be paid one hundred thousand dollars and had to promise not to tell anyone what had happened. He said something funny after that, though; I didn't really know what it meant. It must be American slang."

"Why would you think that?" asked the inspector.

"Well, the guy had an American accent," said Calnan.

"American? Are you sure it was an American accent?" asked the inspector.

"Well, if it wasn't American, it would have to be Canadian," came the reply.

"What was the slang term he used?" asked the inspector.

"Well, it sounded like a threat and went something like, 'Otherwise, you will be going to the big casino in the sky.'"

"I've heard that term before," announced the Inspector. "I'm sure that it was in the cab driver's statement."

Dobie checked his file and pulled the cab driver's statement.

"It says here that Burt had said to the cab driver, 'If he tries anything, he will be going to the brick casino in disguise.' I'm sure that it is the same phrase; the cabby probably didn't hear it correctly. You can continue your story now, Mr. Calnan."

"I didn't know what the gun was to be used for. Honest, Inspector. I didn't know it was going to be used to commit a murder. Otherwise, I wouldn't have gotten involved in it."

When Calnan had finished relating his story, Dobie began to ask the questions. "With such a complicated scenario, how closely did it come to the real thing?" asked the inspector.

"Well, that's the funny thing, Inspector," came the reply. "It was as if the guy who bought the gun was following the same script."

"Who gave you the gun?" Dobie asked.

"I never knew his real name. He just called himself Mr. Smith," replied Calnan. "As I said, he was just a friend of a friend."

"Well, what did he look like?" said Dobie.

"I never saw him. Everything was done by phone," stated Calnan. "One thing did stick out, though, he had an American accent."

Inspector Dobie advised Calnan that he would be charged with selling a handgun to commit a crime—a charge that could put him in jail for a number of years.

Because he had given a statement to the police, it may ease the sentence a little, but Dobie couldn't promise anything. Calnan was then taken downstairs to be formally charged.

"This is the second guy with an American accent who is involved in this case," said the inspector to the two detectives who were also witnessing Calnan's story.

"Of course, they both may be the same person," said one of the detectives.

"That thought had crossed my mind also," said Dobie. "If Burt had wanted to kill Jason and get the money, he could have devised the whole scheme himself. I know that it sounds pretty far-fetched at the moment, but don't forget that there is $8.5 million at stake here."

"Why would it have to be so complicated?" said one of the officers.

"Can you imagine what the chances of such a plan working?" said Dobie. "In the first place, how did this mysterious American know that Burt was going to buy a gun? Also, how did he know the exact time Burt would be looking for a gun and where he would be looking?"

"In most harbor cities, the waterfront areas would be the most logical place to find criminals," answered one of the officers.

"I've spent a few days talking to Burt, and he is one smart person, not one who would be afraid to take a few chances if the need was great enough. And, believe me, $8.5 million is a need that is great enough."

"Maybe I'm too dumb to see it, Inspector, but why would he go through all this trouble of making himself look like the murderer if he really was guilty?" asked the other officer in a very puzzled tone.

"That's the beauty of his scheme," replied Dobie. "He

makes it look like someone has set him up to take the blame. I have a theory of what may have happened. I would like you two to pick it to pieces or come up with an alternative. Suppose Jason and Burt met as soon as Burt arrived in Sydney. He may have even picked him up from the airport. Burt persuaded Jason to find someone who resembled him a little, giving some reason for an impersonation. He then told this person to be at the house at a certain time. His next move was to get Jason to give him half of the money and suggest that Jason should put his half in a safe-deposit box.

"Jason got the money in cash, but before he could deposit it, Burt killed him. Now Burt could have then just taken the money and returned to the States. However, Jason's body would eventually be found, and there would be a lot of questions that needed to be answered—questions that Burt would find difficult to answer. He would then be arrested and extradited back here. The reason he needed another body to impersonate Jason was twofold.

"The first was to throw suspicion on Jason, because he knew that the impersonation would be discovered and Jason would be the most likely suspect, throwing suspicion off of anyone else." Dobie interrupted his story to ask, "Are you with me so far?"

The puzzled looks on both the officers' faces told him that they weren't.

"Well, let me continue in the hope that it will become clearer. The second reason and most important is that if Burt had just killed Jason, he needed to be arrested for a crime that he would definitely be acquitted of. It is very difficult to pinpoint exactly when a person died. Add to this that the impersonator was shot and killed immediately, whereas Jason was shot, but not fatally, and then bled to death. This could have taken, according to the coroner, several hours. So it is conceivable that Jason may have been the first one shot, and that is why Calnan could not pick up the gun until one hour before he was due to meet Burt— Burt had just killed Jason with it."

"One question," interrupted one of the officers. "How could Burt have shot the imposter right between the eyes when he was in a pitch-black house for just a couple of seconds?"

"Good question and one that Burt has already posed to us in his defense," said Dobie. "What if the imposter had been drugged and was lying on the floor right in front of the door? So as soon as Burt went in, all he had to do was to place the gun against the impostor's head and pull the trigger. Simple."

"Why would he have done this?" said the other detective as the two listeners were trying to grasp what Dobie was really getting at.

"Don't you see?" replied the inspector. "Burt knew that he wouldn't be charged with the imposter's murder, because his gun was not the one that did it. He also knew that we would eventually find the gun and would be able to prove that it was not the murder weapon. What he didn't count on, though, is that we would cross-check the gun to the bullet that was taken from Jason's body. However, just in case we did cross-check it, he decided to go through this elaborate scheme to try to prove that it was someone else trying to set him up to take the fall."

Dobie ended his story by saying, "Well, what do you think?"

The two officers just smiled at each other, wondering what planet their inspector had just come from.

"I think you have been watching too many detective stories on TV, Inspector," said one.

"I know it sounds really like a fantastic story," replied Dobie, "but just look at the facts we do have. Number one, Burt had the motive. He knew Jason had $8.5 million on him or, rather, in his possession. He also knew where Jason was going to be at approximately the time of the murder. He admits to owning the gun that killed Jason. And he can be put at the murder scene at about the time both Jason and the imposter were killed. Admittedly, we haven't found the murder weapon that killed the imposter, but we will."

"That's all very well, sir," said the other detective, "but why would he almost convict himself by not hiding Jason's murder weapon?"

"Well, for one thing, the cab driver had already seen Burt with a gun, so he couldn't deny that he had one," said Dobie. "Another reason was that he didn't have enough time to kill Jason, who was found in an upstairs bedroom, since he was only in there for thirty seconds at the most, according to the cab driver. This would mean there would be no way that we could get him for that murder. This lends credence that the gun had been planted on him."

"Of course, this is all circumstantial, sir," replied the officer. "How can you prove any of it, apart from the gun?"

"That's just the problem. I can't," said the inspector. "It's just one way it could have happened. I mean, the American accent on the person who supplied Calnan with the gun, for one thing. How many Americans, who knew Jason, do you think there are in Sydney? Especially ones who would have known that he had $12 million on him."

"So where do we go from here, sir?" said an officer.

"It would be nice if we could track down some of the

money, but I think that's an impossible dream. However, we should check if any large amounts of money were sent to any of Burt's bank accounts in the United States. Apart from that, we will just have to continue looking for other suspects. Jason's wife has disappeared, and she may be a suspect. There may also be a possibility that we will find another body," said the inspector.

The two officers then left to further research their case.

In the meantime Nora had arrived from Las Vegas and was waiting for Burt to be brought to the visiting area. When she saw her husband, she was amazed at the way he looked. The charge hanging over his head was taking a huge toll on him. Burt began to explain the murder charge that the police had on him. Nora just sat there not believing any of it, of course. Burt may be a lot of things, but she knew that a murderer was not one of them. She listened intently but could not see exactly how he had gotten himself into such a mess. Burt could see that his wife was going to be asking a lot more questions later. Her visiting time was up too soon, and she said that she would be staying in Sydney until he was released.

Burt was paid a visit by his solicitor. The solicitor related to him the theory that inspector Dobie had come up with. Burt couldn't believe this latest news.

"This surely must a joke," said Burt. "No one in his right mind could believe such an asinine tale. What proof does he have?"

"Well, he doesn't have too much," said the solicitor. "The only tangible piece of evidence is your gun. However, there are a few other factors that would make you the perfect suspect. For example, you had the motive. You knew that Jason had $8.5 million in his possession—$8.5 million, I may add, that he won at your casino. You also knew where Jason was going to be, and you can be placed at the murder scene at the time of the murder."

"Christ, Tom, it sounds like you think that I'm guilty too," said Burt in a dejected tone.

"Of course I don't think you are guilty. I am just saying what the police have—or, rather, think they have—could be quite damaging to our case," replied the solicitor.

"Correct me if I am wrong, Tom, but is it usual in Australia for the police to give the suspect's lawyer all their information?" asked a puzzled Burt.

"No, it is not normal," stated Tom. "It seems to me that they can't really prove what they are saying and have given us this information in order to scare us. They could also try for a plea bargain for a lesser charge or an outright confession from you before you throw yourself on the mercy of the court. I also believe that they haven't given us all the details that they have. So don't be surprised if, when we eventually go to trial, the crown attorney comes up with some curves."

"I'm not bloody well guilty," shouted Burt, his patience now growing thin. "Doesn't anyone believe in the truth anymore?"

"Well, don't give up yet. We have only just begun to fight," said the solicitor. "All their evidence, apart from the gun, is circumstantial. It would not hold up in a court of law without corroboration."

"I think you should be concentrating on the person who actually did the killings and is trying to blame me," advised Burt. "After all, this person must have been watching me very closely to know the exact moves I made."

The solicitor then proceeded to tell Burt what he had

planned for his defense. He stated that he had a team of investigators trying to track down Jason's wife and the person who gave the gun to Calnan to sell to Burt. He tried to set his client at ease with comforting words, but he knew that Burt was like a caged animal waiting to spring from captivity. Any information that he found would be imparted to Burt as soon as possible, and he would also be kept up to date daily. The police had requested an early date for an inquiry be set, so the solicitor had very little time to prepare.

As Burt sat in his holding cell, he started to think that he would soon wake up from this nightmare. He was about the only one who really knew that the murderer was not him. Who could be trying to bury him?

Since it was not Jason, then it had to be somebody else. *Boy, I must be starting to crack up,* he thought to himself.

In Burt's mind, the most logical suspect would be Jason's wife. However, she didn't really have a motive, because she would get a good part of the money if Jason was still alive. No, it couldn't have been her; it must be someone else. But who?

Maybe no one is after me. Maybe whoever it is just wanted to kill Jason and get the money and needed someone to blame. Like an idiot, I just happened along at the wrong time.

Inspector Dobie was now of a single-minded theory. The voice on the phone to the gun seller had to be Burt himself. He used the same phrase to him as he had to the taxi driver.

"It's still not conclusive, sir," said one of the police officers. "For all we know, everybody in America may use this phrase."

The inspector dismissed this objection. He knew he had his man; there was no question about it.

Inspector Dobie called a meeting with all the police members assigned to the case. He outlined the facts that had come to light, regardless of whether they had hard evidence to back them up. The theory of what may have happened was also put forth by Dobie.

"Are there any other suspects?" asked one of the police officers.

"With all the evidence we have gathered so far, it looks like Mr. Donaldson has the inside track on suspects. So far, we haven't come up with any others," replied the inspector.

"The way you have described how it happened is, of course, only one possible theory of how it may have happened, sir," said another officer.

"This is only one way it may have happened. There could be other ways," the inspector agreed. "It's just that, to me, this sounds like a logical explanation."

The police team then took their assignments and went about gathering more evidence.

Dobie called Inspector Luger to find out exactly what had happened in Las Vegas. Luger was only too happy to fill in all the details about the evening when the casino manager was murdered. He now realized that it was, indeed, murder. The anonymous letter implicating Burt in that murder was imparted by Luger, along with the fact that Burt had insisted that the letter was from Jason. He gladly faxed everything he had on the case over to Dobie.

Dobie's team began to piece together what they believed happened. The evidence against Burt was overwhelming. The inspector now knew that they didn't need a confession from Burt to make a murder charge stick.

It was a long walk for Burt's solicitor, Tom, to make to interview Burt. It seemed a lot longer today, because the news he was about to give Burt was not good news. Inspector Dobie had already given him the evidence that he had received from inspector Luger and the other evidence that had been garnered in Sydney.

Tom knew that Burt was not in a good position, but he had to give him hope and not allow his feelings to be expressed. As soon as Burt saw his solicitor, his gut feeling told him that all was not right. His stomach butterflies began to dance far too much. In the few seconds between his sighting of Tom and the first words spoken, Burt's mind raced along, trying to imagine not who or how they did it, but why.

As Tom sat down to face Burt, it was Burt who uttered the first words. "It's not good news, is it?"

"Not good, but nothing we can't overcome," replied Tom as a slow, forced smile came across his face.

Tom relayed the latest information that Inspector Dobie had released, fully knowing there was probably a lot more that the police were not relaying to him—yet.

Inspector Dobie was pushing very hard to have an inquiry into the two murders to see if there was enough evidence for them to go to trial. Both sides agreed on the date. It was to be in one week's time. Burt's solicitor believed that the sooner, the better, because it wouldn't give the police much time to prepare their evidence.

Nora was present at the inquiry. Showing little emotion, she sat two rows behind her husband as the charges against him were read out loud. The man with whom she had lived for so long was definitely not the one who committed these atrocities.

Burt had so far managed to refrain from mentioning the Las Vegas plan, as he had dubbed the $12-million loss. He didn't feel at this stage that it would be necessary and could probably hurt his case rather than help it.

The evidence that the prosecution put forth was very damaging but not overwhelming, or so Burt thought as he listened intently. The only thing they really had was the gun that killed Jason—his gun. Add to this the statements from the gun seller and the taxi driver, not to mention the fact that he could be placed at the scene of the crime at the time the murders were committed—well, one anyhow. Hopefully, the statements from Inspector Luger would not have much bearing on the case.

Every now and then, Nora would look over at her husband to see what emotion he was showing. She knew that her just being there made him feel there was at least one other person who was on his side. However, upon hearing all the evidence against Burt, Nora was no longer 100 percent sure that he didn't have a hand in this mess. Even so, she still refused to believe that he had committed the murders.

When the prosecution finished giving their evidence, the judge asked if there was anything else they wished to present at this stage. The crown attorney rose and stated that the remaining evidence was not complete yet, as the police were waiting for some confirmation to be received back from the United States.

Burt whispered to his solicitor. "When do you get a chance to say something?"

"Now," replied Tom.

It was the defense's turn. The only defense Tom put up was to give what he thought was the more logical scenario.

Every piece of evidence that the prosecution had presented, except the gun, could be attributed to someone else. The setup theory was the cornerstone of the defense's case. Tom contended that Jason was murdered for his money. The elaborate events that took place, especially the way in which the murder weapon was sold specifically to Burt, were to pin the murders on him.

As Nora listened to this side of the case, she really felt what her husband was going through. To be set up like this and have most of the people think that you are guilty must have been playing havoc with Burt's mind.

Tom stated that most of the hard evidence for the defense was still being appropriated, and at this stage, it would not be prudent to present any more. The judge then asked Tom whether he thought that it was a foregone conclusion that they would go to trial. This caught Tom a little off guard, as he wasn't used to a judge being so direct. He fumbled with the words and managed to come up with an answer.

The judge called the crown attorney and Tom to approach the bench. Burt looked around and smiled a desperate smile at his wife. The smile was returned in kind, as Nora, fearing the worst, had a little tear form in her eyes. There was much whispering by the judge and Tom, and then the crown attorney and Tom returned to their seats. Burt wanted to know what was going on, but Tom just said they were going to trial. The judge then spoke. The trial was set for three weeks out.

Burt couldn't believe that his whole life was now on the line. *This wouldn't happen back in the States,* he thought to himself.

As Burt was being ushered back to his holding cell, he felt so unclean in front of Nora and the others in attendance.

He hung his head like all criminals do, especially the guilty ones. His head hung because he was embarrassed. The closest person to him had to see him being led away like a criminal, and that was very hard for Burt to take.

Tom managed to speak to Burt just before he disappeared through the door. His words were supposed to bring some comfort to Burt, but they failed in that task. The worried look on Tom's face didn't really convey much confidence either.

It was continually dawning on Burt that he was really in a lot of trouble. He was going to have to go to trial. Life in prison was not what Burt had envisaged for himself in his remaining years. It didn't seem real before, but now it was as if he had woken from the nightmare but the nightmare was still going on.

CHAPTER 12

Back in Las Vegas, John had just arrived home from his vacation. He walked into the office looking nicely tanned and beaming. He gave his secretary a little peck on the cheek.

"There is something that I have to tell you before you do anything else," she said as she quickly ushered him inside his office and closed the door. "Now I want you to prepare yourself for some really disturbing news."

"Just say what you have to," stated John, fully knowing that sometimes his secretary was a little melodramatic.

She made him sit down and made him promise not to say anything until she had finished. She stated that while he was away, Burt had flown to Australia and had been arrested for murder.

John just sat there with his mouth wide open, not really knowing what to say. The first thing he wanted to know was who had been murdered. When the secretary said that it was the gambler who had won the $12 million, John just said, "Jason."

"What have Bill and Peter said about this?" he asked, trying to get over his initial shock.

"The only thing I know is that they both rushed in here

as soon as they heard the news. They asked if they could get in touch with you," replied the secretary.

As John started to go to Peter's office, his secretary stopped him in his tracks by saying, "There is one other thing that you should know."

John turned and said, "What could compare with this?"

The secretary then stated that Jane had asked about him the day he left on his cruise. She added that Jane was really upset that he had gone away without telling her. It would probably be in his best interests to call her as soon as possible.

John ignored this latest remark and rushed over to see Peter. Bill saw John coming down the hall and didn't want to miss anything. The two walked into Peter's office together.

"What's all this about Burt being arrested for Jason's murder?" said John in an alarmed tone.

Peter asked how much had he heard.

"Only that Burt was arrested for Jason's murder," replied John.

"Let me fill you in on all the details," said Peter.

John listened as Peter went over the events that had taken place in Australia of which they were now aware. Bill had received continual reports from Sydney. The latest being that an inquiry had been conducted and that a trial date had already been set.

"I don't believe I am hearing this," said John when Peter had finished. "You, of course, don't believe that Burt could possibly have had anything to do with any of this, do you?" John asked. The question was directed at both Peter and Bill.

"Of course we don't believe it," said Peter, speaking for

both of them. "However, the evidence the police have is very damaging.

John asked if any of them should go to Australia as a character witness or something.

"Burt didn't want anyone to go there," Bill said, eager to have a say.

"Nora is already there, and Burt feels that because he is innocent, there should not be any need to involve anyone else," said Peter. "Besides, I'm sure that he wouldn't want any of us there, because we are the only ones who know the real connection between Burt and Jason."

"I suppose someone has to look after his business empire," said Bill.

"We can't just sit around and do nothing," protested John. "No one else knows Burt like we do. Besides being our boss, he is also a friend."

The other two looked at John after this last remark.

"Well, sort of like a friend," John then said, trying to clarify his statement.

"I'm afraid all we can do is wait," replied Peter. "Oh, there is one other thing. The last time Burt called, he specifically asked for one of us three. I took the call. He said that under no circumstances were we to divulge anything about the gambling plan."

The three all agreed not to say anything.

"Well, what's our next step?" said John, eager not to let things just lie like that.

"There's nothing much we can do from here," said Peter. "It's up to Burt and his lawyer now."

John returned to his office, shaking his head as he passed his secretary.

"There is a message for you, John," she said with a little smile beginning to break out.

"Who from?" asked John.

"I'll give you one guess," she answered with a much broader smile.

John knew that the message was obviously from Jane. He decided not to call her straight away, just to make her sweat a little.

Just before eleven o'clock, Jane walked into John's office. The look she had on her face was one of determination. She walked up to John's secretary and calmly asked if John was in.

"Go right ahead," said the secretary. She didn't want to miss any of this. Since her boss had been away, things had been pretty dull. She hoped this episode could salvage some fun.

John looked up as Jane opened the door.

"Nice tan," said Jane.

John just smiled without saying anything.

"How was your trip?" she added.

"Oh, it was pretty good," he replied. John was waiting for this small talk to be over before Jane would state what was really on her mind. He didn't have to wait long.

"Well, it was nice of you to let me know that you were going on a trip," said Jane, beginning to get to the heart of the matter.

"I didn't think I had to clear anything with you," John replied, taking up the challenge.

"No, you don't have to. I just thought you would want me to know where you were so I wouldn't worry," came the reply.

"Look, Jane, I thought that we had already finished with this conversation before."

"You're right, John. You are so right. I have no right to question you like this."

Jane had thrown it back at John now. He had to say something.

She is defying me to disagree with her, thought John, *but I'm not going to do that.*

"I'm glad you see it that way, Jane. What we had in the past were beautiful dreams. Dreams that would not be accomplished," John found himself saying.

He was not really forming the words; they seemed to be coming out by themselves.

"These dreams," said Jane. "Would they be the dreams that we would get married and live happily ever after?"

"Now you are trying to make it sound like a fairy tale," answered John.

"I know it is not a fairy tale, darling," said Jane, using a much softer tone. "While you were away, I had time to think about us. Time to reevaluate my life. I may have been a little stubborn that last night you were at my place."

"Oh?" said John, wondering exactly where this conversation was heading.

"Well, I have decided that you were right, and I was wrong," said Jane. "We did have a great relationship, and it should advance from this stage. If you are still willing, I would be very happy for us to get married. The sooner the better." Jane gave a sigh of relief. This was no easy statement to make. Her whole future had just been laid bare. Jane stared fixedly at John, waiting for some sign of agreement.

John just sat there. He hadn't prepared himself for Jane to have a change of heart. By the time he had gathered his thoughts, Jane had already asked what he thought of the idea.

John had believed that their relationship was over. He didn't really know what to say. "Look, Jane, I'm afraid it's too late to change your mind now," he said.

"You're not serious," replied Jane. She didn't believe John would turn her down. She was always the one who did the dumping. She was not used to being the one who was dumped. "I don't believe that you are throwing a great relationship away so easily," said Jane in a rather pleading but hurt manner. "Maybe you didn't understand exactly what I am saying. I love you, John, and I want to spend the rest of my life with you by marrying you. I thought that was what you wanted."

"That last night at your place, I gave you an ultimatum," said John. "You chose not to marry me and to end our relationship. At the time, I was heartbroken. I have also had some time to think. I realize that I may have pushed you into making a decision, but I believe that the truest decisions are made under pressure. You made that decision then, and so did I. If you have changed your mind now, I'm afraid it's too late. I no longer feel the same way about you that I did before."

"You mean to tell me that you are no longer in love with me?" said Jane, not wanting to believe it.

"Since you put it in those terms, I admit that I am no longer in love with you, Jane," stated John. He was prepared for Jane to get nasty at this stage.

Jane was the type of person who would not let go of something she really wanted that easily.

"There's someone else, isn't there?" she asked.

"There is no one else, Jane."

"Who went on that cruise with you?"

"I went by myself."

"I bet it was that slut Julie," Jane snapped. The claws were now coming out. Jane's pride was hurt, and she was like a wounded animal. John was hers, and no one else had better stake a claim to him.

"If it is the relationship I had with Burt, I want you to know that I have told him I would not go out to dinner with him anymore," said Jane. "There was nothing to our relationship; it was purely business and nothing else. I know you don't believe that, but honestly, darling, it is the absolute truth."

"It has nothing to do with your other relationships. Look, Jane, I don't wish to hurt you. I still care for you; it's just not in the same way as before," stated John, trying to ease the pain a little.

Jane had heard this excuse before. She had used it on nearly all her previous boyfriends. She wondered if it had destroyed them in the same way it was now destroying her.

"Look, John, I realize that you have just come back from basking in the sun on a beautiful cruise, and you probably met some gorgeous women, but you are back now. I wouldn't mind if you had a last-minute fling as long as it was just a fling. I'm sure that the setting sun is very romantic on a cruise, but it is time to come back down to earth now."

John interrupted this speech by Jane, stating that their relationship was over and it had nothing to do with the cruise. Jane rose from her chair and said, "Well, I suppose there is nothing else I can say then."

John didn't answer. Jane simply left without looking back. John knew that this was not the end.

CHAPTER 13

During the three weeks awaiting trial, Burt's solicitor and his team were very busy trying to uncover any new evidence that may help them at the trial.

Nora dropped in to see her husband on most days, mainly to help keep his spirits up. She was curious why he'd come to Australia to meet with Jason. It obviously was not for an investment as he had originally told her. With everything that had gone on, Burt had forgotten the original excuse for the visit and gave her the same one he had given Inspector Dobie. He explained that because Jason had won all that money from Burt's casino, he had invited him Down Under to see his place. After all, Burt had provided so much for him in Las Vegas.

"What did you provide him with?" asked Nora.

"The casino win," said Burt.

That excuse would work on a borderline halfwit like Luger, but Nora had a brain and could see through the bullshit. There was no way that she would let on that she didn't believe her husband, and continued to act like the dutiful wife as she did at home.

When Nora left the visiting room, she was now of a different opinion regarding the murders. She still believed her husband hadn't actually done the killings, but she also knew that he was mixed up in it somehow. Every time Burt's solicitor came to see him, it was as if there was another nail in his coffin. It got so that Burt hated to see Tom at all.

With just one week to go before the trial, Burt was really beginning to panic. Nora's visits had dramatically reduced, and Tom's news was always bad.

The newspapers were playing the trial up big, both in Australia and the United States. It was interesting that although the papers were from different countries, they both had the same slant for the verdict—guilty of murder in the first degree on both counts. The only difference between the two editorials was that the Australian papers could not, by law, identify the suspect by name. This was not the case with the American papers. It's one thing to be tried in a court of law, but to be tried in the papers beforehand was far different and unfair.

The day before the trial, Tom came to see Burt for what might be the last time before the trial. This time, however, he brought good news. The gun that killed the Jason imposter had been found by the police. There were some fingerprints still left on the gun, and although they could not be identified, they were definitely not Burt's.

The other good thing was that the prosecutor was hinting at a plea bargain for a lesser charge. When Burt asked why this was classified as good news, Tom indicated that the police couldn't have as strong a case as they thought they had.

Just out of curiosity, Burt asked how long a sentence he would be looking at if he were found guilty. Tom quoted the law of life imprisonment as being a maximum of twenty years, but with time off for good behavior, it would probably be ten to twenty years. If they accepted the plea bargain, it would be about ten years, and Burt would likely be out in five.

That's still too long for an innocent man to serve, Burt thought to himself. He asked Tom what his chances were realistically.

"To be perfectly honest with you, Burt, I don't think they have a leg to stand on. All their evidence is circumstantial. The only thing they have on you is the gun that killed Jason. I'm sure I can break that down to just a possibility and not a probability. I don't know how they do things back in the States, apart from what is on TV, of course. Down here, we just have to prove reasonable doubt. I must warn you that it is not going to be a cakewalk."

On the day of the trial, Burt did something he very rarely did; he prayed. It was as if he knew that he needed all the help he could get. He made all the usual promises to God—to give up this and that and to be a much better person in the future. His main prayer was to give up his love of money, and he promised that if he escaped the charges, he would no longer look for the money.

It was a bright, sunny day outside the courthouse. The trial was due to start at ten o'clock that morning, and Burt gave himself plenty of time to be ready. Burt was dressed in a charcoal-gray suit with faint light blue pinstripes in it. This day was going to be remembered by Burt for a long, long time.

As Burt was led into the courtroom, he tried to look around. He had been slightly blinded by the flashes coming from the cameras outside the courthouse. Nora was there, and she gave a little wave as Burt passed by.

The feelings that were churning inside Burt at the

moment were of total anger. He was angry at the system that put him, an innocent man, in that courtroom in such a degrading position. He was angry at Jason for taking such a simple task and turning it into murder. Most of the anger, though, was directed at the person who really did the murders, whoever he or she may be.

Tom was waiting for Burt and shook his hand very vigorously. It felt like the handshake of a man who was in an extremely good mood. The smile on Tom's face was another indication of how he was feeling, although Burt had seen many false smiles before. It was the handshake that told Burt of his solicitor's real mood. You can't fake a handshake.

Tom began to discuss his outline of the case as soon as Burt sat down. Burt had heard it before and just went through the motions of listening. Tom did mention that he thought the new evidence about the murder weapon that killed Jason's imposter may be the key they needed for Burt to be acquitted of both murders. At that news, Burt began to pay close attention.

Burt looked over to see what the jury looked like. There were more men than women, and Burt did not know if that was good or bad for him. He wanted to see the people who held his life in their hands. To burn every one of their faces into his mind was his sole aim, just in case something went wrong and he was found guilty. He wouldn't do anything to hurt them; he just wanted to remember them.

The prosecutor, who was the crown attorney, came over and whispered something to Tom. Burt couldn't hear what was said. Tom leaned over toward Burt and said that the prosecutor had offered another plea bargain, one that would guarantee just a five-year maximum sentence. From what Tom had told him before, Burt knew that the prosecution's case was weakening by the minute. Burt shook his head, and Tom passed this along.

There was a distinct look of disappointment on the face of the prosecutor as he returned to his seat. Tom had told Burt the crown attorney would be a worthy adversary as the prosecutor. He stood just over six feet tall and was in his early forties. He was a big man, and Burt knew he would be very intimidating to a jury.

As the trial began, the judge asked that the charges be read out loud. Burt was charged with two counts of murder in the first degree.

The judge then asked Tom whether Burt had changed his plea or would let the not-guilty plea stand as is. Tom stated that the existing plea would stand.

The prosecutor rose and walked over toward the jury. He took a scant five minutes to paint a very disturbing picture of the murder of Jason and the imposter. Burt sat in silence and became intrigued with the description of how the murders were committed, from the prosecution's side, of course.

Tom got his chance to talk to the jury too. He painted a very different picture of how the murders were committed. It was almost in direct contrast to the way the prosecution had portrayed them. When Tom returned to his seat, Burt asked him if he could prove any of what he had just said. Tom put his fingers to his lips as a sign of silence, because the first witness was about to be called.

The first witness was the taxi driver who took Burt to meet Jason. On cross-examination by Tom, the taxi driver gave his evidence, which seemed to help Burt's case rather than the prosecution's. As various witnesses were paraded into the courtroom, it became more and more obvious that Burt was an innocent party to the murders.

When the prosecutor produced the gun that killed Jason, it was the one tangible thing that could really tie Burt to Jason's murder. The explanation that Tom gave about Burt being set up sounded more and more idiotic. Even Burt himself found it hard to believe that someone would go to so much trouble to make him look like a murderer.

The next witness, the person who sold the gun to Burt, testified that the gun was given to him to sell only to Burt. Tom drew out every bit of information from this witness, including the fact that the gun was not available until about one hour before Burt was to meet Jason.

This gave credence to the idea of Burt being set up, the opposite effect of what the prosecution was trying to prove.

After each witness had left the witness stand, Burt turned around to look at his wife. The smile he gave her seemed to become broader after each witness.

By the time the lunch break was reached, the prosecution had already produced half of their witnesses. These witnesses had not helped the prosecution's case very much. Burt was rather surprised at how adept his solicitor was at cross-examining the witnesses. Before the trial, Burt did not think very highly of Tom being his solicitor. The efforts he put forth at the inquiry were, to say the least, pitiful in Burt's eyes. However, here at the trial, when it really counted, Tom was like Perry Mason. Every witness so far had failed to implicate Burt in either murder.

Burt was given permission to eat lunch with his solicitor in the court canteen. Burt told Tom that he was very pleased with the way he was handling the case. Tom said there was still a long way to go, but Burt could see that he was also very pleased with the morning's proceedings.

"Will I have to testify?" asked Burt, hoping to avoid such a thing.

"Only if it is absolutely necessary," was the reply.

When court reconvened, the prosecutor asked if he could produce some new evidence that had just been received and could be vital to the case. The judge motioned both Tom and the prosecutor to approach the bench.

The prosecutor explained that this new evidence was the result of police investigations into large amounts of money that may have been transferred to any of Burt's overseas accounts. The police had obtained evidence that there was a $1 million transfer of funds to one of Burt's bank accounts in Las Vegas.

The money had been transferred on the morning following the murders.

"What hard evidence do the police have?" asked the judge.

"We have a copy of the signed transfer slip and also the bank clerk who handled the transaction," said the prosecutor.

Since Tom had no objections, the evidence was accepted by the court. While they were still at the bench, Tom asked the prosecutor when he was going to bring in the bank clerk as a witness.

The prosecutor smiled before answering. "How about now?" Tom turned to the judge and asked for a five-minute recess to confer with his client regarding this latest information. The recess was granted.

Tom quickly asked Burt exactly what he did on the morning after the murders. Burt stated that he rose early because he didn't sleep very well due to the events of the previous night. He took a shower, had breakfast at the hotel, and went for a walk. Tom asked him where he went for a walk. Burt was a little curious at all these questions but complied by describing where he went.

"You didn't go to any banks, did you?" Tom asked.

"A bank?" answered Burt. "No, I didn't go to any bank. Why?" Burt looked rather puzzled.

"Oh, nothing," said Tom.

The prosecutor stood up and called the bank clerk as his next witness. He referred to the bank transfer slip and suggested that Burt was the one who had sent the $1 million to his own account—$1 million being part of the money that he knew Jason had in his possession.

"Was there anything distinctive about this person who sent the money?" asked the prosecutor.

"Yes, sir," replied the bank clerk. "He had an American accent."

At this statement, there was a hum that went around the room.

"Is that person in this court at the present moment?" asked the prosecutor, turning around to look squarely at Tom and Burt deliberately.

"No, sir," came the reply.

"No?" said the prosecutor with great surprise. "Are you sure you have looked around long enough?"

"I'm sure," the bank clerk repeated.

"Maybe you need a closer look—"

At this stage, Tom objected. "The witness has answered the question twice already. The prosecution is badgering its own witness," he noted.

The judge agreed with Tom.

When asked if he wanted to cross-examine, Tom stated that the prosecution had already done such a good job for the defense with the witness that there was no need for any cross-examination.

Some of the people in the court, who were obviously on Burt's side, began to laugh.

The rest of the day continued in the same vein for the prosecution. As each witness took the stand, none could add any positive strength to the prosecution's case. Just before the trial was to end for the day, the judge asked the prosecutor how many more witnesses he had left to call.

The prosecutor stated there was just one more. The judge decided that it would be in the best interests of the court if that witness waited until the following day to take the stand. Hearing no real objections, the judge ended the trial for the day.

"Well, what did you think of your first day in court?" Tom asked Burt.

"It was very interesting," said Burt. "If that is the best the prosecution can come up with, then I don't think we have much to worry about."

"I'll admit that we are in a much stronger position than we were before this trial started," replied Tom, "but let's not be over confident."

Nora managed to speak to her husband just before he was returned to his holding cell. She threw her arms around him and hugged him tightly. She was feeling guilty about doubting him after the inquiry. Nora knew Burt must have believed that the day's events were good for him, because he joked about returning to his holding cell.

"I've been back and forth so much to my little cell that

they are thinking about installing a revolving door," he noted.

Burt slept very well that evening, very well indeed. He was prepared to face whatever they were to throw at him in the morning. Just before he went to sleep, Burt closed his eyes and thanked God. He hoped it wasn't too premature, but he just wanted to show his appreciation.

As sleep was slowly overtaking him, Burt could see himself on a plane. He was flying back home. There was no way he would miss his cell. One day he would like to return to Australia, but only when he could feel comfortable about it.

It was at this point that Burt began to think of the money. *Who could have it? I think I had better not even try to find out who has it,* he thought to himself. That money—or, rather, looking for it—has brought me too close to spending the rest of my life behind bars.

It was very early in the morning when Burt arose. He was anxious to conclude what he believed would be the final day of the trial.

It was a far different Burt who entered the court this time. He strode like he normally did—with his shoulders back and his head held high. Nora could see that he was confident, and so was she. The thought of the two of them flying back to Las Vegas danced in her head. She knew that her husband would not want to stay for a little holiday in Sydney. He would want to try to put as much space between himself and this place as he could.

The final witness for the prosecution did not throw any damaging light on Burt's case. Now it was Tom's turn to call his witnesses.

Tom had assembled some of the staff of the Menzies

Hotel to serve as witnesses. The night clerk confirmed the time Burt had left the hotel on the night of the murder and also the time he arrived back.

The prosecution had suggested that Burt could have had time to commit both murders. However, they failed to break the night clerk's insistence of the time Burt had left and returned.

The taxi driver who brought Burt back to the hotel around two thirty the morning after the murders was the next witness called. He confirmed the time and place he picked up Burt. Tom had calculated about the time it would have taken for Burt to walk from the murder scene to the place where he was picked up by the taxi. Adding these calculations to the first taxi driver's estimate of the time Burt spent inside the house, there was no way he could have committed both murders.

It soon became apparent that Burt had been set up to take the blame for the murder. At lunch, Tom told Burt that he didn't feel it would be necessary for him to testify.

"Does that mean you think I will get off?" asked Burt anxiously.

"Don't you?" Tom replied with a cheeky grin.

After the final witness left the stand, the prosecutor began his summation. As he walked over to the jury, he knew that his case had been reduced in its credibility. His confidence was not as strong as it had been the day before while addressing the jury. He dwelled on the absurdity that anyone would go to such lengths to put the blame on Burt.

The timing that had to be achieved would be astronomical, except if Burt knew every move himself. He stated that the evidence the defense put forth was inconclusive because there were no corroborating witnesses to back it up.

Burt was impressed by the eloquent words the prosecutor used. He watched to see if it was having any effect on the jury. The rest of the summation dealt with the pinpoint precision that would have been necessary to effect such a frame-up.

Tom patted Burt's hand, as it was his turn to give the jury the defense's side of the case. Burt listened as Tom gave an excellent summation.

Tom made a mockery of the prosecution's case and reiterated what his witnesses had already proven. His words weren't as elegant as the crown attorney's, but the point he was trying to make should have been received more favorably.

After both sides had finished summing up their cases, the judge asked the jury to retire and consider their decision. He first instructed them to vote only according to the evidence they had heard and not with their feelings. He also stated that there was no death penalty in Australia. The maximum term in prison for the defendant, if he were found guilty, was life. The judge went on to say that life usually meant no longer than twenty years.

When the jury retired to reach their decision, Burt was taken back to his cell. His confidence was still there, but it was not as strong as it had been. His heart was beating really fast. *They can only bring in a not-guilty verdict,* he thought to himself. There was no way, judging on the evidence, that he could be found guilty. *The time it takes the jury to decide should be an indication,* he thought. *If they agree quickly, it would mean that I will be free. But what exactly is a short time?*

It was barely an hour when the bailiff came to take Burt back into court.

That's definitely a short time, he thought to himself.

Tom was all smiles as Burt sat down next to him. "How do you feel?" Tom asked.

"Like butterflies are having a barn dance in my stomach," replied Burt. "What do you think the verdict will be?"

"Oh, I think it will be exactly what you think it will be," said Tom.

Burt had noticed that Tom rarely gave a direct answer to any of his questions.

The jury filed in one at a time. Burt tried to read their faces to get some sort of hint of what the verdict was. He realized that they must go through a course to remove all facial expressions in order to be picked on the jury.

The judge turned to the jury and asked what their verdict was. As the head juror rose, Burt could almost see his life flash before his eyes. His heart was pounding so hard against his shirt that he could almost see it. He was afraid he was about to lose control of his bodily functions and embarrass himself.

It seemed like the head juror was taking a long time to give a simple verdict.

"To the charge of murder in the first degree of Brian Cox, we find the defendant not guilty."

That was to be expected, thought Burt. It was the next one that he wanted to hear.

The head juror continued. "To the charge of murder in the first degree of Jason Chard, we find the defendant not guilty."

Burt thought he heard the words not guilty, but when Tom flung his arms around him, he knew that he'd heard right. Nora rushed up to her husband and gave him a big hug and kiss. Tears were streaming down her face, and Burt couldn't hold his emotions in check any longer. He felt that this was the happiest day of his life.

Burt thanked Tom and invited him to Las Vegas.

"When can I get out of here?" asked Burt.

"Inspector Dobie wants to speak to you first," answered Tom.

Burt told Nora to wait around for a while, because he should get out soon. Dobie met with Tom and Burt in the holding cell that Burt had considered home for a short time.

"I would like to congratulate you on beating this charge," stated Dobie. "I had told the crown attorney I didn't really think that you were the one who committed the murders. He wanted to go ahead strictly on the evidence that we had, so I had no choice."

"That's okay, Inspector," said Burt who could now afford to be pleasant. "Now, when can I get out of here?"

"Well, normally you would be held in jail and charged with possession of a handgun. However, because you are from the United States, where you are probably used to a much laxer set of rules, we will dispense with that offence. Besides, you have spent more than four weeks in a cell here, and the paperwork would probably result in too much trouble anyhow."

"Can we get it over with now then?" asked Burt.

"Could you shed some light on who could have possibly been responsible for the murder?" asked Dobie.

"I didn't know too much about Jason," said Burt. "I think that this man probably had a lot of enemies. Since he was a gambler, he may have been in trouble with the loan sharks or something. I know that he was married, but I can't see what his wife would have to gain by killing him.

He seemed to be a high roller and probably mentioned to someone that an American was coming to see him."

"Why murder, though?" asked the Inspector.

"I think it was a setup," said Burt. "They had a perfect patsy—me. And they almost got away with it too. If your guys hadn't found the bullet or the gun, I would be in a really tough spot now."

"I think, Mr. Donaldson, that you were unfortunately at the right place at the wrong time, and someone took advantage of that fact," said Dobie. "The police will now have to try to find who the real killer is. That's our problem, not yours. I'm satisfied that we do not have any case against you."

"Well, I'm sure glad of that, Inspector," said Burt as they shook hands. "As nice as your jails are over here, I didn't really feel like spending the rest of my life rotting in one of them."

Nora was waiting for Burt as he came out. "You can book a flight home for us, darling," he said.

They immediately returned to Nora's hotel where Burt called his secretary and was told that Inspector Luger was looking for him regarding the manager's murder. Even that news was not enough to have any adverse effect on Burt's good mood.

Well, he obviously will change his mind when he is notified that all the charges in Australia have been dropped, Burt thought to himself.

Burt decided to take Nora out to have a nice dinner to celebrate his return from the jaws of endless prison life. He picked a really elegant restaurant—one Tom had told him about earlier.

Food will never taste as good as it will tonight, thought Burt.

As they waited for their food, Nora filled Burt in on what had been happening back in Las Vegas.

"I suppose they have been coping without me," Burt said.

"As best they could under the circumstances," Nora stated half-sarcastically.

"Did any of them think I was guilty?" Burt questioned.

"I only spoke with Bill, Peter, and John, and from what they told me, they were behind you all the way," said Nora. "No one back home believed that you could commit murder. They wondered what evidence the police had on you. One thing puzzles me, though. When I was speaking to them, Bill asked if you had recovered any of the money. When he said that, the other two tried to cover up what he had said by changing the subject very quickly."

Nora stared fixedly at her husband, waiting for him to give some sort of explanation. He only said that they probably thought he wanted to try to get some of the $12 million back.

"Why would they think that?" Nora asked.

Burt did his best to avert her eyes and said, "I don't know, probably the way they think I suppose."

"You didn't have anything to do with those killings, did you?" Nora asked with a very serious look on her face.

"You have got to be joking," Burt shot back. "I was set up for those murders, darling. You heard the evidence at the trial. I was acquitted. Remember?" The last comment was uttered in an irritated tone. Burt was upset at Nora's accusation. He refused to look her straight in the eyes.

Just at that moment, their food arrived.

"There is something that you are not telling me, isn't there?" said Nora.

He realized that he couldn't keep her in the dark about the scheme any longer. She wanted to know how he'd gotten himself into this mess in the first place. Burt could tell that she had not been satisfied with the explanation he had given her before. He knew that if there was anybody he could trust, it was his wife. The hardest part to explain was the plan itself.

"Okay," he said. "I suppose I should tell you the whole story. Before I do, though, you have to promise me that you will not divulge anything I am about to tell you," said Burt.

"Who would I tell?" answered Nora.

"Anyone," said Burt.

The suspense was starting to get to Nora, so she quickly promised that she would not breathe a word to anyone.

Burt suggested that they finish their meal first. He would tell her everything when they drank their coffee. Nora wasn't too pleased with that. She had little patience when it came to listening to gossip.

The conversation over their main meal was just chitchat. It gave Burt some time to formulate a way to tell Nora without it sounding too unbelievable.

When they had both finished, Nora looked at Burt and said, "Okay, I'm ready."

Before he began, Burt asked that she not ask any questions until he was through. He proceeded to tell her the whole story up to the present time.

Nora listened with great fascination. In a way, she was proud of her husband's resourcefulness. It was only when Jason led him on the run and then got himself killed that the idea went astray.

"Why would anyone try to frame you for the murder?" asked Nora.

"That's the strange thing," came the reply. "I have no idea."

"Now that I have heard the truth, I can rest a little easier," said Nora. "You may think I am silly, but not knowing what you were really up to, I thought, well—"

"Thought what?" interrupted Burt.

"I thought that you were having an affair," she answered.

"An affair?" exclaimed Burt. "Why on earth would you have thought that?"

"Oh, just little things," said Nora. "When you came home from that last business dinner, I could smell a woman's perfume on your jacket."

"Only because there were women there," came the reply. "No, I have not been having an affair. Besides, why would I go all the way to Australia to have an affair?"

"I know, I know, it's silly, really," said Nora.

"Look, I know I should have told you the real reason, but I had to keep quiet about it. If any of this got out, I could have been in a lot of trouble," said Burt.

"You mean you didn't trust me?" said Nora.

Burt explained that if anything did get out, he would not know who had leaked the information. It would be far better for him not to have to suspect her. Nora could see, in some twisted way, that his reasoning was logical. She decided to let the matter drop.

"Well, who do you think killed those two men?" Nora asked.

"I must be honest with you, darling, and admit that I have no idea," stated Burt. "That question was on my mind all the time I sat in that holding cell. No matter how hard I tried to think of who could have done such a thing, I come up empty."

"You must have some idea," said Nora in a surprised tone.

"It may not be anyone I know," replied Burt. "Jason could have told someone, a close friend say, all about the scheme. This friend then devised his own plan to get the money and blame me. Now that I think about it, that must have been the way it was done."

Burt made the long journey from Sydney to Las Vegas for the second time in two months. At least this time he had Nora with him.

The thing that nagged at Burt, though, was the question of who had the money now that Jason has been murdered.

One of the mysteries that I will often think about in the future, thought Burt to himself.

He was just so thankful to be out of jail. The loss of the money would have to be put down as experience. At least it could be written off as a tax loss that easily.

Burt knew that the murder trial would haunt him. The identity of the real killer or killers would haunt him even more. As for what happened to the money, well, that could be anywhere.

Chapter 14

When the plane landed in Las Vegas, all three vice presidents were there to greet Burt at the airport.

"Inspector Luger is waiting at your office, sir," said Peter.

Burt made a face but knew that he could get out of this much easier than what he had just endured in Australia. The limousine took all four men to the office. Nora took a separate limo home. Burt related his Australian adventures to the three listeners. After he had finished, it was John who began the questions.

"Do you have any idea who could have killed Jason?" he asked.

"That's the funny part," said Burt. "I have absolutely no idea."

"What about the wife?" said John.

"She was the first one I thought of but realized that she would have nothing to gain. She already had the money in partnership with her husband," said Burt. "She has gone missing, and the police stated that they wouldn't be surprised if her body turned up also. I only hope the Aussie police find the real killer. It would put my mind at rest."

When they arrived at the office, they each went into their own offices. Burt met with Inspector Luger alone.

"Now, Inspector," Burt began, "what is all this about murder instead of suicide again?"

"Well, sir," said Luger in his most apologetic manner. "When you were arrested in Australia for murder, I decided that we should look into the case of the death of the casino manager again. This was just in case there was a connection between the two."

"And what conclusions did you come up with this time, Inspector?" said Burt.

"Well, sir, the final evaluation has been reversed again. I am happy to say that the police department has agreed that the death was, indeed, suicide. Thus, there will be no further investigation."

"Thank you, Inspector," said Burt. "And now we can all get back to normal."

With that, Inspector Luger said good-bye and left the office. Burt told his secretary that for the next few days, he was going to be at his cabin in the mountains. Before he left the office, Burt tried to call Jane, but she was not answering her phone. When Burt arrived home, he found Nora waiting for him. She hugged him and had a drink waiting for him. She had already begun to pack for their little vacation to the cabin.

"You know," Burt said, "this has made me look at things in a different light. I now know what people waiting to go to trial really have to go through. It doesn't matter if they are guilty or innocent, it must still be a very frightening experience."

Nora knew this episode must have had a deep effect on Burt, because it had changed his outlook on things. To stick up for anyone who was about to face a trial was definitely not a typical Burt attribute.

Jane had seen John and the others speaking with Burt at the office. She knew that he had seen her too. For the past few weeks, she had not spoken to John and tried as much as she could to avoid any contact with him. It was not an easy thing for her to do. That last time they spoke in John's office weighed heavily on her mind.

It can't be over. He wants me back. I know he does, she thought to herself. *He is probably using all his willpower to stop from calling me. Oh, it's no use. I have to call him.*

John's home phone rang and rang, but there was no answer. His answering machine had been turned off. Jane slammed the phone down and cursed him for not being there. She quickly calmed down and realized that he may not be home from work yet.

Boy, he sure can be patient to wait for me to come back to him, thought Jane. *I know that when he hears my voice, he will want to see me straightaway.*

She decided to call the office just in case he was still there. John's secretary, who was just on her way out, said that John had left about five minutes earlier.

With that in mind, Jane knew that she would have time to take a shower before he arrived home. She wanted to be prepared for John and look her very best when he came over.

John arrived at his townhouse shortly after six thirty. He walked in and casually took off his shoes, tie, and jacket. He poured himself a scotch, no ice. He picked up one of the daily newspapers that was on the coffee table and relaxed on the sofa. The sound of the shower running could be heard in the background.

John did not show any concern that someone was using his shower. The shower soon stopped, and after a few minutes, a scantily clad woman appeared in the doorway of the bathroom. The light from the bathroom was still on, and as John's eyes moved up from his paper to see the figure, her body was beautifully silhouetted against the light.

John rose from the sofa, slowly walked over to the figure hiding in the shadows, and put his arms around her. He said nothing but gave her a longing and passionate kiss.

When the kiss ended he finally spoke. "We did it, darling. Revenge can be so sweet."

As his face moved away from hers, she stepped out of the shadows, and her face became very clear. It was Debbie.

"Yes, sweetheart, we did it," she replied. "All that money is now ours—$8.5 million just for us."

John picked her up and carried her to the bedroom. Just at that moment, the phone rang.

"Aren't you going to answer that, precious?" said Debbie with a pout that would melt most men.

"No way," said John.

"It rang earlier," Debbie said, "but I didn't answer it either."

"I have an idea who it may be," said John with a cheeky grin.

As he laid Debbie gently on the bed, he smiled. "You know, it must have been fate that threw us together all those years ago."

He then gave her another kiss. He was referring to their meeting at a convention five years earlier when they'd had a brief but beautiful affair. When the search for the gambling candidate began, he'd nearly flipped when her name came up as the wife of one of the candidates. That's when he'd hatched a scheme of his own.

"The murder was a stroke of genius, and to implicate Burt at the same time was icing on the cake," said Debbie.

"You know we can never tell a living soul about this," said John.

"This will be our little secret," replied Debbie.

"You know, you could have had the money anyway," said John.

"Yes, darling, but I wouldn't have had you."

With that, John began to slowly undress.